RAGE

JULIE EVANS

For Mum.

'Rage is a cage without a key.'

ABOUT JULIE EVANS

 After training as a lawyer, Julie returned to her native Cornwall to establish her own law firm and to raise her three children. After years building a successful legal practice it was time for a new adventure and she decided to write the stories she had formulated in her head over the years about her community and the lives of those who find themselves on the wrong side of the law.

RAGE is Book One in Julie's new **CORNISH CRIME** series.

Book Two *A SISTERHOOD OF SILENCE* and Book Three *THE BITTER FRUIT BENEATH* are available to buy now on Amazon. Book Four *A BAPTISM OF FIRE* is due to be released in late 2021.

If you would like to read more about Julie, visit her website at **www.cornishcrimeauthor.com** where you will be given the opportunity to join her readers' club and receive free downloads and inside information exclusively available to members, including a **FREE** novella in the **CORNISH CRIME** series; *THE ROSARY PEA What's Your Poison?*

ONE

CLAIRE

Some people sense when the party's over. Not me, I tend to loiter until the host chucks me out. It's always been a fault of mine not reading the signs; not knowing when it's time to leave. It's why my doctor's words catch me off guard, like a left hook from an overweight bouncer.

'I'm sorry Claire, the cancer's back,' Issy says, bottom lip puckering.

I try to jab back a reply but I'm still reeling from the sucker punch.

'You need to prepare for the worst. We'll make you as comfortable as possible and the medication can be self-administered with supervision,' she says eyes roving over my features; searching for something she can't seem to find.

'I'm here for you,' she soothes as her hand flutters, like a fat white pigeon, from her lap to my arm. Her touch crackles through me like the spark I remember as a child pulling on my nylon nighty when my hair stood on end, and in that static-filled nanosecond, I realise what she's saying. She's telling me I'm going to die.

The odd thing is, I feel almost relieved at the certainty of it. The constant threat of returning disease sitting like a hot coal in the pit of my stomach suddenly feels warm and weirdly comforting. I imagine myself glowing like the child in the old Ready Brek advert, complete with nebulous orange silhouette; the fuzzy infra-red insulation making me different from those who've had a Pop Tart for breakfast and have to take their chances with the weather. I'm free to do what the hell I like, no matter how reckless or misguided or downright loony tunes. I can let rip for once and sod the consequences.

1

I know the smile I feel lifting the corners of my mouth is totally inappropriate but I can't seem to stop it. I need to get out of there, before I break into a fit of hysterical giggles.

Mumbling my excuses, I leave.

Outside, in the driving rain, I'm sorry for being short with Issy. After all, from the very beginning she's gone the extra mile to help me through the chemo and the never-ending crappiness that came with it. More than once she's held back my hair while I retched into a kidney-shaped cardboard bowl.

Note to self; be nicer to Issy.

I seem to hover above the puddled tarmac, barely hearing the splash of my footsteps. Perhaps this is what happens when you're on borrowed time. Maybe the earth senses you're only a squatter.

Some say it's a gift knowing when you're going to die. I wouldn't go that far but it certainly focuses your attention and brings it home to you it's too late to be a slow burner; it's time to go large. Like a broken lightbulb, stamped on then stuck back together Heath Robinson style, I won't last long but I'm determined to burn brighter in the short time I have left. My body might be giving up on me but for a while I'll be invincible; 'The Terminal-ator!,' I laugh out loud.

A young mother pushing a buggy, shoots me a wary glance that screams, NUTTER!

'There are worse things to be,' I feel like shouting after her.

My car drives itself home; it knows the route from the hospital well enough. I suppose I ought to think about who I'll leave it to.

In the house, I discard my dripping coat and glide upstairs to the bedroom.

Waltzing the chair from my dressing table to the wardrobe I step up, stretching my fingers along the top. I pause for a second to examine the dust coating my fingertips. Housework isn't high on my list of priorities. Housework is for people with their whole life ahead of them to worry about what the neighbours think.

Reaching towards the back, I pull down the small white cardboard box and set it down on the bed. I always wait for precisely the right moment; after all rituals are important. Rituals are the stalwart of a civilised society. When the time comes, like an excited child, I tug at the same dull crimson variety of ribbon I use to tie the briefs to counsel and bundles to court; the bindings to the sordid, broken lives my clients bring to me daily for legal healing.

I lift the lid and tip out the contents.

The small balls of paper scuttle across the duvet cover like mice and I hold my breath. I unfold each one, smoothing out the creases, laying them out in front of me. There are four in total and on each one is scrawled a name. The box wasn't my idea. It was recommended by the therapist I was referred to for counselling when first diagnosed two years ago. It was meant to help me sort out the emotional detritus bubbling to the surface. Issy suggested it might help deal with my anger issues.

My 'anger' apparently extends beyond the 'Why Me?' variety. It turns out, whilst I'm a bit of a fatalist as far as my mortality is concerned, I harbour unresolved resentments and anxiety about other things, or rather, other people.

I think my therapist's insightful observations stem from a session where I confessed, I sometimes find myself daydreaming about harming people. People like my ex-husband Daniel, or a particularly aggressive matrimonial client of mine who blames 'lawyer bitches like me' for the crappy life he's managed to carve out for himself. I imagine picking up a paperknife and pinning his wagging finger to my desk. On one occasion, stuck in traffic behind a mindless van driver blocking the road, making me late for my hospital appointment, I thought of getting out of the car and slashing all his tyres.

The images were at the time so vivid and so regular, my therapist warned their suppression was not conducive to my recovery; that I seemed to be carrying a lot of baggage that needed to be exorcised.

'Anger is a natural reaction to your diagnosis,' she said, 'but the suppression of it is a modern response. Think of rage as a cage we build around ourselves to protect us from having to face the root cause of the problem. Rage is a cage without a key and is not helpful. In short, these anti-social chickens are likely to come home to roost.'

I imagined my antagonists with feathery bodies, scratching in the dirt for worms. I tried to avoid the image of guillotining off their human heads with limited success; not very Zen.

'There is a therapy I've had success with in the past which I feel might be helpful in this instance,' she continued. 'I'd like you to place the names of these people in a box. The box should be put somewhere accessible, but not on view every day. When you feel the need to vent your anger, retrieve the box and look at the names. Try and pin down why you feel the way you do about them and then when you've rooted out the problem, acknowledge it and put it away again. Gradually this will diminish their power over you and your negativity towards them. When the name no longer affects you, throw it away. It's a kind of aversion therapy: you see?'

I wondered where I'd find a box big enough.

It all sounded very easy and it worked up to a point. At the start, the box contained over a dozen names: the aggressive client, the neighbours with the yapping dog, Donald Trump, Piers Morgan and the motorist in the red Range Rover hell-bent on driving me off the road every time I chose to cycle to work, to name but a few.

Gradually, most of them ceased to rattle me in the way they once had, and they'd been binned. Looking down at the four names in front of me now, at least one more can move into that category. Louisa, my ex-husband Daniel's 'Yummy Mummy' new wife, who with her postnatal depression and jangling nerves, seems a figure to be pitied rather than detested. The poison chalice has already passed to Louisa - three children under five and Daniel to deal with; poor cow. I'm done with Louisa she's been punished enough.

The same can't be said for the others. There's no time for me to rewrite the lexicon as far as they're concerned. Now I'm dying, they need to be confronted in the only way left. Head on.

I've heard recovering alcoholics search out the people they've harmed through their addiction and apologise to them. It's their way of taking ownership of their actions. Well, my plan is like that only in reverse. As the victim, I intend to force those who have done me harm to fess up and make amends. It's payback time. They won't all receive the same treatment. The lawyer in me will ensure the punishment fits the crime. Daniel, for instance, the serial betrayer I tolerated for too long. I don't intend to harm him, leastways not in a physical sense but I will humiliate him just like he humiliated me. He needs to understand what it feels like and I truly believe in the long term it will make him a better husband not to mention a better father; after all the bar for him is pretty low.

Married for fifteen years we, or rather he, decided not to have children. We'd travel instead, which we did at first until our marriage sunk on a cruise ship named 'Infidelity'. When I caught him having his second affair, with Louisa, I called it a day. After a very grown-up divorce, he remarried and having swept his aversion to parenthood aside, now has a son and twin daughters.

When he rings occasionally to ask how I am; 'what with the cancer and all that' he usually whines about his life, Louisa's disinterest in sex since the twins' birth and how he doesn't get to the gym anymore. Recently, however, he telephoned with a more pressing problem.

'Thought I'd give you a ring, just to see how things are going?'

I didn't want to talk about my cancer, certainly not until I'd been for my three-monthly check-up but he hadn't been at all reluctant to discuss my disease or as it turned out my demise.

'I rang to tell you Louisa and I have made new wills. We thought we should let you know because you have my old one. Louisa said we needed to make them because of the kids; to appoint guardians.'

I noted he hadn't instructed me.

'I got to wondering if you'd made a new will, what with the cancer and all that?' he continued.

'No,' I lied, trying to keep my voice light; my tone congenial. 'I haven't, not yet.'

'I did wonder, because I know when we were together, your old will left everything to me but if I died before you, it all went to your mother. I understand as we're divorced the bit giving everything to me won't stand anymore. The solicitor I saw said it's read as if I'm not there at all like I died before you.'

I let his words hang there for a second like a noose.

'Obviously,' I said, wondering where exactly this was leading.

This was Daniel, after all, it was bound to be leading somewhere in his favour.

'Yes … obviously I do get it but it was the bit about your mother I was thinking about. Isn't it a waste to leave everything to her now she's got dementia, I mean wouldn't it be better to go to someone who could do with the money and would be very grateful for it?'

It slowly dawned on me; he didn't mean charity or some other worthy individual in need of experimental surgery halfway across the world. He meant him. He was putting himself forward as a worthy cause. I decided to play along with him just to see how far this trip down the road to crazy would take us.

'I see your point. Mum has everything she needs now she's sold her house and moved into the care home, but who else is there? I've got no siblings and the rest of the family are much the same as Mum, they don't need anything.'

'Yeah, that's what I thought.'

'Can you think of anyone else?' I said, helping him cut to the chase.

'Well … I wasn't going to say anything, but things are a bit tight for me and Louisa at the moment, with nursery fees and Louisa's therapy,' he moaned. 'I haven't even been able to make the HP payments or renew the insurance on "The Beast".'

'The Beast' is his Maserati GranTurismo, an extravagant present to himself for his fortieth birthday. He hadn't told Louisa the truth about the purchase. Unbeknown to her, he'd borrowed thousands to put down the deposit. Three years on, he was due to make the balloon payment at the end of the month. If he didn't, the dealership would take it back. On top of that, he still hadn't paid off the deposit loan.

I remained perfectly calm throughout the conversation only to find myself smashing the phone against the wall again and again as soon as he hung up. I didn't bother to replace the handset. I have no intention of telling him my prognosis until I'm officially at death's door and probably not even then. I will, however, begin to make plans to meet with Daniel to discuss matters further and to finally deal with the smug egocentric prick, once and for all.

Daniel's name has won its place in the box but I can put him aside for now. He isn't going anywhere. The others have to take priority.

I pick up a square of paper; Jane Donoghue.

The name, not so long ago, seemed destined for the bin. Too much time had elapsed. She must be old and decrepit, if she wasn't already in Hell, calling the register.

Then something changed my mind.

Reading the local newspaper online one morning, I saw Donoghue staring out from the screen of my laptop and felt fate intervene; giving me a chance to settle old scores. The name wouldn't be discarded just yet; not until she'd been dealt with, and now I have my diagnosis, sooner rather than later. I don't have enough laters to go around. Time has caught up with me and time has caught up with Jane Donoghue too.

My mobile judders on the bedside table. It's Sarah. I told her I was having a check-up today and knew she'd call.

'Well … how did it go?'

'Fine, I got the all-clear.' I lie.

'Oh, thank God,' she sighs.

'Yeah, all good.'

'Get the glasses out girl, I'm on my way!'

I can hear the quiver of relief in my oldest friend's voice.

'Do you mind, if we give it a miss tonight, I'm a bit tired. I think I'll just take a bath and have an early night. It's been a long day.'

'Of course, no problem we'll catch up tomorrow … I love you, mate.'

'You too.'

I can't tell Sarah the truth, it would break her heart and besides, I have too much to do. If I tell her I'm dying she'll draw up a bucket list and want to spend time with me; time I need to spend on the names. Holding Donoghue's name in my hand, I lay back on the pillow and close my eyes, too tired to drag myself downstairs.

TWO
ISSY

Issy wrapped herself in the soft pink robe she'd had the presence of mind to drape over the radiator before her shower. She snuggled into it, feeling its fluffy warmth against her damp back. She'd always adored soft things. She still had her old teddy bears and soft toys and gave them a good squeeze now and again when things got stressful. Glancing across to the window seat, she checked they were all present and correct.

The love affair began when she was ten years old and Daddy bought Mummy a mink coat for Christmas. She'd buried her face in it, wanting to stay there forever. Daddy had laughed and promised he'd buy her one of her own for her twenty-first.

Of course, by the time she reached twenty-one, Daddy was dead and Mummy had to sell hers because they needed the cash. She could, she supposed, buy one for herself now, but owning fur wasn't politically correct these days. Every time you wore it you risked some self-righteous animal rights activist throwing paint over you. She grunted in disgust.

Plonking herself down at her dressing table, she leaned in to examine her face in the mirror. She pulled the loose skin under her chin taut, smoothing the jowls she'd noticed lately. If she lost a bit of weight, they'd disappear soon enough, she thought, sucking in her cheeks. Reaching for a pot of moisturiser supposed to tighten and illuminate, she slathered the thick cream over her face and neck and began to dry her hair; pulling her fingers through the pale wispy strands.

She could hear David downstairs making breakfast.

Once, there would have been poached eggs on toast, tea and a croissant smeared with jam, but who knew what she'd get today? The decline began two years before. He'd started getting forgetful so she'd convinced him to go and see a colleague of hers at the hospital. The diagnosis of early-onset dementia was as she'd expected. He'd got worse lately but he needed to keep up the small tasks he could still manage.

He'd always been keen to do his bit around the house after he'd retired. He knew how demanding her job as a consultant oncologist was, after all, he'd been one himself. He'd been her professor at the hospital where she'd trained. He was almost thirty years her senior and in his early fifties when they began their affair; still attractive and at the height of his powers. His wife had multiple sclerosis and Issy had wondered at the time, how a woman in that condition could expect to keep a man like David. High achievers like Daddy and David needed strong, devoted women, like her to support them. She noticed how sometimes his shirts were not as crisp as they should be and he looked tired. She started making him a coffee before he took his rounds and preparing an extra sandwich for him to have with her in the hospital grounds at lunchtime. She liked having him to worry about. It took her out of herself and her life with Mummy in the dingy flat. She knew Daddy wouldn't have let them live there if he'd been alive. He'd have bought her somewhere close to the hospital so she wouldn't have to rub shoulders with the scum riding the tube late at night. Deep down she knew David served as a poor substitute for Daddy but she'd got on better with him than the facile junior doctors who hung around the nurses and got drunk on their weekends off. They were like Claire McBride, hell-bent on having fun and being popular, whatever the consequences.

Pulling her XL tights up over her belly so the waistband rested neatly under her ample breasts, she thought about Claire's reaction the previous afternoon.

She hadn't planned to tell her she was going to die. It had just come out.

She'd had a particularly bad morning. David had been wandering in the night. She'd found him looking through her desk; the desk she was sure she'd locked. He'd needed the loo and they'd only just made it to the lavatory in time. She'd had to physically chastise him. It hadn't been the first time she'd had to do it and she guessed it wouldn't be the last. By the time she'd got him settled, it was almost morning and she was exhausted.

It was clear their housekeeper, Rita, coming in for a few hours every day while she was at work, wasn't enough. There was nothing for it, David would have to go into residential care. He'd started to blub at breakfast when she'd told him, making her late for her first patient.

She'd spent her lunch hour ringing around care homes. She didn't want one on her doorstep. It was clear David would continue to deteriorate, and she saw no point in having him somewhere close enough for her to visit when she had no intention of doing so. Better to be out of sight and out of mind. She didn't want to prolong the agony and liked the idea of a clean break. She was certain if David could make rational decisions, he'd agree.

She'd been frustrated that none of the homes she'd chosen had places available. She'd thought it would be easy to find him somewhere, as cost was no object, but had wondered on reflection whether, given his condition, some of the recreational facilities on offer weren't a waste of money. Modifying the budget to provide only the basics, she'd tried again, but still had no joy, and was told she'd have to join a waiting list.

When Claire arrived later for her routine check-up, something about her cheerful, devil-may- care attitude and her smart business suit got her goat. She knew from conversations they'd had in the past that Claire had managed to get her mother into a nice home with a sea view and it made her want to slap her. She found herself saying the magic words she'd said so often before, usually with devastating effect; 'Your cancer's back.'

That Clare hadn't cried, or said anything at all, had thrown her. It hadn't been the reaction she'd hoped for. There had been no tears, or relentless questions about possible experimental treatments; no sad puppy-dog eyes pleading for help. In fact, Claire had been smiling, actually grinning, like the village idiot.

After she'd left, she'd traced Claire's name on the buff-coloured file in front of her, wondering who in the hell Claire thought she was; up and leaving like that without a bye or leave. She'd been so angry she'd thrown the file across the room before taking a deep breath and rewinding her emotions. She couldn't afford to unravel at the last hurdle. Gathering up the scattered notes, she'd trapped them into a tidy bundle and slipped them back inside their cover, consoling herself with the thought Claire would be dead soon and how that would wipe the smile off her stupid face.

Comforted, by this inevitable truth, she'd drawn a sad emoji on the buff cover; admiring it for a second before scribbling it out with thick black marker.

Having thought about it overnight, she put Claire's reaction down to shock. She guessed she hadn't been prepared for the news because she didn't feel ill, because of course, she wasn't ill. Issy knew she'd soon put that right.

Claire's period of respite had coincided with David's diagnosis and the need for her to concentrate on her own problems. She didn't have the time needed to devote her full attention to both. So, she'd met with Claire on her three-monthly check-ups and though disappointed she'd let it pass. That was, until yesterday.

There wouldn't be any chemo this time and no more remissions. No, this time she just needed to see her off, to expunge her from her life. She needed to rid herself of the things holding her back, including David and Claire McBride.

Feeling better, she made her way downstairs, where David was standing by the kitchen table, cheerily waving a spatula.

'Eggs?' he smiled.

She looked down at the breakfast he'd lovingly prepared. Two scoops of raspberry ripple ice-cream and an obscenely protruding raw sausage.

'Never mind,' she said putting on her coat, 'I'm not hungry, I'll get something at work.'

She thought he looked a little crestfallen; poor old fool.

THREE
DAVID

David waited for the door to click behind his wife, then walked to the table. Retrieving the plate, he placed his foot on the pedal bin and deftly tipped the breakfast he'd prepared for her into it, a wry smile crossing his face. He enjoyed playing the role she'd cast for him, the role of incompetent septuagenarian teetering on the rickety cusp of dementia. It was safer to let her see him that way, to let her believe he wasn't a threat; that he didn't have suspicions about what she really was. He poured water into a shallow pan along with a dash of cider vinegar and waited for it to come to a simmer. Popping two slices of bread into the toaster, he cracked a couple of eggs into the pan and put the kettle on to make a pot of tea. Rita would be arriving soon and liked to have one before she began the mountain of chores Issy set for her.

He liked Rita; and they had an understanding. For the first hour or so after she arrived, they busied themselves about the house. Rita had to do the laundry and prepare the evening meal along with the rest of the housework and then make her way down the weekly list of special tasks Issy gave her; jobs like 'polish silver' or 'clean decanters' or 'dust books in library'. Sometimes he helped her with these, so they could get through them quickly and have an early lunch together watching *Loose Women* on TV.

In the afternoon, he generally went to his study to listen to the radio while Rita studied for her Open University degree in social sciences. In the summer, they went out into the garden to sit sunning their bones and putting the world to rights.

Rita was about fifty-five he reckoned, with all the qualities Issy lacked. She was friendly and kind-hearted and liked to chat about nothing and everything; her life at home with her husband Terry, who worked as a caretaker at the local comprehensive; about her son in the army; her daughter Jackie. They discussed the novels they were reading and Rita's plans to treat her grandchildren to a trip to Legoland.

He looked forward to her arrival every day.

He heard the key in the lock.

'Morning David, traffic's dreadful, there are roadworks on the roundabout from Falmouth causing mayhem.'

She breezed in, taking her mac off in the hall; dropping her shopping bag on the seat next to him.

'I stopped by at Rowe's on the way and bought us a couple of Chelsea buns for our elevenses.'

'You'll be making me fat with all these cakes,' David joked rubbing his belly through his jumper.

'Oh, you only live once and anyway you're alright, you've not got a spare ounce on you. It's me I've got to worry about.'

She moved her hands down her jean-clad hips.

'Mind you, what with Jackie's two and this job, I burn most of it off. What's it today, poached or scrambled?'

'Poached, and done to perfection, if I say so myself.'

He wiped the last piece of toast around the plate, picking up the sticky yellow yolk and popping it into his mouth, then poured Rita a cup of tea as she retrieved the greasy paper bag of buns, placing it on the worktop.

'I'm off to my study to do a bit of reading. Shall we reconvene at eleven for coffee and those?'

'Sounds perfect to me,' Rita replied, shooting a broad smile his way as she tied her apron in an efficient double bow around her waist.

David took his tea through to the room he called his study, but which Issy, rather pretentiously he thought, referred to as 'The Library'. Looking around he conceded perhaps he was being harsh. If a library was a place chock-a-block with books, then technically this was one. The room had shelves along three of its walls, full from top to bottom, a large section containing medical reference books, many of them, out of date. Then there were the rows of classics, books he'd carried around with him since childhood. If he picked one at random, he'd bet he'd find a sticky label in the inside cover awarding it to him as a prize for something or other. He still read them occasionally, Dickens or Keats, a bit of Joyce if he was up to it but at present, he was halfway through something Rita recommended, *My Dark Vanessa*, she'd said it was a game-changer.

He settled in his chair, enjoying the feel of the soft tan leather as he shuffled into the dip made over the years by his backside, and looked around. Nearly all the furniture here came from his house, some even from his parents before that. In consequence, the room felt like his. It was the only one in the house that did.

It was odd given Issy contributed practically nothing to their first place together. He remembered the pitiful box of possessions she brought from the shabby flat she shared with her mother, nothing but a few toys from her childhood.

He'd found it sad at the time but had been happy to let her spend his money to her heart's content on furnishing the flat in town he'd bought for them. She'd continued in the same way, always buying new when they moved, and they moved often. He was, however, always allowed one room where he could keep his stuff, and this was it.

Life had been desperate for him when he first met Issy. He and his wife, Karen, had been married for twenty-five years. They'd met when he was in his first internship and she was a nurse on his ward. They'd lived a happy, social life, with many friends. Karen hadn't been able to have children, although they'd tried, and it was a great sadness for them both, but they supported each other through it. They'd channelled their parental instincts into their nephews and nieces and the children of their friends, and in time, they'd managed to overcome the sense of loss and had stopped letting it monopolise their lives.

Then Karen, out of the blue, was diagnosed with multiple sclerosis.

They'd sought advice from their medical friends who put them onto the latest treatments. He'd managed to pull strings to get her on some experimental trials, but the disease was unpredictable. For some it was a slow-burner, taking years to develop fully, and giving the patient long bursts of remission, but for others, like Karen, it meant a persistent, unrelenting decline and over a couple of years he witnessed his vivacious, lovely wife crumble away. She lost her mobility, her independence and eventually her ability to communicate. He felt powerless and guilty to be grieving for a wife not yet dead, but most of all he felt desperately lonely. Issy had lifted him out of his grief.

She'd been different then, young of course; so much younger than him. Kinder too with the softness of youth still intact. He'd been flattered by her attention. It was nice to have someone caring about him for a change. Karen had a full-time nurse, but he still felt the weight of her disease upon his shoulders. Issy was a welcome distraction and then there was the sex. He missed the intimate touch of another's skin against his. Issy gave that back to him. It was not the same as with his wife. They had enjoyed the intimacy of equals, of two young people who'd grown up together and moulded into a mutual fit. Issy expected him to take the lead and guide her through their lovemaking. She liked him to flatter and cajole her and constantly tell her how sexy she was; how much better than anyone else he'd fucked. She wasn't, of course. Karen had and would always hold that trophy, because he'd loved every fibre in her body. If truth be told, sex with Issy was formulaic and, after a while, downright dull. He put her need for constant praise down to her unhappy childhood and her longing for a father figure.

She'd told him early on about 'Daddy', who'd died of a heart attack in prison. He'd been shocked at first, even with the benefit of the spin she put on the whole episode, but he'd never held it against her and it had given him insight into why she was so damn needy. She'd had to plough her own path; had learnt to rely on no one but herself.

Her mother by all accounts was hopeless. He'd never met her, but Issy told him about her addiction to anti-depressants and sleeping pills. The picture she painted of a pitiful, vapid woman trapped in the past, who gave no help to her struggling industrious daughter, filled him with sympathy for Issy. He understood her drive to succeed despite everything she'd suffered. She wanted to get back what she'd lost, and he accepted he was a stepping stone and was happy to oblige. It wasn't difficult. She was talented, hard-working and his most promising student. He'd never been able to fault her learning skills or her capacity for hard work, but she had two dangerous flaws in her character. She was arrogant and lacked empathy for the vulnerable, as if acknowledging another's weakness re-enforced her own. He believed these traits had enabled her to become a killer. Now he feared she had a new victim in her sights and, given her increasing intolerance of him, he wouldn't be far behind.

Up until now, he'd chosen to ignore certain things worrying him about his wife rather than run the gauntlet of having to face up to them. Challenging her would cost him. He was forgetful, it was his age but often his absent-mindedness was a self-imposed defence mechanism. He knew what Issy was capable of, so he'd play along with the diagnosis of dementia for now.

He'd gone with her to see her friend at the hospital and deliberately flunked the mini-mental test. He'd told Rita not to talk about what they got up to on the pretext Issy wouldn't like her studying on her time. He'd also shown her the marks where Issy had tied him up at night, explaining he tended to sleepwalk and Issy did it for his own good.

He'd said it with just enough lack of conviction to arouse her suspicion and had seen the pity in her eyes as she snapped a photo of his wrist and penned the note on the pad she used for her shopping lists.

So, for now, there would have to be two versions of himself; the elderly buffoon, the other the real him, sharp as a pin. How long the charade could continue, he wasn't sure. He knew, however, he couldn't stand by any longer and do nothing; it would be far too dangerous for everyone, particularly him.

FOUR

CLAIRE

Standing at the front of the group of WI ladies, photographed by the local paper for an article on 'Loneliness in Old Age,' a stony-faced Jane Donoghue radiated all the warmth of Norman Bates's mum. My old insecurities swell like a wave. The year is nineteen eighty-five and I'm eleven years old again.

I remember vividly the first day I met her. Having sat the exam on the recommendation of my primary school teachers, to Mum's delight, I'd won a scholarship to St Bridgit's School for Girls. I'd have preferred the comp where all my friends were going but never said. Instead, I barrelled up on my first day; my oversized blazer resting heavily on my shoulders like the high hopes that came with it. Settling into my seat, next to a girl with bottle thick glasses and uneven bunches, I was a fish out of water.

'Don't worry, you're a good mixer,' Mum had reassured that morning, helping me negotiate the mystery of my school tie; 'and don't forget unlike most of them you don't have to pay for your education.' The inference was, I had an advantage; I was clever.

Choking in my tight collar, it didn't feel like it.

Donoghue stood before us, rocking on the soles of her sensible shoes; a comic book drawing of a teacher in her high-collar Laura Ashley dress. She was perhaps in her mid-forties but her bare face was unlined, her hair pulled back in an uncompromisingly tight bun. Despite the cloak of plainness she could not hide her good looks. She was beautiful; the stripped back variety you don't see very often. To me, she seemed perfect. I longed to be taught by a dedicated spinster, who kept in touch with her old pupils and sat at home at night marking books, but Donoghue was no Jean Brodie and what came after she called the register revealed her ugliness.

'And your father; his profession?' she questioned every girl.

The enquiry at first seemed innocuous enough. A form teacher getting a bit of background on her pupils; what was wrong with that? The problem was, for me, it wasn't innocuous at all.

One by one, each girl reeled off their father's profession; GP, bank manager, company director.

I felt the crawl of embarrassment as my name moved up the list.

'Claire Penrose; and your father?'

'He's ... he's dead,' I mumbled, picking at the zip of my new pencil case.

'Are you sure?'

The woman hovered over me like a beautiful moth. I shuffled in my seat, suddenly needing the bathroom.

Bemused heads turned. Unlike them I guessed where this was going. Like Mum said, I was no fool.

'I ask, Miss Penrose because it says in your file that your father is "UNKNOWN".'

There was a snigger from the back of the room.

'I don't know, I just ... I just,' I floundered.

'You thought you would take the course of least resistance in the way the lazy always do. Here is a lesson for you Claire Penrose. The truth will always out.'

The words hung in the air like damp washing.

No one laughed, no one said a word; it would have been better if they had because their cold contempt felt infinitely worse, as it slowly dawned on me, I'd been publicly and routinely humiliated for being illegitimate.

I was angry at myself for feeling ashamed. I was proud of Mum, who'd raised me on her own. I'd never once missed having a father and had the teacher asked me what my mother did for a living, I'd have used Mum's midwife mantra and answered: 'She delivers bundles of hope into the world every day.'

I never told Mum about the incident or the persistent attacks that followed. I knew if I did, she'd march me up to the school and make things worse.

Instead, every morning of the first year, I woke with a squirming dread in my stomach. Attempts to stay home with a headache or stomach pain were given short shrift by Mum with her medical nous. I devised ways to avoid the teacher's unwanted attention; to dodge her x-ray eyes and cutting tongue, but it was no use. The woman seemed to feed off my fear.

There was no logical reason why she'd singled me out other than my illegitimacy, and for a while, I began to believe maybe she was right. She wasn't a nun like some who taught us but the rumour was she had once been one and spent all her spare time in the school chapel. From that I deduced she must know good from evil and began to think perhaps I was bad, wondering if it was something to do with the father I didn't know. Maybe he was a bad man and that's why nobody talked about him. What if he'd forced himself on Mum and I was the product of an unholy union; the spawn of a monster and Donoghue could see it in me?

I lay awake at night dreaming of faceless men, looming over me; monstrous men with dark unnatural thoughts. I convinced myself I was damaged goods and too stupid to have an opinion. I stopped answering questions in class in case I drew attention to myself and others began to see the badness Donoghue saw.

I think Mum noticed me becoming withdrawn because she asked outright whether I was being bullied by the other girls. I didn't have to lie; it wasn't the girls doing the bullying.

Mum talked of going to see my form teacher, but after my desperate pleas for her not to, she instead had a word with Sarah's mum, who taught art at the school. She suggested I sign up for drama club to get some confidence. I did and loved it, but Donoghue's attacks escalated, as if, like some dark angel, she'd been delegated with the task of hammering my feet to the ground.

It was the tedious regularity that affected me the most; the bad grades and the constant disparaging references to the lack of a father figure in my life; the awful inference I was tainted.

The tipping point came one afternoon when the teacher called me to the front of the class to collect my exercise book. As she leaned over, she muttered in a low laconic whisper,

'B, for bastard and don't you forget it.'

The rest of the class were oblivious to the slur.

After school, I tossed the exercise book in the hedgerow and ran all the way home.

I found Mum, just back from her shift, washing dishes. My jaw felt stiff; my chest tight with raw paralysing anxiety as I blurted out the question haunting me for months.

'Were you raped ... am I the daughter of a rapist?'

Mum calmly reached for the tea towel to dry her hands.

'Shush, shush, come on now, what on earth's brought this on?'

Mum pulled me in; held me tight before whispering, 'You wait here a moment.'

Moving to the sink, she poured me a glass of water. 'Drink that. I won't be a minute.'

I sipped the water, relishing its coolness on the back of my throat. I dipped a finger in and ran it over my eyes, swollen and sore from crying.

When she re-appeared, she was carrying a photograph which she handed to me.

It was of a group of young men and women, outside a pub on a summer's evening. I immediately spotted Mum, her dark curls resting on the shoulders of her denim jacket, a short summer dress underneath. The group looked relaxed and happy; tanned arms wrapped around each other, pulling silly faces. From the cheesecloth shirts and *Charlie's Angels* hairdos, I guessed it was taken in the seventies and from the white coats and green uniforms they were all young doctors or student nurses.

'Your father could be any one of the men in that photograph. It was taken when I was a student nurse in London. We were all great friends at the time until we went our separate ways. I loved them all, but I loved the idea of having you to myself more. Whoever's baby you were, never mattered to me. All that ever mattered, was you were mine. That's why I've never discussed who your father is. He's one of them and it doesn't matter which one. They knew I wanted a child but didn't want a relationship and the deal was they'd have no claim on either of us. They were medical students and I was a nurse. They donated their sperm anonymously and we all knew our way around a syringe. It took a few attempts but we got there in the end. There would be no paternity test and no maintenance. We didn't stay in touch because it would have been too difficult, but that doesn't mean I was any less grateful to them for giving you to me.'

My eyes bounced between the photo and Mum's face.

'So, you see, you're very special. You're the product of the greatest gift. Friendship without judgement.'

Shocked though I was, the way Mum delivered the bombshell didn't invite questions or comment.

'I intended to wait until you were older before I told you, but I can't let you go around with these ridiculous ideas in your head. This, I guess, is the lesser of two evils; you might think badly of me but at least you know your father was a good man.'

I remember my heart filled with relief and a strange kind of pride.

I didn't dream of faceless men again. I had a face in mind now, in fact, I had several. I could take my pick. Now and again, I'd go into Mum's bedroom and retrieve the photograph from the drawer. One time I even ringed the names written on the back with crayon, but I never really wanted to know any more about them, I didn't want to spoil the story by finding out which was my father. I was Eileen Penrose's baby and that was enough for me.

I've never told anyone about the photograph, or what Mum revealed to me that day. It stayed our special secret. I did, however, sometimes imagine what a field-day Donoghue would have if she knew the truth, and wallowed in her ignorance. The less I took notice of her attempts to belittle me the less she bothered. Eventually it stopped altogether, but the scar it left, a mistrust of those in authority, has never healed. Perhaps it made me a better lawyer; someone prepared to take the bullies on, who knows? But the truth is it could have crippled me if not for Mum and Sarah.

All these years later, the sight of the teacher made my stomach churn but as I rushed to slam my laptop lid that morning; to shut her out, I noticed someone else towards the back of the group in the WI photo; the face of a much younger woman. It was a pleasant face with a hesitant yet genuine smile I recognised. Once, when young, it had been delicately pretty, framed by pale blonde hair. It had held expressive green eyes that spent most of their time examining the floor.

Donoghue cast her net widely. There had been others she terrorised both before and after me, others without love to sustain them. One of those sad creatures looked out from the screen straight at me; Maureen. The lost youth and quiet resignation only served to strengthen my resolve.

I knew in that moment this was no longer revenge; this was a rescue mission.

FIVE

CLAIRE

I plan to give a talk on wills and powers of attorney to the local WI as part of my law firm's drive to provide pro-bono work to the elderly, and when the tea and cake are served, take Donoghue aside and give her a piece of my mind. The problem is, she's not here.

I speak to the woman who'd organised the event.

'I couldn't help but notice the group in the paper seemed larger?'

'Yes dear, a few of our ladies had another engagement. A flower arranging competition in Taunton. Ten of them have gone in the minibus, and Maureen, of course, the driver. She's one of our ladies' carers.'

Maureen ... poor Maureen.

I feel cheated. I'd psyched myself up for the big showdown; the moment I'd berate my old teacher for the damage she'd done and tell Maureen she had options. I hoped then, I could finally close this sorry chapter of my life and one way or another remove Donoghue's name from the box for good. Now all I can do is hand out plenty of vouchers for free consultations in the hope those interested will ring my office to make an appointment, and pray Donoghue's one of them.

Several weeks pass and many of the group, including those not present for my talk, make contact. I scrutinise the names and pass them over to my trainee with increasing frustration. I'm about to give up on the whole idea when out of the blue I get a request for a home visit. A woman calls for an appointment for her aunt.

'She has a voucher from your talk. She can use it, can't she, even though we weren't there?'

I reassure her she can and Maureen rattles on as if any chance for conversation needs to be wrung out.

The appointment is eventually arranged for the following

Tuesday at two o'clock. Maureen will be there to show me in but will have to leave as she helps out at a local charity shop in the high street on Tuesday afternoons between two and four.

I know we'll be alone, me and the wicked witch of the west, and wonder whether I should take a trip to town myself to invest in a pair of ruby slippers.

SIX

Yellow wallflowers stand to attention as I walk up the path to the tidy terraced house at precisely ten minutes to two. I spot the net curtains twitch in the front bay window and thirty seconds later the door opens. It's Maureen, coat on, ready to take advantage of the only day in the week she can probably escape the four walls without her aunt in tow. I search for remnants of the girl she once was, but there are none. Her skin, scrubbed to a rosy glow, is framed by a thinning grey bob that has been on the receiving end of a home trim. She has the look of a woman who doesn't eat enough veg or get enough exercise and the soft curves of youth have settled into a matronly dumpiness belying her age. Only her eyes hold any hint of hope, apart from them, Maureen looks like someone used to defeat.

I'd first met her when she'd been introduced to the class as Donoghue's niece, brought along on the school trip to the V&A to help her aunt marshal us girls.

She was about eighteen and frumpish in her baggy clothes. The teacher barked orders, eviscerating the girl with her vicious tongue. In consequence the day was remembered for its cutting put-downs and red-faced apologies rather than the miniature portrait of Mary Queen of Scots.

That Donoghue had any warm-blooded relatives came as a shock to me. That she had one even halfway normal who wanted to visit her seemed too farfetched to be true. I imagined she must have been kidnapped and held for ransom. I'd heard of Stockholm Syndrome and it seemed the most rational explanation.

I'd felt immediate empathy for Maureen. I'd been on the receiving end of Donoghue's spitefulness and suffered the same ground-opening humiliation. Like Maureen, I'd sucked it up because I had no choice.

I have to know why Maureen is still here after all these years; what's made her stay?

I'm surprised how nervous I am about being recognised. I need to remain incognito long enough to be able to confront the old woman.

These days I wear my naturally curly hair straightened into a sleek dark bob. I've worn my specs for good measure. Polished and professional, my high heels give me height and my dark suit fits like a glove. I understand enough to know first impressions count, even if they're rarely accurate.

Donoghue's sitting in the dreary eighties kitchen when I arrive.

'This is the nice lady from the solicitors, Auntie Jane.' Maureen articulates the words loudly and precisely reminding me of the way Matron speaks to Mum in her care home. I wonder whether I'm doing the right thing, or whether I'm going too far.

The old lady sits at the table, looking straight ahead, her drawstring mouth pursed tight. The beauty she once possessed has been scoured away, I assume, by years of scowling so all that's left is a scavenger-sharpened bone structure.

'She's come to talk to you about …' Maureen stumbles over the words, 'what will happen when you pass.'

Donoghue's head flicks upwards; shooting a defiant glare, before jerking back to hold its position. The gesture reminds me of the staccato stutter beloved in Japanese horror films and I imagine her long grey tresses tumbling over her face.

Maureen invites me to sit and pours me a cup of tea.

'Hobnob?' she offers brightly.

'No thanks.' I know it will stick to the roof of my mouth like wallpaper paste.

The old lady's hand shoots out like a missile to grab a biscuit but the barrel is pulled away.

'Now, Auntie, you know you're not allowed,' Maureen scolds gently, before turning to me and whispering from the corner of her mouth; 'she's diabetic, I have to watch her. I keep the biscuits for visitors. I've got a sweet tooth and love cake but I never have it in the house. It wouldn't be fair to Auntie.'

She looks lovingly at the old lady and I'm thrown. Perhaps Donoghue has changed, maybe living with her kind, doting niece, has meant she's already seen the light and mended her ways?

Retrieving my notebook from my bag, I look up from beneath the rim of my glasses, just in time to see Donoghue grimace as Maureen bends down and kisses her on the head before returning the biscuit barrel to the top shelf.

'I'll leave you to it,' she smiles.

I hear the front door close behind her and finally, I'm alone with my withered nemesis.

I resist the impulse to get this over and done with and confront her straight away. First I need to make sure 'Auntie Jane' hasn't earned a reprieve so I decide to steady my nerves by starting as I would with any other client instructing me to make their will.

I crack a fake smile that makes my jaw spasm.

'Shall we begin? Before I take your specific instructions, I assume I'm right in thinking you'll want as a priority to benefit your niece, Maureen?'

'Why would I want to do that?' the woman croaks.

I'm taken aback.

'Because, as I understand it, she's your only living relative and has been your carer for many years, since she was quite young. I assumed you'd want this house to go to her for instance?'

'Certainly not. She's lived here rent-free for years, she's had enough out of me. It's time for her to stand on her own two feet. She was lucky I took her in. Not many would have, I can tell you; not a girl in her condition; with a swollen belly.'

'Maureen has a child?' I ask surprised.

'Not anymore she doesn't. All the arranging I had to do to get rid of it, to make sure it went to a good Christian family who wanted a baby from a trollop like her. She was lucky I had contacts in the church and was held in such high regard. If I hadn't been, then she'd have had to pay for not keeping her legs together; for giving up her virtue to the first boy that came along.'

Her dreadful words to me flood back like it was yesterday; "B for bastard and don't you forget it."

Maureen hadn't been able to forget it. The girl had no doubt paid over and over again. I imagine the cruel taunts; the lewd accusations and demands for her to be grateful for her servitude.

I want to smash the teacup I'm holding over the evil cow's head but know it won't solve anything. It's not enough to confront her treatment of me and her other pupils in the hope of an apology, that's a lost cause and looking at her now; this bitter withered shell of a woman has no power over me. This is about Maureen. I have to free her; if I don't, who the hell will? I have to adapt.

I write down the woman's instructions including the appointment of my firm as Executors and the provision giving Maureen one month to vacate the property before it's sold and the proceeds of sale along with all Donoghue's other assets are given to St Andrew's Catholic Church.

I finish just as Maureen arrives back, jollied up with gossip from the charity shop.

'Did everything go okay?' she asks. 'I hope Auntie wasn't too upset by the process.'

It is as much as I can do not to shout, *Leave now. She's had the best years of your life. Leave now and don't look back.*

I don't, of course, because I've already decided Maureen will get every damn penny of Donoghue's money.

I've always adhered to the rules of my profession; never dreamt of breaching my solemn duty as an officer of the court but right now there's no option and I'll be using the law as a weapon for good and there's not a lawyer alive who can hand on heart say they've always done that.

'I'll bring the will back for signature next Tuesday. Can you arrange for a couple of neighbours to attend as witnesses?'

'Of course,' Maureen smiles, clearly pleased to have been entrusted with such an important task.

***

Back at the office I don't follow my usual practice of opening a file on the database or dictating an attendance note. Instead, I set to work preparing two drafts, the first following the instructions given by the old lady, the other appointing Maureen as Executrix and sole beneficiary. The two must be interchangeable so I'll be able to swap the first two pages leaving the attestation clause intact so Donoghue will read the first will, see it follows her wishes and sign. Later, I'll replace the first two pages of the signed will with my own in favour of Maureen and no one will be the wiser. I'm confident the old biddy is too secretive to have told anyone of her intentions.

I'll add a clause expressing Donoghue's wish her much-loved niece uses her inheritance to take the opportunity to travel, make new friends and broaden her horizons.

I don't have long left for new adventures but I'm determined Maureen makes up for lost time. After all, time is the most precious commodity of all. I know that better than anyone.

SEVEN
ISSY

Claire had missed several appointments and hadn't requested further prescriptions. All she complained about was a touch of insomnia. Issy couldn't imagine why; what did she have to lose sleep over, as long as she did as she was told and took the medication?

What a waste of time fretting was; self-indulgent and pathetic. It showed a lack of self-control and somebody had to take control. If you left it to the waverers, then where would we be? That type complained about the cuts in the NHS and the lack of resources. They had endless meetings about elderly patients clogging hospital beds but they didn't have the guts to do anything about it. They wanted their house fumigating but didn't want to sweep up the bodies afterwards. They were prepared to spend hours debating whether smokers and those who scoffed their way to diabetes should be treated. Not her; she talked less and did more. She'd made sure over the years, she only treated those who deserved it. She didn't spend valuable resources trying to put right what had taken those lowlifes years to put wrong.

No one questioned her. For every whistle-blower; every enquiring mind, hundreds of jobsworths left their whistles and their conscience at the breakfast table.

The patients were glad to be given any chance at all. Some even felt better for a while believing in the fake treatments she gave.

The placebo effect always fascinated her. She'd learnt it was best to begin by over-emphasising the severity of their illness, so from the very start they held little hope. Even the natural fighters needed hope. Once she got fed up with them, she'd look them in the eye and tell them they were terminal and watch the hope melt away. It was something she never got tired of. She reckoned at that point, they began choosing the hymns for their funeral and she always accepted the invitation. When they died it was expected and their relatives felt relieved and thanked her for all she'd done.

Sometimes, when she felt the disease was not progressing quickly enough, she had to take a more proactive role. She'd prescribe medication to speed things along and increase their dependency. Then, eventually, she'd administer an overdose of morphine or, on one occasion, to a morbidly obese diabetic, insulin. She was doing society a favour. If you weighed up the benefits of not having to spend any more time and money on these lost causes it was a no-brainer. She didn't hate them; she just didn't see the point in them.

Claire McBride was different though; with her it was personal.

The name McBride had meant nothing to her two years before when she'd shouted it from her patient list into the waiting room, but she'd immediately recognised the woman with striking blue eyes who answered to it. Had she been another blast from the past, she might not have known her, but Claire's face was indelibly fixed in her mind although it was abundantly clear from her expression, Claire didn't recognise her.

Issy conceded she had changed a lot. She'd been fifteen when she'd last seen her and time hadn't been as kind to her as it had to Claire. She'd felt a rush of pure rage and considered confronting her, but it suddenly dawned on her that obscurity could play to her advantage. Fate had brought Claire to her after all these years and she'd make her suffer. When she'd had enough of that, she'd have the added satisfaction of watching her die an unnecessary and demeaning death. Only at the very end would she tell her why. She'd goose-bumped with delight at the thought of it. She'd introduced herself as Issy Moran. She always liked to be on friendly first name terms with her patients; even those she murdered.

Claire Penrose as she was back then would have known her as Elizabeth Major; never Issy or even Liz. Daddy always insisted on the use of proper, given names. Had Daddy still been alive she probably would still be very much an Elizabeth.

Claire had been referred by her GP following a biopsy on a suspected melanoma. An operation was scheduled, and she'd met with her to go through the options for her subsequent treatment. It had helped that the melanoma had proved malignant. It was real enough. It was the treatment that followed; the months of chemo for the non-existent secondary that gave her control over Claire. She'd wanted to see how she'd cope, not knowing what was going to happen next; to lose control and find her life on hold, just as she had, when she'd been forced to live an unpredictable and depleted existence. Claire McBride may not have recognised her and forgotten what she'd done, but she hadn't. She'd had to live with the repercussions.

No amount of being clever or popular would help Claire. Disease, like old age, was a great leveller. Cancer was indiscriminate, it wouldn't spare the successful or the gifted. The wealthy couldn't buy their way out and being a smart lawyer like Claire McBride couldn't beat it either.

She'd spent hours talking through her progression. She'd even referred her to a therapist, taking pleasure in the fact she'd needed one. It had all been very rewarding, taking Claire down and becoming central to her life. She'd been so pleased with the way their relationship had developed she'd given Claire a present too; a short period of remission and had imagined they might even be able to develop a relationship beyond that of doctor and patient, making Claire's final goodbye even more poignant, but things had not turned out as planned. Once she'd got the all-clear Claire had soon forgotten everything she had done for her. She didn't even send her a Christmas card. So now phase two had to come into play.

She'd prescribed oral morphine to be taken for the pain. The usual progress of the disease necessitated pain relief but as Claire would feel no pain because she wasn't ill, it was necessary to create a dependency; the morphine addiction Issy planned for her. She wanted Claire to fade away; drift into soporific oblivion. She wanted to replace the woman she was, with a sleep-walking zombie, numb with medication. By the end she'd be nothing. But, two weeks after Claire was supposed to have begun the medication, she'd met her, by chance, in the local supermarket looking perfectly fine.

She'd walked up behind her and tapped her on the shoulder.

'Oh hi,' Claire breezed, tossing her curls so they flicked Issy in the face. 'Sorry, didn't see you there.' She was dressed to the nines; choosing a bottle of wine. 'Must dash I just popped in for a bottle to take to a friend's party,' she beamed.

'You really shouldn't be drinking you know, not with your medication,' she'd reprimanded, a hot flush of irritation blotching her neck. She'd felt matronly and frumpy, standing next to Claire in her jeans and strappy top.

'Oh, I'm not taking the medication. I don't see the point until it's necessary.'

The ground began to fall away beneath Issy.

'But you must take it,' she'd stuttered, 'you must start gradually. You shouldn't wait until the pain is intense, because the effectiveness of the morphine relies upon building your tolerance so eventually, we'll be able to predict the perfect dosage.'

She'd watched with growing annoyance as Claire's eyes glazed over.

'Maybe we can talk about this some other time when I'm not in such a rush,' she said unconvincingly before turning her back and walking away.

Issy had been incensed. She wanted to bellow down the aisle after her; *You fucking come back here ... I'm the doctor; you listen to me!*

Instead, she'd run from the supermarket, abandoning her trolley in the frozen food aisle.

She couldn't sleep at all that night and the next morning she'd made a point of ringing Claire to reiterate the advice she'd given her the evening before.

Claire sounded sleepy when she answered the phone and for one moment Issy's heart leapt, thinking she had been listening after all and had taken her meds.

'It's me; Issy.'

'Hi, sorry ... I had a bit of a heavy night last night, I had a few too many and didn't get to bed until three in the morning.'

'You do need to do as you're told or I'll have to revise the medication so it's administered another way ... for your good.'

'Okay ... but I feel so well?'

There was something about her tone Issy didn't like one bit. It smacked of *I hear what you're saying but I don't give a damn.*

She needed to keep closer tabs on the situation; to nip this defiance in the bud.

She'd follow Claire. The more she knew about her life, the easier it would be to rip it from her.

EIGHT

CLAIRE

Tuesday arrives and armed with Donoghue's will, I leave the office at lunchtime. I don't know why but passing the bakery in the high street I get the overwhelming urge to stop and buy Maureen the largest sickliest cake I can find; all cream and hundreds and thousands. She deserves a treat. It'll be one in the eye for the selfish old biddy.

The witnesses are in the living room and I guess from their bemused faces, they've never witnessed an official document or been invited into their crotchety neighbour's house before.

I'm ushered into the kitchen by Maureen.

'My glasses,' orders Donoghue, pointing to a handbag resting on top of the tired-looking units.

Maureen rummages about and retrieves a pair of spectacles which she wipes with a tea towel before kneeling beside her aunt and gently manoeuvring them so they rest comfortably on the bridge of her nose.

'There you are, is that okay, they were a bit grubby but I gave them a wipe for you.'

'Yes …yes, now get out of my face and go next door with the others.'

I shudder as I hand Donoghue the will, watching her examine it word by word, mouthing each syllable until she's happy her perverse wishes are reflected in the document.

When she's finished, I invite the witnesses in. Maureen remains in the other room, getting ready for her Tuesday afternoon jaunt, then when the formalities are over leaves with the neighbours. I tell her I'll not be long and will close the door behind me once I've tidied up my paperwork. Picking up my briefcase, I lift out the striped cake box, placing it on the shelf out of Donoghue's reach.

It's petty I know but then who was even pettier than her?

'I nearly forgot, this is just a little something for Maureen, a thank you for all her help in arranging the witnesses.'

'What is it?' the woman asks, her voice filled with childish peeve.

'Just a cake, with cream and chocolate and bits, nothing much.'

'She can't eat cake, she's dieting, to get rid of that fat backside of hers.'

'I didn't know, what a shame, never mind I'll throw it in the bin.'

'No, don't do that,' the old woman squeals. 'That would be a waste and waste is a sin.'

'Okay, then I'll leave it here for Maureen, she can always restart her diet tomorrow, she deserves a treat don't you think?

The woman said nothing.

'Goodbye Miss Donoghue, it's been lovely meeting you,' I lie, wanting desperately to add; *and by the way, you know the will you just signed? I'm altering it, so Maureen gets the lot.*

There is so much more I want to say to her; about how she's treated Maureen and how she made my young life a misery but I don't. It would spoil everything if the woman knew who I was and how I planned to unravel her poisonous legacy. No, I'm playing the long game.

Back at the office, I'll change the pages of the will and imagine the old woman spinning in her grave. I might not live to see the fruit of my labours but I know looking at the decrepit creature in front of me, it will come soon enough.

'I'll see myself out,' I say as I close the door and walk down the path to my car. I feel a deep sense of satisfaction, a comforting warmth like a cup of soup on a winter's day.

I wonder if Maureen will be pleased with the provision Auntie Jane has made for her and book a trip to Machu Pichu. Then again maybe she'll be so affected by the loss of her captor, money will provide no solace at all. Maybe it was Stockholm Syndrome all along?

NINE

ISSY

Issy had been following Claire for almost two weeks and still found it impossible to tell if she was taking her medication. When she telephoned her, (every day since the supermarket incident) she said she was, but given the excessive dose she'd prescribed, she'd anticipated incapacitation sooner. She was still working, even if only mornings, suggesting she wasn't taking the morphine in the prescribed dose, if at all.

She'd got into the habit of getting up early to park at the end of Claire's drive just to check if she was heading for work, which she did most days other than when she went to a spa at a local hotel, emerging with wet hair carrying a kit bag. Issy would sometimes ring and ask to speak to her to check she'd gone home at lunchtime or, if she was in the vicinity, drive past at one o'clock to see if she was still at the office.

That day, she arrived as Claire was leaving the carpark and followed her, expecting her to drive home. Instead, she took a left-hand turn at the roundabout and pulled up sharply outside a local bakery.

Issy hovered outside until minutes later Claire emerged swinging a small candy-striped cake box tied with a ribbon. It was galling to see the spring in her step. She followed her in the car to a terraced house a few streets away and, parking at a safe distance, watched her walk up the path and knock on the door. She caught a glimpse of the middle-aged woman who let her in and for a moment thought she recognised her but couldn't quite place her. Another patient maybe? The last thing she wanted was Claire comparing notes with anyone. She dismissed the idea. No, she'd remember a patient and most of the relatives who hung around like bad smells with them at the hospital.

Annoyed Claire was still carrying on as if nothing was wrong with her, she decided to leave and give her a home visit over the next few days. She'd take morphine with her and give it to her by injection. When Claire dropped off to sleep, as she knew she would when the drug took effect, she'd be able to check the house and see exactly what medication she'd taken over the previous weeks. It would be a bind, but she'd have to do this for several days until she was happy, Claire was hooked. Her patient needed to start to rely on the drug and in turn, on her.

She was just about to drive off when she spotted three people leaving the house, two women and a man. The man and one of the women veered left into the next-door drive. The third, the woman who'd opened the door to Claire, carried on walking along the pavement towards Issy's car. What on earth was Claire doing there? Was it some sort of club, another group Miss Popularity had joined instead of doing what she was told?

Was it a party? she wondered; that would explain the cake. Whose; no one she knew obviously. She hadn't been invited to a party for a very long time. Party invites only came when you had friends. Who was important enough for Claire to find time to party with when she was dying? She'd been watching her and the only friend she had much to do with was Sarah. Issy knew her from school. She was keeping an eye on her too. She knew where she lived.

Issy was still running through a mental list of candidates when Claire emerged, got in her car and drove away.

She would normally have followed but couldn't bring herself to. She had to know; was this someone she should worry about, someone who might interfere with her plans?

She couldn't shake the feeling Claire was up to something.

She made her way up the path towards the house turning over in her mind what she'd say when the front door opened. She could always pretend she worked with Claire and had been told to meet her there. She could apologise for being held up in traffic and be sorry to have missed her.

She knocked. No one came. She waited, then knocked again,

louder this time. Still nothing. She was about to walk away, annoyed she'd wasted her time when she heard a voice from behind the door.

'Alright, alright. I'm coming. No need to bang the door down.'

The voice had a cracked, reedy quality and Issy wondered if it was one of Claire's mother's friends? The door opened and Issy's mind went blank as her words caught in the back of her throat.

Luckily the old woman barrelled in before she could say anything.

'Are you from the council, to assess my Attendance Allowance?'

Issy hesitated then, using every effort to compose herself. 'Yes … yes I am.'

'Well about time. We filled the forms in months ago. My niece has been on to you lot to come for weeks. Now when you do, she's out. If you'd taken the trouble to phone first she would have been here.'

Issy prickled with annoyance at the attack, even though it wasn't meant for her. She didn't like criticism, least of all from decrepit invalids looking for handouts. She could always turn-tail but then she'd never know why Claire had been visiting this obnoxious old harridan?

'Where's your badge thing? I don't let anyone in, you know. Just because I'm old it doesn't mean I'm stupid.'

Issy had her hospital pass in her bag. It looked official enough but she'd have to bank on the woman not looking too carefully. She flashed it, before slipping it back into her pocket.

'Not so fast. I didn't get to see the photo. Show me again?'

Issy lifted the badge from her pocket and held it up again.

Magnified bush-baby eyes squinted out from behind thick bi-focals as a skeletal finger reached to grab it.

Issy snatched it away.

'Look if you're worried, I'll rearrange the appointment but you'll go to the back of the list I'm afraid.'

'No, no it'll do,' Donoghue said grudgingly, 'come in and mind you shut the door properly behind you, you're letting a draught in. I'm not made of money.'

The woman turned, motioning her to follow. As she snailed along the hall towards the kitchen, Issy had a feeling she was making a meal of it, to demonstrate her limited mobility. She'd seen malingerers like her before, she couldn't fool her.

Entering the dismal kitchen, Issy spotted a low stool propped against the units. On the worktop rested the cake box she'd seen Claire carrying. A huge creamy chocolatey cake sat on a plate next to it untouched.

'That looks nice.'

'It's mine,' nipped the woman, snatching the plate and sitting at the table.

'It looks very fancy. Is it for a special occasion?'

'You could say that; I made my will today. It was a gift from my solicitor.'

'Was it indeed? That was very kind of her.'

'Not really, that lot make more than enough money putting a few words on a bit of paper.'

'Nevertheless, it was good of her to do a home visit. Not many go to the trouble these days. Has she been your solicitor long?'

'How do you know it was a she?'

Damn, Issy thought, I didn't see that coming, the old biddy is as sharp as a tack.

'I thought I saw an official-looking woman in a suit leaving just as I was arriving and I just assumed that was her when you said. What's she called, your solicitor? I've got an elderly relative who needs to make a will but he's housebound too.'

Donoghue shot her a glance, 'I'm not housebound. What gave you that idea? I'm very lively for my age.'

'Oh, are you. It was just with you applying for Attendance Allowance and the obvious difficulty you had walking back from the door, I thought …?'

Worried she might not get her money, Donoghue backtracked.

'I meant, I try to get out when I can. My niece helps me and I can just about manage with a stick and the use of a wheelchair lent to me by my church. I do my best but my eyesight is not too good. It's been affected by my diabetes.'

'Diabetes? Should you be eating cake if you've got diabetes?'

Typical, thought Issy. Another drain on the NHS. Diabetic; dependent on medication, eating sugary foods she shouldn't and then, when her insulin levels are all over the place or she goes into a coma, she'll expect people like her to put her right and afterwards it'll be, 'I can't think how that happened, I'm so careful what I eat and test my levels every day.'

Liars … liars the lot of them.

The old lady sucked at her lips before responding. Issy could practically see the cogs spinning.

'I said it was a present for me. I didn't say I was going to eat it. I'll give it to my niece Maureen. She's the one who'll get the Attendance Allowance too. She's an angel.'

A sickly gummy grin spread across the woman's face that made Issy want to throw up.

'Where's your niece today Mrs …?'

'It's Miss … Miss Donoghue. She's gone to help at a charity shop. As I said Maureen's an angel.'

Issy's heart began to thump so much it hurt as she felt the sweat gather in the creases of her neck; the name buzzing in her ears like the detonator on a time bomb.

Why hadn't she recognised the woman as soon as she'd opened the door? It was obvious now as she imagined her younger and better looking without the beer bottle glasses and the stooping gate, and the younger woman she'd seen leaving the house earlier was her washed-out niece; the one Donoghue had trailed around the school like a beaten dog.

Why was Claire visiting Miss Donoghue? Issy didn't believe the story about making a will for a second. Lawyers, like doctors, didn't routinely do home visits, especially senior lawyers with a full caseload. No, Claire must have stayed in touch with the teacher over the years and to do that she must have a bond with her. It had never crossed her mind that Claire and Donoghue had acted together all those years before but now, she realised it was the only explanation.

'Well, Miss Donoghue. I think I have all I need. I'm more than satisfied you should get help. I'll put in my report and you should hear in a couple of weeks.'

A self-satisfied smirk buckled the old lady's lips.

Issy gritted her teeth. 'I tell you what, why don't you have a slice of that lovely cake to celebrate. A tiny bit can't hurt surely? I feel that the council has taken so long with your claim, you deserve a bit of spoiling. I won't tell if you don't.'

'Well, I wouldn't usually, but if you think it would be alright?'

'I won't watch. It'll be like it never happened. I'll just wash up these cups for you, then I'll be off,' Issy cajoled, as she moved towards the sink and carefully pulled on the rubber gloves draped over the taps.

By the time she'd run the water and squirted the Fairy Liquid into the bowl, Donoghue was scoffing the cake, cream oozing from the corners of her wrinkled mouth.

Issy left the sink and walked behind her to get into position.

Donoghue's eyes never left the gooey confection.

Waiting until the woman's mouth was full, Issy swiftly clamped one hand over her sticky lips, holding her nose with the other as spindly fingers clawed at the suffocating soap-slicked gloves.

'Remember me, Elizabeth Major?' Issy whispered in her ear above the squeak, squeak of wet rubber. 'If you and Claire McBride, or should I say Penrose, think you can get the better of me, think again.'

For one moment, there was a flicker of recognition, then the old woman's button eyes rolled back into her head and she slumped onto the table.

Issy's mind whirred with the jingle to an old washing-up liquid advert from her childhood where the mother walks from the sink and lovingly daubs some soap suds on her child's nose; "For hands that do dishes can feel soft as your face …"

She was jolted back to reality with a sharp rat-tat-tat at the door.

She froze, hands clammy in the pink rubber gloves, hanging like two dead lobsters at her sides. What if it was someone Donoghue was expecting; what if Claire had forgotten something?

Adrenaline pumping, she walked to the sink, quickly swilling the gloves in the soapy water before returning them to their spot over the taps. The knocking sounded again, making her jump. Whoever it was, wasn't going away. She reprimanded herself for her panic, desperately trying to regain control. She thought of Daddy.

'Pull yourself together, Elizabeth.'

Tucking in her blouse, she adjusted her skirt and jacket. Whoever it was, they were less likely to want to come in if they thought they were intruding on official business? She had to look the part.

Licking paper-dry lips, she made her way down the hall towards the silhouette pressed behind the frosted glass and opened the door. She recognised the woman as the neighbour she'd seen leaving the house earlier.

'Can I help you?' Issy asked officiously; used to getting the upper hand through her demeanour alone.

'Oh, I'm so sorry. I hope I'm not intruding, I'm Miss Donoghue's neighbour, Mrs Thompson. I was around earlier and left my cardigan on the chair in the kitchen and … you are?' She asked, craning her neck to look around the stranger keeping her on the threshold.

Issy was determined to proffer nothing unless she had to.

'If you wait here, I'll get the cardigan for you,' she smiled, moving to shut the door.

Before she could, the woman was inside.

'Oh, don't trouble yourself, I know exactly where it is,' she said pushing past like a determined shopper at the January sales.

Issy had to think quickly. She blocked the woman's way, placing one hand against the wall so she couldn't pass.

'I'm from the council. I'm here going through some paperwork with Miss Donoghue about possible disability benefits and as I'm sure you are aware; she is a very private person.'

She raised her eyebrows in a conspiratorial gesture of mock exasperation, met with approval.

'Oh … yes of course,' the neighbour replied in a semi-whisper; 'I'll just wait here. It's a mint green M&S angora mix.'

Issy strolled back along the hall, glancing over her shoulder at the woman to check she wasn't following. She walked into the kitchen, grabbing the hideous pastel green cardigan from the back of the chair. She spoke loudly, so the woman outside could hear.

'It's only Mrs Thompson, Miss Donoghue. She forgot her cardigan. I'll just give it to her and I'll be right back.'

She waited a few seconds before returning, closing the door behind her. To her relief, the woman was now hovering near the porch, examining the ornaments on the shelf above the radiator as if assessing them for *Cash in the Attic*.

'There you are,' Issy said handing over the cardigan. 'What a lovely colour.'

Ushering the woman out she glanced at her watch. She'd wasted precious time and now needed to get out of there.

Returning to the kitchen she took one last look at Donoghue, head flopped to the side, chin covered in hundreds and thousands and was grateful she'd always preferred fruit cake.

TEN

Her hands felt shaky on the steering wheel. It had been a different kind of murder from the sort she was used to; too messy for her liking but satisfying nonetheless and she was pleased she'd saved the public purse some expense in the bargain. She'd never felt a rush like it; not from her other killings. Maybe it was because of the risk? Could it be that after all these years she'd become bored with her *modus operandi* or maybe this was something else. Maybe this was all about Claire? She was so close now to ending this thing. She had Claire in her sights but to have bagged that hideous witch in the bargain was beyond all her expectations. She could still smell the rubber gloves and the woman's ancient biscuit breath. She imagined all the laughs she and Claire had enjoyed at her expense over the years. Well, she had the upper hand now. She was the one plotting Claire's death and if the old lady wanted in on the deal, it was fine by her.

An image returned of the woman back in her teaching days and Claire in her uniform. Claire Penrose was a scholarship girl.

It had always seemed unfair to Issy to expect girls like her, fresh from their council houses to fit in. On open days their overweight mothers shuffled around, trying to look smart in their catalogue clothes and cheap shoes; smelling poor. Back then she left them to it. She could afford to be generous; she'd never have to be one of them or so she thought.

She'd always felt, as Mummy did, they were to be tolerated but it wouldn't do to make friends with them. You couldn't invite them home after school because they'd be bound to feel uncomfortable. That, Mummy said, would be unkind. So, she'd stuck to her prep-school group.

If she were truthful, she might never have been interested in Claire if not for the fact she was fatherless. This, Issy remembered, was established on day one of senior school when Donoghue told everyone in the class, Claire was illegitimate.

It had shocked her. She couldn't imagine how anyone could manage without a father. Daddy meant the whole world to her. He was her rock, her mentor; her champion.

She'd become increasingly fascinated by Claire and had made it her business to go out of her way to engage with her in one way or another.

It hadn't been easy because her friend Sarah was always hanging around, but eventually, she'd managed to get Claire to herself in drama club.

She was never really interested in acting, which was for vain shallow types with no glamour in their lives, but volunteered to help with the lighting. She took pleasure in the fact she could ruin the whole thing if she had a mind to; lay waste to hours of rehearsal with one flick of a switch on the big night. The thought always excited her and she had on occasion had to stop herself doing just that.

Claire was always picked to act.

She managed to speak to her sometimes when there was a break in rehearsals. She'd sit beside her watching her drink her drama club squash and felt her fascination turn to obsession. She tried out for the choir and attended after school netball practice just to be near her and they got on well, all things considered until the day her whole world fell apart and she realised Claire was to blame.

It was just like any other day. She'd gone to maths, taken by Donoghue, that sad scrawny spinster Daddy referred to as 'old vinegar knickers.'

She'd noticed her friends giggling as she walked into class; whispering behind their hands. They stopped when they saw her. Her fifteenth birthday was on the horizon and she guessed they'd been plotting some surprise for her. She was having a big party with a professional entertainer so she'd anticipated they'd be equally generous. She'd given an invitation to Claire, but when she told Mummy she'd said Claire couldn't come. She'd told her to make some excuse but to be clear it was not negotiable. When she'd approached Claire to tell her earlier that day, she'd been with Sarah in the changing rooms huddled over a magazine. She'd nervously explained Mummy had told the catering staff there were a certain number of guests and unfortunately, she'd not told her about inviting her. She'd said she was very sorry, but it was too late to do anything about it. She'd expected Claire to be as disappointed as she was. Instead, she said it was fine, that she'd forgotten all about it and was doing something else that day and wouldn't have been able to come anyway.

She'd thought she was the best person in the world for putting on such a brave face when she must have been devastated to miss her closest friend's party.

As she'd waited to be seated, she'd noticed Claire staring at her as if she was trying to see something, craning her neck and leaning backwards. She'd hadn't known why but found out later, when the class ended, and she'd been called back by Donoghue.

The woman had prowled around her like a cat for what seemed an eternity then suddenly stopped, and pushing her face close had said,

'He who breathes out lies will perish.'

Those were her exact words; she'd remember them forever.

She'd not been able to fathom what on earth the woman meant; what small fib she'd told or whether someone had wrongly accused her of cheating. The teacher picked up on her confusion and with one hand, deftly tugging at her jumper removed a square of lined paper with the word LIAR written upon it in bold red letters.

She'd left the room and walked to her next lesson in a dream wondering how Claire could have done this to her after all the kindness she'd shown her. It was just a party; a stupid, stupid party.

It had been her last day at the school; the end of everything she loved and all of it was Claire's fault. She had found out about Daddy somehow, then let the whole world know.

Later that afternoon she'd been called to the head's office. Mummy sat bolt upright in the chair opposite and she could see she'd been crying. She was told, that unfortunately next term she wouldn't be able to pay her school fees and, in the circumstances, it had been decided it would be best for her to leave. There were only a few weeks left until the end of term and as the exams were over and her mother could do with her help at home, she wouldn't have to return after that day.

It was the beginning of the end.

Mummy admitted Daddy hadn't been working abroad but was detained pending an investigation into alleged misuse of client money and fraud.

Daddy, though innocent, was convicted and sent to jail for a term of five years. They had to sell the house because the bills couldn't be paid and had to file for bankruptcy.

She and Mummy took a grotty flat in Gloucester near to the prison and Mummy paid the rent from a small inheritance from an elderly aunt. Later she'd contributed, with a weekend job in the local newsagents.

Day in day out, she'd attended the grotty comprehensive school, concentrating on getting the grades to get her to university to study medicine.

Daddy hoped to serve three years and once released would clear his name but he died of a massive coronary eighteen months into his sentence. No one came to the funeral.

Her husband's death left Mummy shell-shocked. Life hadn't prepared her for reduced circumstances and she found it impossible to budget. So, she'd had to take control of the money. In the sixth form, she'd worked an extra job as a waitress in the pub around the corner. Every night she came home smelling of chip fat and onions and had to wash her hair in the kitchen sink with boiled water from the kettle so as not to run the immersion heater.

Mummy became increasingly dependent on the mix of antidepressants and sleeping pills prescribed by her GP, staying in her dressing gown all day until she got home from college. When awake, she spent her time looking through old photo albums full of pictures of her other self, standing in the driveway of a beautiful house in her fur coat. Issy remembered how she couldn't bear to look at the photographs and increasingly couldn't bear to look at Mummy.

When she won her place at Guy's to read medicine, she moved them to London. The flat was even smaller and they'd had to share a bedroom. Her studies were too demanding for her to work and she'd gone to local charity shops to furnish the place. She'd done her best to make it homely, but it never was, with its mismatched furnishings and peeling paintwork. Mummy didn't seem to notice, so long as she had her pills and when she'd graduated with first-class honours she didn't attend. In the end, she'd decided it would be better for everyone if Mummy joined Daddy and one night, she crushed her tablets into her cocoa giving it to her before she left for dinner with David at Quagalino's.

The autopsy recorded Mummy had taken her own life. She had a history of depression and the means to end it all sat in her medicine cabinet. She'd closed the door on the council flat and never looked back.

She thought about Mummy occasionally but saw no necessity in remembering her as she was in the end, a pitiful, drug-addicted albatross around her neck. Nor did she think about her last moments. She'd had no compunction about killing her because she'd done what she knew was best for everyone concerned and for the same reason she felt no compunction about any of her killings. She certainly didn't feel guilty about killing the old woman. She, like Claire McBride, had it coming. She just wished she'd sought her out and done it sooner now she knew they'd been in cahoots all along.

ELEVEN
CLAIRE

At about five that evening I get a call from my secretary, Jan.

'Hi, Claire, sorry to bother you but someone called Maureen telephoned about a Miss Donoghue. She said you went to her house this afternoon for a will signing. I told her I couldn't find any record of a will under that name and you don't work afternoons or do home visits. She was in a bit of a state so perhaps she's confused and it was someone from another firm but I thought I'd better check with you?'

My ears are ringing as my tongue thickens in my mouth. I can't deny it; I'm bound to be found out.

'Yes, she's right. Jane Donoghue's an old friend of my mum's. She's one of the ladies I gave a talk to at the WI. As it was pro-bono anyway and I was seeing her on my own time, I didn't bother with all the paperwork. Sorry, I forgot to tell you.'

There was an uncomfortable silence on the other end of the phone.

'Jan, are you still there?'

'Yes, yes it's just if that's the case I've got some bad news for you. I'm afraid your mum's friend is dead.'

'What ... that's impossible ... I mean she was fine when I left her?' My knees buckle.

'Apparently, when her niece got home from the charity shop where she helps out, her aunt was slumped on the kitchen table. The paramedics were called but it was too late and this is the horrible bit, she'd choked on a slice of cake!'

No way, the cake?

'Oh my god,' I gulp.

'I know, imagine it. What a way to go. What's more her niece, who by the way, took ages to get off the phone, had no idea how it got there? She hadn't bought it because she was dieting and her aunt wasn't allowed cakes. She was diabetic. There's a lesson to follow doctor's orders if ever there was one.'

I don't know what to say. I'm having a hard time processing all this.

'Jan, I really ought to call Mum to break the bad news. Thanks again for letting me know.'

'Of course ... such a shock for your poor mum.'

'I'll catch up with you at work tomorrow morning ... thanks again.'

I put the phone down.

My mind's racing. I have to admit I left the cake half-hoping Maureen would give in to the old woman's complaints and give the greedy bitch a bit in a bid to inch her nearer to death, but I hadn't thought for one moment it would kill her on the very day she'd signed her will. That was bound to raise questions and was the last thing I needed.

I debated whether to ring Maureen and fish for more information. Would it look suspicious, would I do that if this was just another client? Then again, I couldn't ignore the cake. Why did I buy the stupid cake? I put it on the shelf, how the hell did she reach it? Maureen must have given it to her. I had to ring to find out.

The phone was answered by a tearful Maureen who relayed the whole story again.

'Maureen,' I took the deepest breath I could as if it would help blow out the truth, 'it was me who left the cake there. I put it on the shelf beside the biscuit barrel. I told your aunt it was for you and I didn't think for one moment she'd reach it let alone eat it because of her diabetes.'

Maureen began to sob. 'You bought a cake for me?'

She sounded pitifully grateful.

'Yes, for being so helpful with the witnesses and everything, I thought you deserved a treat.'

'That was so nice of you to think of me.' Maureen began to cry again then, almost as an afterthought, 'You mustn't blame yourself.

She must have climbed on the stool to get it. She's done it before. It was a nasty accident, that's all. You weren't to know auntie would eat it, no one can blame you.'

She was right. No one could blame me. I wasn't there when it happened and as far as the will was concerned, I've meticulously covered my tracks.

***

The next day the police telephone for some background because they've been told I was the last person to see the woman alive. I tell them Maureen is the beneficiary of the will but stress as far as I'm aware she didn't know the contents.

I freely admit to buying the cake and leaving it on the shelf as a thank you for Maureen and explain how mortified I am the old lady, who I understood to be a diabetic, helped herself with such tragic consequences.

It's the final question that surprises me.

'Thanks for putting us in the picture. The coroner may need a statement but we probably won't need to speak to you again unless you can cast some light on the identity of the visitor who came after you.'

'I'm sorry, a visitor?'

'The lady from the council who came to assess Miss Donoghue, I was wondering if she arrived while you were there?'

'No … no she didn't. She must have arrived after I'd gone.'

'Ah well, it was a bit of a long shot but at least we have a timeline now from what you've told us and the information from Mrs Thompson who met the woman when she came back to collect her cardigan. We were hoping for a name that's all because the council have no record of sending anyone. Then again you know what they're like, they've probably mixed up the records or something.'

The relief is overwhelming. I wasn't the last person to see Donoghue alive. That had been someone else's pleasure.

TWELVE

I arrange to collect Mum from the home and take her on an outing the following weekend. I need to see her. Donoghue is dead but Mum is very much alive and deserves to escape, if only for a couple of hours. She can be difficult to manage on her own, so I phone Sarah to ask if I can borrow her girls for the afternoon. If I need to take Mum to the loo, or if she became anxious and I have to pack up in a hurry, they can carry the picnic and the rest of the beach stuff. Sarah is glad to oblige.

'That would be great. I'm stacked with work and could do with an afternoon without distractions to complete a well overdue job. Lerryn's out with friends but Chloe would love to come.'

I make a proper picnic; sandwiches, cheese straws, scotch eggs, a flask of tea and a smoothie for eight-year-old Chloe. I put the whole lot into the back of the car with a blanket and a lightweight metal-framed deck chair for Mum to sit on.

Chloe chatters about her new guinea pig, Mr Grunt, who Mummy hasn't let her bring with her. As we descend the hill into the seaside town she lifts in her seat, craning forward.

'I see the sea and the sea sees me,' she sings.

I glance in the rear-view mirror, pleased I thought to bring her.

Walking through the carpark, we pass two old boys sitting on a bench in the spring sunshine, engrossed in the pages of the *Racing Times*.

I punch in the number on the keypad. I'm glad the place is secure but it doesn't make the whole palaver any less tedious. I'm a regular but it makes no difference, I still have to sign the visitor's book.

I'd told the home in advance I'd be taking Mum out. 'Not far, just to the beach for a picnic,' I'd said brightly.

'Just as long as you're careful what you give her to eat. We don't want to ruin her appetite for her evening meal, do we?' the curt voice spiked on the other end of the phone.

Don't we? I thought, bristling, the way I always do when faced with petty power-play dressed up as concern. Nurse Ratchet was clearly alive and kicking, working in a care home near me.

'I perfectly understand,' I said, thinking all the time; she's my mum and she'll have two cheeseburgers and a bloody knickerbocker glory if she fancies it.

Activities are going on in the communal areas on either side of the corridor. I spot a couple of easels set up for an art session and in one corner a trio of old dears playing Scrabble. I'm glad, I hate those places where the residents are lined up around the walls like ducks for shooting at a funfair. I pay extra for Mum to have a large room with a sea view. She has her own TV and the place is impeccably clean; no whiffs of boiled veg and pee wafting through the corridors.

Mum's already dressed.

'Hello dear,' she says, looking up as we walk in.

I've noticed she increasingly uses 'dear' as a catch-all address for anyone who comes to see her, so she doesn't have to struggle for a name.

'Hello, Mum,' I say bending to kiss her. Her cheek feels as powdery as a butterfly's wings against mine; 'I've come to take you down to the beach for a picnic. I brought Chloe along to help.'

Gleeful eyes fix on the little girl. I look out of the window at the weather. It's a fine spring day, but the wind could turn. Weather never settles on the coast like it does inland.

'Come on then, let's get a move on so we can catch the sun.'

Mum stands up, sprightly as ever except for the bit of arthritis in her shoulder that means I have to help her with her coat. We make our way back to the entrance, sign out and walk past the two old men still sitting where we left them.

'Afternoon Eileen, looking smashing today my love,' one croaks, creasing a rheumy eye into a dramatic *Carry On* wink.

'I'm going out with my daughter and Chloe here, for a picnic. Have I introduced you to my Claire; she's a lawyer?'

The man wobbles to his feet and holds out an age-spotted hand. I hate it when Mum pulls the lawyer daughter card. It always feels as if I'm expected to slip on a curly white wig and begin a cross-examination.

I hold out my hand. 'Very nice to meet you … I'm sorry, I didn't catch your name?'

Mum interjects. 'Frank, this is Frank. He's my dance partner when we have sixties night.'

Frank laughs, struggling to keep his clickety false teeth within the confines of his mouth. 'We show the rest of 'em don't us Eileen?'

I have a vision of the couple strutting to Mick or Otis, wiggling arthritic hips, twisting the night away; well at least until Matron calls time at eight-thirty.

'We've got another one next Wednesday, haven't we Frank?' smiles Mum.

The old boy hesitates, then grins like a naughty schoolboy caught snogging behind the bike sheds. 'It's a date.'

He swaps my hand for Mum's and with a gallant little bow plants a kiss on it.

Chloe giggles and Mum blushes as she demurely withdraws her hand and walks away, a smug smile playing across her lips as if to say; *Still got it.*

Not only has she remembered where we're going and Chloe's name, but she also has a date the following Wednesday. It's official, my mother has a better social life than me. I feel a swell of affection for her but my heart aches for the woman I've lost. I hate to think what it must feel like to be plugged in and out of reality and can't bear the thought of her waking when I'm gone, alone and afraid, not knowing where she is or why she's been abandoned there.

Carrying the picnic, we walk along the sandy path to the beach.

'Can I take my shoes off?' Mum asks.

'Of course, you can. We'll need to roll your trousers up so you don't get them wet.' A pale sandy carpet spreads out in front of us. Mum stops dead in her tracks, inhales and begins to laugh; loud guttural chortles. She drops the bag she's carrying and, before I can stop her, plonks herself down on the sand, tugs off her shoes and races off, skipping and whooping towards the sea.

'Mum! … Stop!'

I push the flask I'm carrying into Chloe's arms, drop the deck chair and chase after her, afraid she'll run into the freezing water.

She stops just short of the water's edge, lifts her arms and spins around, head back, laughing. Breathless, I join her. Grabbing me around the waist, she gives me a big bear hug. She places her head on my chest, closes her eyes and whispers,

'Thank you, thank you.'

'Mum, are you alright?' I pant. 'I thought for a moment you were going to go in.'

'Don't be silly, I haven't got a bathing costume and it's freezing. It's not had the chance to warm up yet, this early in the season.'

I feel foolish.

'No … no of course not. Look, we'll come back down again but we need to go back now to help Chloe with the stuff.'

Mum shrugs and turns to walk back up the beach, striding out like a five-year-old, pausing now and again to bend and pick up a shell or a piece of Cuttlefish washed up by the tide.

I look around to see if anyone is staring at us, after all, I'd acted like a lunatic, but there was no one. The beach is empty other than for a couple walking a pair of skittish spaniels in the distance.

The beach, backed by dunes, tufted with couch grass and yellow patches of gorse, is an old friend. My mates and I always cycled there in the school holidays once we hit ten or eleven. Armed with a towel, a can of coke and a packet of crisps each, we'd head up to the dunes. We knew it could be dangerous, faded wooden signs sunk into the sand and barbed wire fencing told us as much. Just like virgin snow, the sand could, without warning become unstable and shift, avalanching down to the beach below, burying everything in its wake. Although we liked to tell tall tales of kids buried alive, we generally took no notice of the risks. Like marine gypsies, we'd construct makeshift camps from junk collected from the shoreline; plastic crates to sit on, blue nylon rope to tie it all together.

The sea was good for surfing, but for swimming we preferred

the clear calm water of the tidal pool hewn from the rocks, in the middle of the beach.

Later, as teenagers this beach had been the place where Sarah and I would go to hang out with boys, whose lithe bodies, nut brown with the sun, seemed beautiful now, looking back. We girls would beachcomb for holiday romance, flirting with the lads from Manchester or Liverpool, agreeing to meet them later; knowing we wouldn't.

When the sun went down, us local boys and girls would reunite to light a bonfire, both tribes telling tipsy tall tales of their exploits as we sat cross-legged drinking cider. I remember I had my first kiss on this beach, with a boy called Ross Trenear. Thinking back, he looked like a young Greek god; sun-bleached curls skimming his neck. I remember the first electric charge of teenage sexuality, intensified because my bikinied body allowed me to feel his warm flesh; skin on skin; his soft salty lips as they touched mine.

I'm still friends with Ross. He's a gentle, lovely man in the same way he'd been a gentle, lovely boy, but he's no longer a god: a career in the police force, four kids and two ex-wives had seen to that. I've never asked him what it feels like to live the life of a mere mortal when he'd been a superhero. I wonder if he ever thinks about his glory days or our first kiss.

Chloe is standing where we left her, looking like a refugee waiting to be rescued. I oblige, walking her and Mum to a sheltered corner close to the rocks at the back of the beach.

I lay out the rug and delve into the bag for the sandwiches, wondering why I bothered with the wretched deck chair. Mum has planted herself down on the sand and is already tucking into the cheese straws from the picnic box.

'I'm parched,' she smiles, holding up the flask.

I pull out the salad dressing bottle filled with milk and pour a splash along with the tea, into the lid of the flask for her.

'We lost a dog here once,' she says, 'my sister's dog Netty; in the dunes.' She pauses to sip her tea. 'She went down a rabbit hole.'

'What, right down the hole?' Chloe asks, wide-eyed. 'I'm glad I didn't bring Mr Grunt.'

Mum shivers. 'Yes, right down. We called and called all afternoon; stayed until it got dark then Dad came back with a torch but he didn't find her. My sister cried and cried for Netty. She kept coming back day after day, but we never saw her again. Dad said she'd probably got stuck down the tunnel and couldn't turn around even though she could hear us calling. He said she'd probably just given up in the end.'

I watch her face as she vividly re-lives the loss of the dog as if it were yesterday and wonder if she'll remember our picnic and her run to the sea tomorrow, or whether tomorrow will be the day she finally ventures down the rabbit hole never to turn around, unable to come back.

'Can I go down to the rock pools, Auntie Claire?'

'Yes, yes of course you can, but be careful, the tide's only just gone out and the rocks will be slippery.'

'I know, I'll be okay. I want to look for anemones. I like anemones, they look like flowers, but they sting and they're coniferous, they eat creatures you know, tiny things in the water. My teacher says.'

'That's right, they are *carnivorous,* I correct. Remember, pretty creatures can be just as dangerous as monsters.'

'Watch out for the Weavers,' says Mum, 'they're the same, but they're masters of disguise. They'll get you, given half the chance.'

'Weavers,' I explain, 'are bony spikey fish that live in the rock pools buried just under the sand. If you stand on one its spines can go into your foot and it's really painful, so be careful. They're well camouflaged.'

'Okay,' chirped Chloe. 'I'll be careful.'

We sit in silence after Chloe leaves. Mum eats a sandwich and we share a KitKat, but Mum's distracted and seems to have drifted somewhere else. Attempts by me at conversation are met with short, monosyllabic responses until she makes a move to get up and says;

'I'd better go and get Claire; she's been down there on the rocks for ages. I need to get her home for her bath. It's a school day tomorrow.'

'It's okay,' I say, touching her arm gently. 'You stay here and finish your tea. I'll get her.'

'If you don't mind,' she replies. 'I am a bit tired. I did a long shift at the hospital last night. Two new babies in one evening, a boy and a girl.'

Leaving her to finish her tea, I walk down to where Chloe is dragging a large piece of driftwood through the wet sand, writing something in giant capital letters. As I get closer, I see she's tried to write my name.

C L I A R

'Well done Chloe but there's an 'E' on the end and the 'A' and the 'I' are back to front, you've put them the wrong way around, the 'A' comes first.'

'Have I?' Chloe says, tilting her head quizzically at the name she's written before dropping the stick and running back up the beach to join Mum.

I lift the discarded stick and begin to scratch away at the letters to start again but find myself crossing through the 'C' leaving the word L I A R in the sand.

I draw a line under it.

As the tide licks away the letters, an image of a piece of paper, LIAR, written in bold red capitals crawls like a crab into my thoughts and a sense of dread washes through me. At first, I can't put a name to the feeling but as I slowly walk up the beach to join the others, I recognise it as shame.

THIRTEEN

The purple clouds bundle in from the sea as we leave the beach. After we've settled Mum, I drive Chloe home to Sarah's house.

Sarah; my refuge; my port in a storm, and let's face it, my life lately has been a regular tsunami.

Since Issy told me I'm terminal I've wavered between anger and despair, never knowing which will gain the upper hand on any given day. The raw, destructive energy of both, drive me forward on a bare-knuckle ride, with little time to take stock. Now Mum's lost to me, all I have to cling to is Sarah's friendship and a box of names.

The rain begins to spit and I turn on the wipers. The motion sends my mind drifting back to something long forgotten until today when I saw the word laid bare in the sand and it flooded back.

Unlike most of Donoghue's victims who evoked a kinship spirit in me, I didn't much like the girl on the receiving end of the incident brought to mind. Elizabeth Major was a snobbish prig. By the time I arrived at the school, she already had her entourage of sycophantic 'mean girls'. They did their level best to make us scholarship students' life a misery. They were privileged, callous types with access to their parent's bank accounts and a free pass to success in their back pockets. However, in the fifth year Elizabeth's stockbroker father was found guilty of embezzling client funds and sent to prison, although it wasn't common knowledge at the time because she told everyone he'd been promoted overseas.

One of the girl's so-called friends got wind of the truth, and just before one of Donoghue's lessons, pinned the word LIAR in bold red capitals on the back of Elizabeth's school jumper.

Having arrived before her, I didn't notice at first but hearing the crawl of whispers knew something was up. All eyes were focused on the girl, who stood oblivious to the charge nailed to her back. The room fell silent as Donoghue slithered her way between the chairs. When she reached Elizabeth, she paused to examine the note for several seconds but made no attempt to remove it or extract the identity of the perpetrator who had put it there.

I knew at the time it was unforgivable for a teacher to allow a child to be publicly ridiculed in such a targeted, cynical way but to my shame, fear of reprisal from the teacher made me party to the girl's humiliation. I'd gone home that evening, locked myself in the bathroom and cried.

I never knew how or when the girl finally became aware, or whether the sign just dropped off and she was none the wiser. Donoghue kept her behind after the lesson so perhaps she dealt with it then? Soon after, Elizabeth left. Chloe's misspelling of my name raked up the memory. I've dealt with plenty of lies and liars since but suppose it's natural I should think about my school days following my recent encounter with Donoghue and more importantly, her death.

The word LIAR crackles and sparks like a broken neon sign in my thoughts and I'm glad when I pull up outside Sarah's house and can finally switch it off.

The heavens open as Chloe and I run up the path and we're drenched when Sarah lets us in.

'Put the kettle on, Ben. I've got two drowned rats on the doorstep who look like they need warming up.'

'I'm not a drowned rat, I'm a drowned guinea pig, I don't like rats,' scowls Chloe.

'Well, Miss Piggy, up the stairs and run a bath. Put your wet clothes in the laundry basket.'

Chloe does as she's told and we walk through to the kitchen, where Ben's pouring hot water into the teapot.

Sarah's lucky with her choice of husband. The opposite of his firebrand wife, he exudes calm. They were always a good fit but once their daughters arrived, they were the complete package.

Their home is welcoming in an artsy, casual way. The terraced cottage has a jumbled, eclectic feel to it; the girl's stick-men pictures pinned to the walls alongside Sarah's watercolours and Ben's architect's blueprints.

Today there's a piece of batik laid out on the kitchen table.

'So, did you get your work done?' I ask running my fingers along the silky fabric as I help Sarah move it to one side. I notice a furtive glance pass between husband and wife and guess they've taken advantage of a few hours alone for some quality time not involving a sewing machine or a drawing board.

'Yeah … thanks, did you have a good time, was Eileen, okay?'

'She was pleased to see Chloe and remembered her name, and … get this, I met her new boyfriend!'

'What?' squealed Sarah.

'She has an admirer, although she's playing it cool; treating him mean to keep him keen,' I laugh.

'There you go; hope for you yet,' Sarah grins.

I change the subject quickly.

'Do you remember a girl at school called Elizabeth Major?'

Sarah looks puzzled. 'You mean that odd girl who used to follow you around like a lost sheep; whatever made you think of her?'

I'd forgotten she'd done that but I remember now for a short time I couldn't get rid of her. Every time I looked around she was there.

'I don't know. It was just the beach, being there with Chloe and remembering us as kids and I got to thinking about school for some reason and thought of her.'

'Well, I can't think why, she wasn't one of our crowd, and she left, didn't she? Wasn't there a scandal; something about her father?'

'Yeah, I think so,' I shrug.

I don't tell Sarah about the word written in the sand, or the memory of the label pinned to the girl's back.

Chloe reappears in her dressing gown.

'Can I go outside and get Mr Grunt to show Claire?'

'Not today, it's getting dark. Show Claire next time she comes when it's not so wet.'

'I've got to get going anyway,' I say. 'Some of us have got real work to do. There's a court bundle sitting on my desk crying out for attention.'

I kiss Chloe on her damp head. 'Thank you for a lovely day

sweetheart, and for helping me look after Auntie Eileen.' Chloe beams at the compliment.

I shout goodbye to Ben and leave the warmth of my friend's happy home, not relishing the thought of driving back to my cold, empty house.

***

The rain is heavy now and I need to concentrate on the road, watching out for large puddles that might send me aquaplaning into oncoming traffic. I don't much care if that's how I go. It would be quick at least; I wouldn't know about it. I wouldn't have to face the prospect of dying alone without a special someone to hold my hand but then I might take others with me and I wouldn't want that.

My isolation is largely down to me if I'm honest.

After I split from Daniel, I went on a few dates with men I'd met through work or had been set up with but I was over-cautious, not wanting to be hurt again. Then two years after the divorce I got diagnosed with melanoma and everything changed. I know my friends would deny treating me differently if I challenged them but nevertheless, they did, whether consciously or not.

Only Sarah continued to distinguish me from my disease and treated me as she always had but as far as the others were concerned, my cancer quickly cut me out of the loop and I'd come to feel like an outsider. I was excluded from their WhatsApp conversations about juicing or drinking green tea. There was no need for me to bother with the latest fad diets, the weight fell off me relentlessly throughout my treatment and detox wasn't an option, when my chemotherapy required me to regularly take a cocktail of drugs that would have made Lindsay Lohan blush.

I put up barriers; turned down invitations to barbeques and Sunday brunches where long prosecco-fuelled afternoons were spent talking about Brexit and Trump. It all seemed so irrelevant. I kept away from them, all except Sarah.

Sarah and I have been friends since the day Donoghue worked her venom and humiliated me in front of the class. I thought the girl next to me a complete geek with her childish bunches and thick glasses but something miraculous happened to change my mind. As Donoghue finished her gratuitous attack and I was feeling at my most desolate, Sarah's hand slid across the desk and she whispered, 'what a bitch.' At that moment I knew I had a friend. We've been inseparable ever since.

Sarah hadn't stayed a geek. At fourteen she'd returned from a summer holiday with her mother's family in the Vendee, having ditched the glasses and with her sun-streaked hair cut into an edgy asymmetric bob. It was as if *Joe le Taxi* had taken a wrong turn and dropped Vanessa Paradis on the wrong side of the Channel. She drove the local boys crazy.

Luckily, whilst we loved the same clothes, the same films, the same music – we never had the same taste in men. I always fancied the good-looking confident ones, like Daniel, with their perfect smiles and well-practiced chat-up lines. Sarah on the other hand fell for the serious, studious boys; the skinny gangly ones with glasses who listened to Nick Cave and read Dostoevsky. I'd watch her zoom in on them at parties, cornering them as they stuttered and blinked their earnest eyes, not believing their luck.

Sarah never really took to Daniel. At first, I thought maybe she worried he'd taken her place but later I came to learn she knew long before I did Daniel was a womaniser and not to be trusted. She'd known this partly because she'd heard about his affairs on the Cornish grapevine, and partly because he'd made a pass at her. I knew the minute she told me, the play for her had been genuine, and it had been the final straw on the night I learnt about Daniel and Louisa's affair.

I'd sat in the car that night four years ago for at least an hour. My phone, on the seat beside me, lighting up intermittently with text messages from Daniel, I couldn't bring myself to read.

Several times I'd tried starting the engine but every time I took the wheel, my hands locked around it and I froze. Angry tears skewed my vision and I had to wait until they stopped. In the end, with nowhere else to go, I stayed at Sarah's and that's when she dropped the bombshell.

I started to think about all the evenings Daniel had been late home, the constant 'Louisa said' conversations and it all pieced together like the plot of a predictable soap. Why had he done this to me ... not once but twice? I hadn't had a clue about the first affair. I had begun to wonder whether the late appointments with patients and the dental conferences in York and Manchester might not be completely innocent. Even then, I hadn't considered anything serious. I thought about nights on the lash with the other delegates.

Then one Wednesday evening he was so late home after a course, I half-jokingly confronted him asking him whether he was 'having an affair or something?' He without pause for thought, admitted he was. She was called Gina and was a dental technician. It had been going on for six months. He'd then spent the next hour telling me how wonderful Gina was whilst I, dumbfounded, tried to come to terms with the gut-wrenching reality my husband had strayed. Worse still, that day I'd done a test and found I was pregnant and was so numbed by his revelation I couldn't bring myself to tell him. When I eventually plucked up the courage rather than see the error of his ways and pledge his commitment to me and our unborn child, he said it was probably best for everyone if I had a termination.

'You have to understand, this could devastate Gina,' he protested.

'Devastate Gina? What about me, don't you think this devastates me?'

'But she's delicate and easily upset and she doesn't ...' he paused, looking at the kitchen floor.

'What? She doesn't what?' I questioned, my voice breaking.

'She doesn't think we still sleep together.'

I wanted to pull my broken heart from my chest and lay it in his lap; wanted to see it there all bloody and beating so he couldn't ignore it.

'Don't worry, Daniel. If I do this, I'll do it alone just like my mum. I just need time to sort out a few things first. You owe me that at least. I didn't get the chance. The following week I miscarried and spent the next couple of months in a daze. I cried all the time; great big salty tears as I sat in the park eating my lunch or woke alone in the dark, in the spare room trying to work out what to do next.

Oblivious to my pain, Daniel behaved like a lovesick teenager. He bought new clothes, changed his hairstyle; became a stranger.

Then, one day he came home after work and told me he and Gina had split up. It all seemed in a day's work for him. Just one of those things.

'Look, Claire, I can't turn the clock back, it happened, now it's over, don't let's go on about it.'

We never spoke of the miscarriage, although I thought about it all the time and strangely the loss put Daniel's affair into perspective, a one-off; a mid-life crisis. I was so relieved, so raw with grief, I carried on as before. Until it happened again.

Daniel's dental practice had been undergoing a revamp. New equipment, new website and an expansion into cosmetic dentistry, teeth whitening and veneers; sexy stuff, as far as Daniel was concerned.

He'd employed a PR consultancy. They in turn had recommended a life coach, Louisa, on the premise that the partners needed to crystallize their goals and develop a good work-play relationship. This involved self-exploration and 'team bonding'.

As part of this process, they went on activity weekends to discover what type of people, they were by completing multiple-choice questionnaires and paint-balling. They were colour coded into 'purple leaders', 'red doers' or 'green thinkers.'

Daniel came home bragging about his achievements, how he scored better than anyone else and, as the weeks of tedious navel-gazing continued, Louisa's name was gradually dropped into the conversation more often.

'Louisa says I need to learn not to feel bad about indulging myself.'

'Louisa says I need to recognise and have the confidence to show off my qualities.'

'Louisa says I need to learn to demand support when I need it.'

The last of these was a dig at me, who found it difficult to provide support to someone who finished at four o'clock most days when I was often still at my desk at seven in the evening.

I had, in the moments when I bothered to listen to the life-guru nonsense, begun to wonder what this Louisa was like. So, when Daniel told me she'd be at the Christmas party, I was intrigued.

I was late. My case overran because the Judge hadn't wanted to adjourn just to come back after Christmas, so I'd texted Daniel saying I'd meet him there. I'd been home, showered and slipped into something remotely festive and by the time I arrived, the party was in full swing.

The practice had rented a room in a local hotel and laid on a buffet and free bar. I was greeted by Daniel's partner, Jonathan.

'Claire, how are you? When are you going to leave that ugly Irish sod, and run off with me?' he grinned, planting a kiss on my cheek.

Jonathan and his wife Polly had been happily married for thirty years but we went through this routine whenever we met.

'One day, Jonty, one day.'

'Can I get you a drink? Daniel's around somewhere, I saw him a few minutes ago ... yes, over there,' he said, pointing towards the bar where Daniel was holding court.

'No, I'm fine thanks,' I said giving him a parting peck on the cheek.

I decided not to join Daniel right away, wanting to observe from a distance the woman standing to his left, her arm pressed against his as he spoke. I watched as she touched his shoulder, allowing her fingers to linger on his neck. It lasted only seconds but was intimate, unguarded, and had a routine quality about it. I didn't recognise the woman but guessed who she was; Louisa.

I moved back into the shadows, wanting to get a good look at her before my cover was blown.

She was in her mid-thirties and wearing a red halter neck bandage dress that crisscrossed her stick-thin body, ending above the knee. She was angular, pointed and eager as a whippet. Not pretty exactly, her face was too sharp for that. I noticed she'd availed herself of the practice's new teeth whitening equipment as she smiled a perfect flash of shark white choppers at no one in particular but for everyone's benefit. Pivoting on sky-scraper stilettos, her legs crossing and uncrossing, she perched on the barstool fiddling with the swivel stick poking out of a glass containing something pink, I guessed was a Sea Breeze.

Now and then, she ran her fingers through her mane of expensively highlighted hair as her eyes popped like a child's at Christmas. The ocular acrobatics were accompanied by wide-mouthed laughs; head thrown back in good time girl affectation. She scanned the room as if to check she was the centre of attention, as if she needed to know all the posturing and posing was worth it. She was exhausting to watch; like a marionette on crack.

As Daniel reached across the bar to pass around the drinks, Louisa touched his hand, and I knew with absolute certainty from the gesture, that this woman, this strange, self-absorbed, fidgety freak-show was sleeping with my husband.

I felt a hand touch my arm and turned to face Ruth, the practice manager.

'Hello Claire, love.'

I'd known Ruth for years. She'd worked with Mum at the hospital when young but had eventually left the NHS to join Daniel's dental practice.

'You've got to watch that one.'

She cast her eyes in Daniel's direction, but the comment was aimed at Louisa.

At first, I thought this might be a reference to the obvious turmoil she was causing Ruth and her carefully ordered surgery, coming in with her new ideas, but then I caught that look in her eye, the look I'd seen before when people talked about Daniel, that 'poor cow' look. I had to get away from her before I betrayed myself.

'Excuse me,' I smiled apologetically, 'I really do need to go to the loo.'

I left the woman with her knowing looks and made a run for the toilets.

Opening the cubicle door, I pulled down the lid and sat,

listening to the piped music drifting through the speakers as I perched, not knowing what to do.

I could have marched into the room and taken back possession of my wayward husband, put the usurper in her place, but I knew that wasn't going to happen.

I could walk out nonchalantly, as if I didn't have a worry in the world, be charming and vivacious, play her at her own game, but then thought about all those prying eyes, like Ruth's, and unlike Louisa, for me, the attention would be mortifying.

The cloakroom suddenly filled with a hubbub of chatter and the pumping sound of 'Valerie' being played through the sound system, as the door to the ladies opened and closed and two women entered.

'Did you see that terrible dress Georgia's wearing? Oh My God!'

They both collapsed in fits of laughter.

'Don't … don't make me laugh … I can't stop and … I need a pee.'

I hoped beyond hope no one tried the door.

I heard the cubicle next to me open and the latch twist behind one of the girls as the other hovered by the mirror. I listened to an aerosol being sprayed around and a whiff of overpowering perfume seeped through to where I sat.

I heard the loo next door flush; the latch open again and the conversation continue.

'And what about Louisa?'

'It's sooooo embarrassing; what's she like?'

It was then I vaguely recognised the voice of the girl speaking. Nicky, one of the practice dental nurses.

'She's nothing but a slut, and she's not even that pretty, I don't think, do you?'

'No, not pretty at all,' said the other girl spraying the aerosol again. 'Sort of skinny, and not in a good way, and too made up.'

'Yeah, I think his wife's prettier, don't you?'

Oh please, please go; just go now.

'Yeah, I think so. She's nice, she's here you know. I saw her earlier with Jonathan. It's such a shame.'

69

Part of me wanted to open the door, just to see the look on their shocked gossipy faces.

'Yeah but that's men for you. It doesn't matter what you look like, look at Cheryl Cole! Men will always cheat on you given half a chance. My mum says all men are the same, cheating bastards.'

'Not my Darren,' said Nicky.

'No, not your Darren, he'd be too scared you'd chop his bloody balls off!'

With a burst of laughter and to my huge relief, they left.

I had to get out of there before I got trapped again. I decided to push through the crowd and leave before Daniel saw me, then text him once I was outside, say I had a migraine and had gone home.

I rushed out of the cloakroom into the party which was now bustling with noisy chatter, the clink of bottles and people having a good time. The lights had dimmed and to my left people were dancing.

Head down I made a run for it, bumping into Daniel on the way.

'There you are,' he said, 'Ruth told me you'd arrived, but that was ages ago, where have you been?'

'I don't feel well, I need to go home,' I mumbled.

I couldn't bear to look at him. I'd been watching his every move from a distance before I'd bolted to the loo, but now, as much as I tried to meet his eye, I couldn't.

My eyes stayed fixed firmly on the floor. I'd heard people say the words 'get out of my sight I can't bear to look at you!' it was a common enough phrase, but I'd never realised what they truly meant before. It was the most peculiar feeling, this magnetic draw to the ground.

I assumed everyone who knew about him and Louisa, including Louisa herself, was watching and suddenly the shame and disgust I felt for him turned to embarrassment for us both. How could he do this to me; why bring me here just to humiliate me?

'I've got to go, let me pass.'

'Claire what's the matter?' he said grabbing my arm as I finally drew my reluctant eyes up to meet his. He must have seen something in the look that brought a realisation the game was up because he dropped my arm and stood aside. As I passed, I caught a glimpse of a red dress. For once Louisa was perfectly still.

As I lay awake that night in Sarah's spare room, taking stock, amidst the boxes full of material and sparkly trimmings I realised that despite my meltdown in the car, this didn't hurt like before. I knew then Daniel would carry on having affairs because he felt entitled; that he was worth it. All those months of grief; and it had been grief - a bereavement - had prepared me for this and by the time I finally fell asleep I knew I could let Daniel go.

I fell out of love with him as quickly as that. It was over, and it was a huge relief. The next morning, despite his pleas to be given another chance, I threw him out and consulted a colleague about getting a divorce.

I swing into the drive and make a dash for the front door thinking about Louisa and how you don't have to be alone to feel lonely. Louisa is as lonely as me, in her way. She has Daniel and her children but she has lost herself. Not long after the divorce Louisa's blonde hair reverted to mousy brown and these days the white teeth rarely get an outing. Since having the children, she's looked increasingly like a woman under siege. Whenever we meet the look in her eyes is one of resentment, as if she thinks I've pulled a fast one. I, on the other hand, won't be lonely for much longer. I won't be anything for much longer come to that and until then, I have plenty of things to distract me. I have a new absorbing hobby for one thing.

Inside, I pour a large glass of wine and walk upstairs to get out of my damp clothes.

There's a text from Sarah;

Hope you got home ok. Thanks again for today. Ben says thanks too!! Sarah X.

Work to do; yeah right, I text back.

My own work, piled high on the dining room table, can wait. I can feel the anxiety building, the need to fill the void. The box sits on the bedside table. There is no longer any need to keep it out of sight or to control my feelings. These days it serves as a reminder of the promise I've made to make the most of the time I have left.

My whole life I've believed in second chances; shouldn't everyone be allowed to redeem themselves? As a defence lawyer, I have to believe that. It has been a huge disappointment most don't take the opportunity.

I gave Donoghue and Daniel a second chance and they both blew it. The second chance I thought I'd been given; the chance to be well again has been snatched away. If there is no second chance for me, why should there be one for anyone else?

Taking a large swig, I plonk my glass down and lift the box. I untie the ribbon and lifting the lid shake the contents, as you would for a raffle draw, before tipping the screwed-up scraps of paper out, laying them flat just as before.

Now Donoghue's out of the picture it's clear to me who is next. Fergus Jennings. The foul man's name stares up from the piece of paper and it's as much as I can do not to spit at it. He deserves no pity. He is a piece of filth that needs to be disposed of. No one will miss him. I'll be doing the world a favour the day I get him taken off the streets.

The rain persists all evening, sheeting down in relentless torrents as an unyielding wind rattles the window frames and the gutters overflow, sending mini-waterfalls splashing and clattering onto the pavers outside.

I remember as a child I could smell rain on the way and how after a long dry spell flying ants rose from the cracks in the steaming crazy-paving. They'd fill the heavy air, settling on the sheets hung out to dry and wander listlessly into the house to die. Seagulls making the most of the ready feast became dizzy and disorientated sometimes; crashing into things. Mum told me once something toxic in the ants made the birds drunk if they ate too many.

These days a temple-throbbing migraine arrives, only disappearing when the storm breaks.

I take the sound of the rain and these memories with me as I crawl between the sheets exhausted, leaving the names strewn across the bedclothes.

The storm resurfaces in my dreams.

An ant floats, drowned in a discarded glass of orange squash on the draining board. The childhood version of myself stands with Mum, young again, staring out of the kitchen window. She looks down at me and says; 'There's a storm coming, gather in the washing, Claire, there's a good girl, before the rain comes.'

I follow her gaze upwards to where the clouds bundle together, vying for space in an overfilled sky. I'm in my grandparents' house close to the harbour in St. Ives; the acid yellow slick tracing the horizon giving the Atlantic an ominous nicotine glow.

With a rolling drum of thunder, the sea darkens, like a monstrous beast, herding the frothy white breakers like sheep. Seabirds caught in the tumble of the wind take to the hollow cliffs for shelter. Fishing boats strain on their moorings as the sky bubbles and flashes of white lightning engulf the bay, silhouetting the lookout perched on the tip of the harbour wall.

I stand in the garden, the rain beating down, drenching my summer dress as I hopelessly scrabble to pull the billowing white sheets from the line. Mum comes from the house to help, one arm raised above her head, shielding herself from the rain. Then, as we struggle together to keep the sheets from the mud, as if from nowhere, a huge wind blows and strips the black paint from the sky to reveal a small patch of vivid blue that grows and grows, as Mum takes my hand and looking upward says,

'Look Claire, blue sky ... blue sky.'

When I wake, my sheets are damp with sweat. The storm has come and gone. The black clouds have gathered, the thunder has roared, and I have heard its message. I am ready.

FOURTEEN

I don't despise Jennings for the reasons most do; because he's a serial offender; up in front of the magistrates at least twice a year. As a lawyer, I've dealt with worse; sad, often mentally disturbed individuals who find their way into the prison system, only to become so institutionalised they can't hack it on the outside. They end up sleeping rough, shambling from hostel to hostel, reoffending to feed a drug habit they can only service through petty crime. That alone would never have earned his name a place in the box.

Whilst on the outside Jennings seems to be one of those people, he's not. Despite a stable start in life, he's chosen violence and crime as a lifestyle. An aggressive, unpredictable sociopath and chronic alcoholic, he's a piranha in a pond full of goldfish, dominating and bullying his vulnerable followers. In the murky water, he's achieved celebrity status, rewarding his most loyal groupies with the occasional free hit of meth or whatever he happens to be peddling that week. In his mind, he's a full-blown gangster, like Escobar or Gotti but in truth he's an inadequate destroyer of lives, including my mum's.

One night two years ago, Mum and her friend Pam went to the cinema and asked to use the carpark behind my office. There was a concert in the Hall for Cornwall and so the multi-storey was bound to be full. It was around the back of the building at the end of a narrow street and after the film, the two women headed back there to the car. Pam, when re-telling the story, said she'd been vaguely aware of a group of rough-looking men and women, down at one end, drinking and laughing. It was a freezing night and as Mum took off her gloves to fumble for her keys a dog came from nowhere; a snarling bull terrier type. Mum shouted and swung her bag at it and it ran off, tail between its legs, but then a tall man in an oversized army coat and boots laced up to his calves, lumbered from the group towards them, shouting obscenities.

'Hey, you ... what the fuck did you do to my dog?'

Pam said he had a shaven head and a tattoo saying FERGIE on his neck. Mum apparently squared up to him.

'That dog should be kept on a lead. It could do real damage if it attacked a kiddie.'

'Why don't you mind your own fucking business, you nosey old cow?'

'It is my business. It's everyone's business and that poor dog looks like it's not been fed for weeks. You're not fit to keep it.'

Seething at the dressing down from the pensioner, Fergie began to prod Mum in the shoulder. 'You can shut your trap; you old bag.'

'Go on then, big man hit me, that's what you want to do, isn't it? I've seen plenty of men like you in my time as a nurse, men who use their fists instead of their brains.'

Pam reached in her pocket for her phone to call 999 but it had been turned off in the cinema and she didn't use it often enough to turn it on again quickly. In any event, the man then reached over and knocked it out of her hands.

'Fucking piece of ancient shit. You, and the phone, I mean,' he said spittle foaming his twisted lips.

The phone landed at Mum's feet and as she bent to pick it up, Fergie lifted his leg and shoved her from behind with his boot to the floor. She lay on the cold tarmac for a second before crawling to her knees, grabbing the car handle to pull herself up. Pam moved to help her but before she could get to her, the man unzipped his flies and proceeded to urinate over Mum, before running off laughing as he went.

Pam could barely say the word, 'urinate' as she relayed the story to me. With tears in her eyes, she said she'd been hysterical, but Mum got up from the ground and told her, quite calmly, to get into the car. Pam thought Mum would call me or drive them to the police station or A&E but instead, she drove them back to Pam's house and parked up. She made Pam promise not to tell anyone, especially me. They weren't hurt, and she said she'd replace Pam's phone if it wasn't insured and that would be that. Mum hadn't let Pam leave the car until she'd sworn not to tell or take the matter further. Pam said she'd agreed because she respected her oldest friend and because by this time the overpowering smell of pee had begun to thicken the air in the heat of the stationary car. The next day, Mum called a garage to collect the car to sell.

Pam only told me about the incident eighteen months later when she called into the office to drop a birthday card off for Mum. I had, in the days after the cinema outing, wondered why Mum had decided to sell her car but accepted her explanation she no longer felt confident enough to drive in the heavy tourist traffic. Bit by bit she began to feel less and less confident about a lot of things; no longer wanting to come to mine for Sunday lunch, or into town on a Saturday afternoon for a mooch around the shops. When I happened to meet her friends, they started to say they hadn't seen her for a while or they'd telephoned and got the answerphone but were never called back. I noticed she began to talk more about the past and less about the future and often when I saw her, we sat together in virtual silence other than the repetitive monotony of her questions which rolled off her tongue on a loop.

She never asked about my illness or my treatment and never got to share the relief I felt when I was told the chemo had been successful. I knew this wasn't because she suddenly didn't care. She'd forgotten about my cancer and I didn't have the heart to remind her.

Had Pam not called into my office I would never have known about the incident in the carpark. I'd immediately recognised the pitiful scarred mongrel whose name I knew was ASBO and his master Fergus Jennings as Mum's attacker.

That callous bastard had thrown my wonderful, capable mum into the void. I knew it would be useless to report him to the police for it now; what could they do? There would be no physical evidence and Pam would be understandably reluctant to put herself out there as a target. I knew I had to deal with Jennings myself and relished the thought of making him pay for what he'd done and protecting others from him in the bargain.

FIFTEEN

ISSY

Issy decided to turn up unannounced. She didn't want to give Claire the chance to make excuses not to see her. She followed her home from work; gave her enough time to settle in, then knocked on the door. Claire answered immediately.

'Issy?' she looked bemused. 'Sorry, did I miss an appointment. Am I meant to be expecting you?'

'No … no, I was passing and thought I'd call in to see how you were getting on with the meds?'

'Mmm … well,' Claire hesitated, 'Oh look come in.'

Claire led the way to the sitting room.

The last time Issy had been there she'd been so preoccupied with Claire's lack of commitment to her treatment, she hadn't really looked around. Now she could see it wasn't to her taste, in fact it seemed rather spartan with its wooden floors and minimalist furnishings. She preferred something cosier.

'I thought I'd examine you here; save you a trip to the hospital.'

'I'm fine, really there's absolutely no need.'

'I'm afraid there is, Claire. I know it's difficult to accept, but things are not going to get better this time. I'm not trying to be a party-pooper, far from it. I don't want you to suffer unnecessarily. Years of research have gone into the development of drugs that will allow you to be virtually pain- free until the very end. Are you really turning your back on that? It would be foolish of me not to take legal advice from a professional like yourself if, heaven forbid, I ever found myself in trouble with the law. I hope you'll afford me the same courtesy?'

'Well yes of course, but I feel fine.'

'Feeling fine is not the same as being fine. Please, take a seat and roll up your sleeve.'

Claire's reluctance was obvious and Issy knew her suspicions were well founded. Claire hadn't been self-administering the morphine as instructed, if at all. She was pretty sure she'd find the packets of pills intact.

'I'm going to take some blood for the lab and give you some meds by injection. I told you before it's important we build up your tolerance to the drugs. It's extremely dangerous to use them only in response to severe pain. Patients can easily overdose on oral morphine if they're not used to handling the tablets and I'm simply not prepared to have your death on my conscience. I appreciate it's a big step for you; to face up to the inevitability of your prognosis but trust me you will have a better quality of life this way.'

She leant in. Reaching to touch Claire's face; she pulled down the bottom lid of her left eye.

'Mmm, I thought as much,' she said. 'The whites have a yellow tinge; jaundice could be an indication the disease has taken hold in the lymphatic system.'

Claire's face dropped, and Issy felt a tremor of delight.

'Not to worry. Your blood count will tell us where we are on that score. I've been your doctor and I'd like to think your friend for a long time. I hope you know I'd never recommend a treatment I didn't think necessary.'

'No, no of course not.'

Issy heard a delicious catch in the back of Claire's throat as her eyes glassed with tears.

'Now lie back and relax, this won't hurt a bit.'

Claire laid back. Issy inserted the needle, filled a phial with blood; stuck a label on it, then placed it in an envelope. She'd dump it in the bin when she got home.

'That wasn't so bad, was it? Now for the morphine.'

A single tear trickled from the outer corner of Claire's eye as she choked back a sob.

'There, all finished,' Issy soothed, pulling down her victim's sleeve.

'Now lie back and rest. I'll let myself out.' She watched Claire unsuccessfully try to peel open her lids and speak.

Issy knew given the dosage she'd administered; Claire would be out for the count in a couple of minutes. She'd be lucky if she woke this side of midnight.

As predicted Claire was soon fast asleep. Issy began her search.

She started upstairs, pausing as she climbed to inspect the gallery of photographs decorating the half-landing. Photos of Claire and an older woman she assumed was her mother. One of Claire in her twenties smiling to the camera, on holiday somewhere hot she guessed by her tan. Two little girls; God only knew who they were. And finally, one of Claire and Sarah both in fancy dress, grinning like Cheshire cats. She felt like knocking that one off its hook.

She paused at the top. She could see the bathroom door was open but her eyes were irresistibly drawn to the room opposite which looked as if it might be Claire's bedroom.

The room was painted duck egg blue. She didn't like blue, not for a bedroom. Her bedroom was painted pink. 'Sugar Mouse,' it said on the paint chart and it always made her laugh when she thought of it. She liked yellow too; yellow was a nice sunny colour.

The furniture looked like it had been reclaimed. It was what people referred to in the magazines as shabby-chic. She'd had a gut full of shabby when she lived with Mummy in the council flat. Shabby was not an interior design look she intended to revisit.

There was nothing particularly personal on show; cheap prints on the walls and the shelves above the bed were empty of books or ornaments.

She opened the wardrobe, scanning the ditsy print dresses and floaty skirts with a growing aggravation. She pulled out an expensive-looking size eight silk blouse, holding it up against her ample size sixteen frame before rattling the hangers so a couple of tops slid to the floor, when she shoved it back on the rail.

She slammed the wardrobe door and was about to head for the bathroom when she spotted a small white cardboard box sitting on the bedside table. She walked over and lifted it. It felt empty and she would have left it had it not been tied with the pink ribbon she'd seen wound around the legal documents that occasionally landed on her desk in her capacity as head of department when some chancer decided to sue the hospital. She untied the ribbon. At first, she thought the scraps of paper inside were the remnants of packaging. Then just as she was about to replace the lid, she glimpsed handwriting and reached in to take a closer look. Daniel. Daniel was Claire's ex-husband's name. She lay the name down on the bedside table and dipped into the box again, pulling out another slip; Fergus Jennings. Who the hell was Fergus Jennings when he was at home? Next she lifted out a sliver of paper with Jane Donoghue's name on it. Well, she knew who she was; *was* being the operative word. It was like some bizarre lucky dip; three names in a box; a Secret Santa.

Then something flashed through her memory from when Claire was first diagnosed and she referred her for therapy. She'd spoken to the therapist after her first session on the pretext she needed to know if she'd prescribed any anti-depressants that might impact on her cancer treatment, and the woman told her she'd decided instead to try out a therapy involving putting names in a box as a means of treating Claire's anxiety. She'd never trusted psychologists. She'd never been convinced they did any good, not compared to proper doctors like her. Any fool could sit and listen to people harp on about their troubles. They ought to spend a day listening to David's inane ramblings then they'd know about troubles.

She looked down at the names again. So, these were people Claire had a problem with. Her ex-husband; that was predictable and Donoghue, but who was this Fergus Jennings. He sounded Scottish. Perhaps Claire had a problem with Caledonians?

She knew the therapist would quote patient confidentiality or other such nonsense. No. she'd have to do a little bit of research herself to see what Claire was up to.

Intrigued at the prospect she completely forgot about checking the medication. She wandered back downstairs where Claire snored gently.

Issy decided her patient looked so peaceful, she'd make a point of coming back every other day to administer her injections from now on. A little more each time should do the trick.

Back in the car she scribbled down the name, Fergus Jennings.

No one was a stranger these days. One click on the internet and you knew everything about a person from their cat's name to what they had for lunch. The whole world wanted to be your friend. Morons, the lot of them.

SIXTEEN
CLAIRE

I wake at about eleven-thirty, mouth dry and feeling nauseous. It's a falling away sensation like nodding off on a train. The streetlights cast shadows across the room through the open curtains. The last thing I remember is Issy giving me the injection. It must have completely knocked me out. I make a cup of tea and go up to bed. I'm not sure if the morphine has done its job or not? I haven't got any pain but then I didn't have any before.

I left the office yesterday with every intention of spending the afternoon finalising my plans for Fergus Jennings. I've lost time I can ill afford. Some things I've already mapped out. It's a fairly straightforward plan as plans go. I meet with Jennings, give him my prescription drugs on the pretext I've stolen them from my dying mum's medicine cabinet, and I want to swap them for weed. I anonymously tip off the police who, if they do their job, take him in for questioning. Generally, it seems to me they show a marked disinterest in his dealing small quantities of weed to the motley crew of addicts he supplies. He sticks to his own and keeps his skanky house in order.

Mostly they only bother with Fergie when he starts mouthing off when drunk, vandalising property or hassling local cafe owners or tourists. I imagine for those set with the task of keeping the peace, there is an element of better the devil you know but lately, I've heard he's been peddling other stuff, Molly and Spice, and he's on their radar after several teenagers ended up in hospital after taking a bad batch of MDMA at a local festival. That being the case, I hope they'll be interested if I say he's offered me prescription drugs.

I'm not counting on them charging him with possession. They just have to take him in then I'll put the word out to some of my risk averse criminal clients I've heard on the grapevine Jennings has spilled his guts to the police and let them do their worst. A grass is a grass after all. It won't matter if the charges stick, the mud I sling will. His life won't be worth living.

The whole plan hangs on him not recognising me. I've brushed past him in the courts more times than I care to remember as the duty solicitor representing one or other of his flunkies. He'd know me in an instant but Ross Trenear once told me an interesting theory about identification; there were two ways to avoid it, either you looked so average in every way you became invisible or you created something about you so obvious it became a distraction. Either way, you were hiding in plain sight. I've decided to deploy a combination of both in my plan to punish Fergus Jennings.

***

The following morning, I telephone Pam and offer to look after Barney, her Golden Retriever. I've helped previously with walking him when she had her knee op and know she's planning to visit her daughter in Bristol next week. She doesn't drive and taking the dog on the train is a nightmare. Barny will be my decoy; my shaggy accomplice and hopefully the only thing about me anyone will remember. I'll have to change my look as well. I need to look rough enough not to stand out, but not so bad the man won't have anything to do with me. In the end, I settle for black leggings, a pair of cheap trainers, a bobbly grey fleece and a parka with a fur-lined hood, I buy second hand off eBay. I decide not to wash my hair for the week and practice pulling it up into a topknot.

That afternoon I take a trip to the chemist and buy a foundation two shades darker than usual and an eyebrow make-up kit to give me the thick dark caterpillar brows unfathomable to me. Once I've finished my transformation, I'm shocked at the result.

The final touch will be to take Barney's name tag off his collar and tie a bright yellow Cornish tartan scarf in its place.

Issy's meant to be calling on Monday afternoon to give me another injection but I ring to tell her I've an important case coming up I need to work on; probably my last. I say I need a clear head and can we postpone any treatment for a couple of weeks? Reluctantly she agrees on condition I take the tablets if I get the slightest twinge. I agree but have another use for the tablets I don't divulge.

I'm relieved she's let me off for now. The prospect of not being able to have my usual couple of glasses of Rioja in the evening is another reason I haven't taken any of the tablets to date. The maintenance of old habits is important to me, I want to feel normal for as long as possible before pain and misery take hold.

I line everything up for the following Friday night.

I intend to make my way down to the underpass where Jennings hangs out at about ten o'clock. The shelter enables him to deal in all weathers and there are always rough sleepers he can force to take the drugs off him if the police turn up. Several times this week I've parked near the entrance, out of view but close enough to be able to see the comings and goings of the junkies who meet there. If I wasn't convinced I had to do something before I am now. People like Jennings leave broken lives in their trail.

SEVENTEEN
ISSY

Issy spent most of Sunday searching for information about Fergus Jennings on the internet. He appeared in the local paper several times in the court section for a catalogue of petty offences including drunk and disorderly and breaches of the peace stretching back over a decade. What Claire had against him she didn't know. Claire didn't appear in any of the articles as the solicitor representing him. Her connection to him remained a mystery.

When Claire rang to cancel her Monday appointment saying she had a big case in the offing she wondered if the man was connected to her excuse but had no way of finding out. So, without other options she decided to keep following Claire.

Finding the names in Claire's house had taken things to another level. She didn't want any more surprises. She decided to keep tabs on Claire, who continued with her usual routine; spa, work, care home visits to her mother. By Wednesday, Issy was getting decidedly bored, but then that evening, driving by Claire's house to check she wasn't out partying, she arrived just as she was pulling out of her drive and followed her into town where she parked up in a particularly rough part of the city by the underpass.

Issy parked a little distance behind and waited for her to get out, wondering where she was heading but Claire stayed in the car, lights off for a good hour. She seemed to be watching the comings and goings of the dissolute rabble who frequented the place. Issy knew only too well what types they were; the sort who arrived at A&E on a Saturday night out of their tiny drug-addled minds expecting help. What fascination such a place could hold for Claire she couldn't imagine; until she spotted a familiar face, a face she had seen coming out of the magistrate's court in a back issue of the *Western Packet* online; Fergus Jennings. She stayed until Claire left then followed her home and watched her go inside. She waited twenty minutes and when she didn't come out again, left.

Thursday evening, she followed Claire a second time to the underpass where once again she sat in her car watching Jennings and his customers do business. What the hell was she up to? There was nothing for it. She needed to get this from the horse's mouth. She didn't mean Claire, that was too close to home. No, it was clear from the press coverage Jennings was a chronic alcoholic. She'd purloin a bottle of David's whiskey from the drinks cabinet and use it to discover Claire's connection with Jennings. She didn't relish contact with the disgusting creature but needs must.

She'd had to work a late surgery on the Friday evening and had not finished her paperwork until about eight when she'd gone home, relieved Rita had packed David off to bed with a light sedative in his cocoa. Once she was sure he was asleep she headed to McDonald's for a burger. She took a detour past Claire's house, where she parked up to finish off her skinny fries. She wasn't sure if Claire would pull the same stunt this evening as she had the previous two. If she did, she intended to follow her and hang around when she left to have a word with Jennings. As it was, she had about an hour to kill.

Swigging the last of her Coke, she glanced down at the bottle of whiskey in the passenger well. She half hoped Claire would stay put tonight. It would mean she could get the job done earlier and get back home in case the sedative wore off and David went roaming. She'd told him if he got up and wandered again, he'd find himself in incontinence pads. He must have taken something in, as there hadn't been a reoccurrence of the desk incident.

An hour and a quarter later she was about to turn on the ignition and head down to the underpass when she saw Claire emerging from her house walking a Golden Retriever. Her clothes seemed strange, not at all her usual style, but it was the dog that caught her attention because around its neck it wore a scarf: a yellow tartan scarf. Claire had never mentioned a dog. She'd asked her about pets when planning her treatment, as certain animals had to be avoided during chemo.

It was strange for Claire to be going out on foot at this time of night. It was dark, and what's more she'd turned down the old railway track which was badly lit and could be dangerous. Down-and-outs were known to gather there taking drugs and getting into fights. It was no place for a woman to be walking on her own at night. Maybe the dog needed to relieve itself and Claire didn't want it to do its business in her precious garden? She waited to see if she turned back but after half an hour she still hadn't returned to the house. It didn't matter. Issy knew where the lane came out; by the river, next to the entrance to the underpass.

EIGHTEEN
CLAIRE

I leave the house with Barney alongside, wagging his tail in furry anticipation of his unexpected walk. I decide to take the route into town along the old railway track. It's deserted at night. I know the path well. Daniel and I always took it when we cycled into town to pick up the papers and fresh bread from the farmer's market on a Saturday morning when we were together. During the day it's used a lot; it's a pretty walk which follows the track until it hits the river running through the city centre. At night, it's poorly lit and people avoid it.

As I walk, I play out various scenarios. Any number of things could go wrong, but I can't turn back. I can see the street lights of the Riverside Walk ahead. I know there is CCTV at the entrance. I pull the hood of my parka around my face and check the tablets in my pocket. I've taken them out of their outer packet. My prescription is written on the side and I don't want them traced back to me.

I bend to stroke Barney. 'Good boy, you're George from here on in.'

The shaggy bear of a dog wags his tail.

'Okay, here goes,' I whisper, walking slowly towards the underpass. I know the CCTV will pick me and the dog up and in the days to come, the footage could be scrutinised by the police. I make sure Barney is on my near side so he will be in the frame and stand out in his tartan scarf. I, on the other hand, look ordinary. Nothing will stand out about me. The cameras inside the underpass will be broken. They always are. No matter how many replacements are fitted, they get smashed within a matter of days by those sleeping rough there who choose privacy over security.

As I get closer, I spot two figures. One, a boy of about eighteen with the waxy pallor and emaciated body of a heroin addict. I've seen him busking outside the library on Saturday mornings. He isn't half bad but I've always resisted dropping anything into his guitar case because I know it will end up in his arm or up his nose. Fergie stands next to him. ASBO begins to growl and I pull Barney closer.

Walking further in, the place takes on a murky hue, half-light seeping from the few stuttering unbroken bulbs. The tiles running along one wall form a mural of a nineteen fifties style beach scene, complete with swooping seagulls and two smiley-faced children. Despite the council's best efforts, the tiles give off the feel of a public convenience. The other wall is plain concrete, but the budget has stretched to the Cornish flag with the word KERNOW written above and the county motto; 'One and All' underneath. Some wit has graffitied it out and written 'Fuck 'em All'. Next to it, among the other obscenities, is a pink sprayed heart declaring RE loves JN. My eyes begin to smart with the thick musky scent of unwashed bodies and I wonder what kind of messy romance thrives in this god-awful place, amidst the discarded needles and overpowering stench of piss.

'Is your dog okay with other dogs?' I shout.

'He is if I want him to be. If I don't, he'll have its fucking leg off.'

My heart flaps like a bat in my chest.

'You want something or you gonna stand there all bloody night?'

'I might,' I shout back and then deliberately and provocatively, 'depends what you're offering.'

The men laugh and just as my courage is about to fail, the younger man heads towards me.

'I like your dog, he's lovely.'

'Yeah, he is,' I say.

'Are you fucking coming in or what?' shouts Fergie, obviously jealous the attention has moved away from him. 'Your dog will be alright. ASBO does nuffin less I says so.'

He gives the animal a swift kick with the side of his boot.

I walk towards them. The boy shuffles forward and bends to stroke Barney.

'What's he called?'

'George, you know like George Clooney,' I say trying to crack a smile, 'If he'd been a Pitbull, I'd have called him Brad.'

The boy looks bemused, incapable of getting the pun.

'Brad Pit-Bull'! It's a joke, you fuckin' moron,' Fergie taunts.

The boy laughs nervously. 'Oh, yeah, I get it, funny.'

I'm not sure he gets it at all.

I suspect Fergie keeps him on a tighter leash than he keeps the poor cowering creature at his feet.

Barney, AKA George, isn't remotely fazed by the other dog. He knows ASBO's bark is worse than his bite. After a while, the dog lies down put out by the attention the Retriever is getting from the boy who is now tickling Barney's ample belly.

'Who's a good boy then, who's a good boy, George?'

The dog licks his hand.

'He likes me,' he grins, delighted. I don't have the heart to tell the boy the soppy animal likes everyone.

I move closer to Fergie.

I nod to him.

'What you after then?' he asks.

'Weed, but I've got something to trade.'

I reach into my right-hand pocket and pull out a foil blister pack of Oral morphine.

He smiles; eyes fixed on the silver foil.

'Where's it come from?'

'My mum, she's got the big C. She's got way more than she needs. She's on the way out. There's nothing anyone can do about it. Any stuff left over has got to go back. I might as well get something for it. They haven't got a clue how much she's taking. They just keep writing the prescriptions, glad they haven't got to pay for the hospice. It's strong stuff.'

'Yeah, I can see that. Can you get more of it?'

'I've got six packs like that one with me.'

'You're not into it then?'

'No.' I say; that much is true.

'That's what happens when you take this shit,' he gestures

towards the boy who is still engrossed with Barney. I look up at Fergie through my lashes, and smile.

'You don't mind me taking a sample, just to check?' he says.

'Course not, as long as you give me discount on the weed but like I said it's strong stuff.'

'Don't worry, I'm a big boy,' he brags.'

He pops a 50g tablet into his mouth.

I wait for a reaction but then remembered Issy telling me the tablets unlike the injections are slow release, designed to give an extended period of pain relief rather than a quick hit. It was why the inexperienced overdosed, they thought they weren't working and took more.

'See nothing,' said Fergie who seemed to think his ability to be unaffected by the strong dosage made him a man.

'But they are the real thing,' I say, acting as if I was worried he wasn't going to take them in part-exchange.

'I think we can do something, and as long as we stay friendly like, we can do business again,' he grins through tombstone teeth.

He snarls at the boy impatiently, 'Leave that fucking dog alone and go and get some gear.'

Claire knows Fergie's an expert at delegating risk.

'Hey, Shaun,' he shouts after the boy, 'take your time. We're alright here, aren't we darlin'?'

'Course we are,' I smile, trying to suppress the urge to run.

Fergie moves his face closer to mine and I smell his hot tobacco breath on my cheek as he mumbles in my ear. His words are slurred. His rolling gait and the empty cans on the floor tell me he's probably been drinking all day. Even so, he isn't done yet. He drains the can in his hand then throws it to the ground, just missing his dog who moves instinctively to avoid the missile.

I busy myself rolling a cigarette. Not having smoked since university, I don't find it easy, but it steadies my nerves and gives me an excuse not to get closer. I hope the boy gets back soon. Even though Fergie has given him orders to take his time something tells me he won't be gone long. He'd be worried Fergie would start to fret about his merchandise. I wonder if he might be there already, hiding in the shadows, hoping to sneak a peek at what he thinks might be going down.

He arrives two minutes later with a leather holdall he hands to his boss.

Fergie unzips it, then roots around inside pulling out two small bags of weed which he hands to me.

'There you go, knock yourself out.'

'Thanks,' I say, shoving the weed into the pocket of my manky parka as I hand him the rest of the tablets. I know he's secretly rubbing his hands thinking what a poor trade it is from my point of view but I'm not there for the deal.

I look down at Barney dozing to the side of the blanket next to ASBO.

'Come on, George time to go.' He gets up and shakes himself as I pick up his lead. I don't look back.

'Hey,' Fergie shouts after me, 'give my love to your dear old mum.'

'I will, you bastard, don't you worry.' I mutter under my breath.

When I get home, I stash the clothes in a plastic bag along with Barney's scarf. I feed the dog who seems tired after his adventure and call the police on the pay as you go phone I've bought for the purpose. I tell them I'm calling because my fifteen-year-old son has just been offered drugs by a man calling himself Fergie. I say he's admitted he went looking for cannabis but was offered something called 'Mandy' and even stronger stuff called 'Miss Emma' and that when he said he wasn't interested the man threatened him; that no, I wasn't prepared to give my name for obvious reasons but I expected them to do something about it or I was going to tip off the local press. I put down the phone satisfied the uber posh accent I laid on meant they took the threat seriously.

I shower; scrubbing myself practically raw in my desperation to get the smell of the filthy man off me. After washing my hair for the second time the odour is finally gone. In bed, I lie awake thinking about Mum and the night Jennings urinated on her like a dog, marking his territory.

'For you, Mum,' I whisper into the darkness.

NINETEEN
ISSY

'That's a single malt you know, it's meant to be appreciated, ' Issy said watching Fergus Jennings down David's bottle of Glenmorangie.

'You can come again,' said the filthy lout taking a breath, 'what was it you want to know?'

'Claire McBride; how do you know her?'

'Claire who?' he slurred.

The man is clearly a cretin, Issy thought.

'McBride, Claire McBride … she was here tonight. You met with her about an hour ago.'

'Eh … and who are you?' he asked swaying.

'I'm her doctor, I need to know what she was doing here?'

'I dunno what you're talking about?' He took another large glug from the bottle which was now practically empty.

'She's a lawyer. I thought perhaps you'd had dealings with her?'

'I fucking hate lawyers … not as much as the pigs but almost, fucking lying bastards.'

'But do you know her? For God's sake man she was just here. She had a Golden Retriever with her.'

Fergie started to laugh uncontrollably.

'That weren't no lawyer. She was some stoner selling me her mother's gear.'

Issy listened as the laugh morphed to a deep guttural cough which in turn rolled into a succession of lung-rattling wheezes. Before reeling, he fumbled in his pocket and pulled out a blister pack of tablets Issy recognised even without its packaging as the brand she'd prescribed for Claire.

Sinking back against the wall, the man's eyes widened as he slowly slid to the ground.

Issy was rooted to the spot.

Rivulets of sweat crazy-paved down his greasy cheeks. Dropping the foil packet into his lap, his hands pulled at the neck of his filthy t-shirt as he gulped for air like a dying goldfish.

Issy watched transfixed as his grotesque face turned puce then blue.

She felt nothing but fascination and had to resist the urge to reach into her pocket for her phone to film the whole thing so she could play it back later and make notes.

With one almighty heave, his body juddered then slumped forward.

He was dead and she knew why Claire had given him the tablets. She could see four of the tablets were missing. That amount of morphine with the whiskey was a lethal combination.

What a dark horse her patient was turning out to be and how thrilling to be part of her journey.

She bent to pick up the packet resting in his groin and felt a sharp pain as nicotine-stained fingers clamped themselves around her wrist. Holding onto the packet she frantically tugged her arm away, panicking he wasn't dead, worried in her torpor she'd misread the signs.

She kicked his shin then grabbing his mop of filthy hair with her free hand, pulled back his head. She could see no hint of life and was reassured the lunge was a defensive reflex, something primal, stemming from his years of sleeping rough, keeping one eye open against the threat of someone pilfering his stinking possessions.

His terrified dog slid on its stomach to the corner of its filthy blanket. Not once had he so much as growled.

TWENTY

CLAIRE

I'm woken next morning by Barney licking my face. After breakfast I'll take him back to Pam's flat. She's due on the midday train so he won't have long to wait. In any case he's had more than enough adventure for one weekend. On the way back I'll pop into the office to ring a couple of my less than worthy clients to tell them I've heard on the grapevine Jennings has been taken in for questioning and is I understand, being very co-operative. I'll tell them I thought I should let them know because I have health issues and won't be available to represent them if there are repercussions. It'll be like pressing a panic button.

Wandering barefoot to the bathroom. I notice the dark circles under my eyes, testimony to the toll of sleepless nights, have faded a little.

People talk about wrestling with their conscience; my conscience is less physical. It doesn't grab me by the neck in a half-nelson. It pokes and prods, trying to break down my resolve. It won't win. After all my years as a lawyer, I feel qualified to mete out the appropriate penalty. I've weighed the evidence and found guilt. Conscience has no place loitering once Justice has delivered her sentence. There will be no clemency.

After dropping Barney off I take the route back into town to make the calls, only to be faced with a diversion at the roundabout. Three or four police cars necklace the junction leading to the underpass. I spot yellow tape across the entrance and two men dressed in the protective gear worn by SOCO, before I'm waved on by a young officer redirecting the traffic.

I hadn't expected that. I know I laid it on pretty thick last night, but my phone call hardly warranted this level of attention.

I wonder if Fergie put up a fight when they went to arrest him;

pulled a knife or something. Or maybe it was totally unrelated? What if the police got distracted by some other incident and my complaint got bumped? I'd have to re-think the whole thing.

I need to find out what the hell is going on.

I park up in the office carpark and walk back towards the underpass to where a small crowd has gathered some distance back from the police cordon.

'What's going on?' I ask a man to the left of me who looks like he's been here some time.

'They've found a body. They brought it out in one of them body bags about half an hour ago.'

I feel hot, adrenaline racing through me like lighter fuel.

'Whose body?'

'Who knows, some junkie I expect if they found him down there? They ought to put a bloody match to the whole place if you ask me?'

Someone sidles up to me and I look around. It's Lisa, one of the clerks from the magistrate's court.

'Hi,' I say trying to manage a smile; hoping she doesn't get close enough to feel me shaking.

'My brother's in the police, he says it's Fergus Jennings,' she whispers in my ear. 'Couldn't happen to a nicer bloke. It'll reduce my paperwork that's for sure, now that little shit is out the picture.'

I say nothing. What can I say; I'm glad the bastard's dead, and I'm glad he died badly, but I'm petrified I had something to do with it. He only took one tablet. Yes, he'd been drinking but one tablet?

***

There's nothing on the TV or local radio on Sunday morning and I begin to doubt he's dead at all, but then the early morning bulletin on Monday reports a local man Fergus Jennings has been found dead in the underpass and the public should take an alternative route to work as the police have cordoned off the site. Nothing is said about an ongoing investigation or that foul play is suspected, and I guess it's assumed Fergie overdosed.

Two days later, the police announce they're looking for a woman with a Golden Retriever who was seen in the vicinity around the time of death to help with their enquiries. No description of the woman is available but the dog is believed to be called George and there is footage of him on CCTV wearing a yellow Cornish tartan scarf.

The following Saturday on my morning shop, I see the boy, Shaun, busking in his usual spot. Beside him, curled up in a blanket-lined dog bed; ASBO fast asleep.

For once the dog looks well fed and relaxed. As I pass, I throw a fiver into the boy's guitar case. 'For your dog,' I say.

'Thanks very much,' he replies looking straight at me.

Whether it's the drugs or my disguise, I don't know but he clearly doesn't have a clue who I am.

TWENTY-ONE
ISSY

Issy read the headlines with a degree of excitement she'd rarely felt before.

A local homeless man had been found dead in the underpass and as part of their general enquiries, the police were looking for a woman captured on CCTV at the time of death. The woman's face was obscured by a hood, but she had a distinctive dog with her. A Golden Retriever wearing a yellow tartan scarf.

'Ha, I knew it!' she shouted loudly, making David jump.

She'd played her part of course giving Jennings the whiskey but how was she to know Claire had given him the drugs before that?

She wondered whether she'd got it wrong about Donoghue too. If she remembered correctly the teacher had picked on Claire at school; constantly berating her for one thing or another. Maybe Claire intended to do the old woman in as well, but something stopped her. She imagined how thrilled she must have been when she heard she was dead and how grateful she'd be if she knew it was her who had finished her and Jennings off.

Whilst at first, she'd been frustrated things weren't going her way, she now couldn't help but think it was no coincidence Claire's activities had started after her terminal diagnosis. She marvelled at the impact she'd had. For a long time, she'd thought Claire was underwhelmed by the news, treating her advice with total disregard but she'd been wrong. She'd provided the impetus for all this; she was responsible for making Claire wake up. It had brought them closer, even if Claire didn't know it. She'd not felt this kind of connection with anyone since Daddy. Everyone's shine eventually wore off. She'd been close to Claire all those years ago, until Mummy had banned her from her party. Now fate had brought them back together. They were members of an exclusive club. They shared a common interest and were prepared to go the extra mile to get a job done. Not everyone was as committed, not everyone had the stomach for it. Eventually, of course, she'd have to tell her she knew everything but that her secret was safe with her if they could be friends. She might then also tell her that, despite all the odds, she'd been cured. She'd have to give her some treatment to make her believe it. Claire was no fool, but there was plenty of time for that. Claire wasn't ill and as she wasn't taking the meds, what harm could come to her? She'd be able to pick the right time. She was proud of her apprentice and pleased she'd been able to help her reach her full potential. She'd stop hassling her about her medication, after all, things had become more interesting when she wasn't taking it. All the psychosomatic studies showed you could convince patients of anything if they trusted you. She'd always known the power she wielded when she gave people the devastating news they were dying, but not in her wildest dreams could she have hoped for this metamorphosis.

Maybe, all those years ago, she'd been right to want to get to know Claire, maybe even then she'd sensed a kindred spirit.

She'd wait and see what unfolded. She knew things about Claire now, things she admired but other lesser people wouldn't understand. Things that could wreck her cosy life and destroy the respect she'd earned over the years from her clients and friends. No, she wouldn't kill Claire McBride. She would nurture her talents, groom and manipulate her. She was her creation and might yet prove her masterpiece. If things didn't turn out the way she hoped she always had other options.

If she and Claire were to become firm friends she'd have to make the first move. Perhaps she could join the hotel spa so she could get to know her socially; after all killing was hard work and both would benefit from some R&R.

Ideally, she would have liked to have lost a bit of weight before buying a new bathing costume but then again, the exercise would do her good and when she'd shed the pounds, she could go for something racier; something she could wear abroad if she and Claire went on holiday together. She hadn't had a holiday for a while, what with work and David being the way he was, but once he was out of the picture, she'd have far more leisure time and as Claire was single too it would save a fortune if they booked a double room instead of paying the ridiculous surcharge hotels always added for singles.

She realised there was a danger she was letting everything else slide. She was having difficulty concentrating. Dealing with David wasn't helping, having to restrain him and put up with his silly antics. It was all too much. Everything seemed to be getting on top of her. She'd had to cancel several appointments with patients. All she thought about was Claire. She needed to rid herself of all the other obstacles holding her back and causing her grief.

TWENTY-TWO
DAVID

David first became suspicious of Issy when he started doing some basic arithmetic and discovered, statistically, the people she treated were five per cent more likely to die than the national average.

There was always a slight variant between hospitals and regions of course, but he'd accounted for that. He then considered perhaps she'd been unlucky with her patients or because of her seniority, been given difficult cases and the odds were stacked against her. He made it his business, unbeknown to her, to call up her files on the computer and he'd noticed a clear pattern. The five per cent had things in common.

They were obese or had a history of drug or alcohol abuse or were smokers with other health issues unrelated to their cancer. The drugs didn't seem to work on them no matter how successful the treatments were on others or their chances of recovering statistically. It was almost as if they hadn't been treated at all for all the good it did them.

Then David began to wonder whether they had, in fact, been treated at all.

Their decline was generally so extraordinarily rapid despite the records indicating Issy was following the recommended treatment to the letter. He couldn't put his finger on one thing making him think the worst of her, rather it was a combination of factors.

Firstly, her dispassionate approach to medicine, her inability to be upset even by the most traumatic of cases. He had, throughout his career, come home disheartened and depressed at the futility of it all, after losing a patient. He knew not every doctor was as affected as him. He'd met cold fish before, who had Issy's approach. He worked with one professor who couldn't look his patients in the eye and could not empathise at all. He seemed callous and relatives complained about his terrible bedside manner. With the power of hindsight, David suspected he'd been on the autistic spectrum but back then consultants were often standoffish, and in any event, David had an inkling he'd seen him walking the wards in the evenings to check on his patients, long after every other consultant had gone home.

Issy was different. Outwardly she was kind to her patients and their families but in private she almost seemed to take pleasure in the drama surrounding a patient's decline and eventual death. She'd talk about how this or that one's treatment was failing and how their relatives were so grateful for all she was doing, but she didn't hold out much hope. David occasionally looked at the case file and often thought the patient should, on the face of it, recover, despite what Issy said but she was generally proved right. On the one occasion, he'd searched her desk for clues and questioned her, she hit the roof, accused him of spying and pulled out a bundle of thank you cards from grateful relatives. After that, he'd left well alone but continued to worry his wife attended far too many funerals for his liking.

When he discovered an old chest of drawers full of drugs in the attic when looking for his fly-fishing kit, he knew his suspicions were well-founded. That she'd logged out the drugs prescribed for her patients, led to an even more pressing question. Why was she keeping the drugs, why hadn't she just thrown them away? It was then he began a second investigation into his wife's activities and to his horror realised, not only was she practising selective euthanasia by withholding treatment from those she thought lost causes, but she was also killing those she thought undeserving or who annoyed her. People like him.

By the time he'd concluded his investigation into her activities over the previous fifteen years; scrutinising coroner's reports and medical records online he was almost certain she'd killed not only her mother but also his dear wife Karen, and once he had hard evidence, he'd make her pay. By God, he'd make her pay.

TWENTY-THREE

DI Ross Trenear hadn't had a day off in three weeks, not since Fergus Jennings had been found dead in suspicious circumstances. Jennings was one of his informers; part of a much bigger investigation underway relating to a lowlife by the name of Jem Fielding. They knew Fielding was behind a number of seedy operations in the county; prostitution and drug trafficking to name but a few, and believed he was funded by an organised crime group operating out of Bristol and Cardiff.

Jennings was on the bottom rung; a lowlife with an alcohol problem and delusions of grandeur. He'd been recruited originally when caught red-handed bringing two vulnerable teenage boys across county lines. Jennings who was never the brightest had hired an Uber to collect them from Plymouth. He hadn't reckoned on the driver being an ex-copper.

The boys jabbered on in the back of the cab about not only the care home they'd been recruited from in Cardiff but also Jennings, the gear they'd be selling and whether they'd get the chance to go to the beach before being carted off somewhere else. Jennings had been passing information to save his own scrawny neck ever since, but alchys were never the most reliable sources. Like druggies they had a tendency to blab. It could be Fergie's whiskey-soaked voice box had got him into trouble.

If Jennings was murdered there was a real chance the whole operation involving months of work by the combined team of the Devon and Cornwall Police and the Avon and South Wales forces might have been compromised.

The autopsy revealed he'd taken a large dose of prescription morphine and that if that wasn't enough, he had sufficient alcohol in his system to knock out the average man twice over. Nothing new there. His addiction to alcohol was well documented but something didn't ring true. Jennings was due to meet up with him on the Monday morning to deliver important information he had about Fielding. He died on the Friday night. They could pinpoint the time of death almost exactly because they had a statement from one of his flunkies; an eighteen-year-old addict called Shaun Randal who told them Jennings had met with two women that night, one looking to buy weed, and the other who'd bought him a bottle of posh whiskey. All the boy could tell him about the first woman was that she'd come via the riverside walk and had a fluffy Golden Retriever called George. He hadn't seen the second woman's face. She'd come from the other end of the underpass near the main road. She'd had her back to him. He'd seen Jennings drinking the whiskey and knew enough to stay away. He'd gone to get a burger while she was there and when he'd come back Jennings was dead. He'd found the broken bottle afterwards and chucked the pieces in the river because he didn't want Fergie's dog ASBO to get glass in its foot. The boy knew nothing about the morphine Jennings had taken or how it had come into his possession. It was not anything he'd come across before while working for his boss. Hopeless.

Jennings was no amateur. He knew all about the stuff he peddled. An expert mixologist he'd been able to concoct you a cocktail to order if you asked and the price was right. For all his faults he was no junkie. He had no history of drug abuse at all; so why was the stuff in his system?

He and his colleagues in the Devon and Cornwall police force had been relegated to the grunt work, interviewing everyone who had connections with Jennings. Other than Shaun, no one admitted to having seen anything. The CCTV cameras had picked up the woman with the dog who was wearing of all things a Cornish Tartan scarf but cameras at the road end were broken and they had no second woman. The request for the woman with the dog to contact them in order to eliminate her from their enquiries had been met with stony silence.

They also had footage of the riverside carpark. During the day the private carpark was packed with the cars of those who worked in the converted ships chandler's and waterside warehouses that served as offices. At night it was generally deserted. On the nights leading up to Jennings' death, however, a car parked there. On both occasions the driver parked in the far corner under the trees facing the underpass. The individual or individuals inside (it was impossible to tell from the grainy black and white footage) stayed in the car, waited for about an hour then left. Whilst they could make out the make, the number plate was indecipherable. It was lucky for them the camera on the roundabout was better quality and picked it up. The car belonged to Claire McBride.

When he'd come across Claire's name on the database, two things crossed his mind. Firstly, they were barking up the wrong tree and secondly, he'd like to see her again and this was the perfect excuse.

He was surprised she'd been referenced more than once.

There was a record on the database of an interview given by Claire a few weeks earlier, when she'd been one of the last people to see a Miss Jane Donoghue alive.

Foul play had not been suspected in that case but routine interviews were carried out before the inquest because the woman had apparently choked to death on a piece of cake; the cake Claire had bought for the woman's niece. Claire was not a suspect because the woman was alive after she left. There was a note on the file about a council employee having had a meeting with the woman later, although the note was incomplete because the officer in charge had not been able to trace her, which Ross thought odd seeing as there should be a paper trail for something like that.

He decided the incidents, though totally unlinked, were reason enough to get away from the station for a couple of hours and visit Claire.

He called her office, only to be told she was taking time off and so he'd looked up her home address. Pulling up outside her house, he felt nervous and knew it was nothing to do with the interview. He didn't expect she could be of any assistance at all but he was intrigued as to what she was doing sitting in a dodgy carpark late at night.

He'd always carried a torch for her. She'd been his first real girlfriend. Neither had dumped the other. Life had intervened. She'd gone off to university to study law and he'd gone to Hendon to train for a career in the police force but two marriages hadn't stopped him keeping tabs on what she was up to over the years. Whenever their paths crossed, as they did occasionally, at court or at some mutual friend's bash, he felt the tug of nostalgia and a lingering, *what if?*

She answered the door dressed in a red check shirt tied at the waist; baggy jeans resting neatly on her hips, exposing the tiniest piece of trim flesh; her feet bare. Dark curls piled up on top of her head to keep her hair out of her face, had fallen loose and corkscrew tresses brushed her cheeks. She was holding something wrapped in tissue paper.

He felt like a drowning man.

'Ross?'

She looked surprised but not unpleased to see him.

'Hi Claire, long time no see,' he said trying to control the waver in his voice not to mention the snaking in his stomach.

'Come in, come in,' she smiled. 'The place's a bit of a tip I'm afraid.'

There were a couple of heavy-duty cardboard boxes on the kitchen floor and around them piles of crockery. She'd obviously been wrapping and boxing up.

'Are you moving?' he asked, worried.

'No, this is mostly Mum's stuff from her house. I don't need all this china. I'm taking it off to the charity shop, these are the last two boxes.'

Ross had heard Eileen Penrose had dementia and had gone into a home. He felt sorry for mother and daughter. They'd always been so close. He was also aware Claire was divorced and single just like him. He'd heard back when she'd first split from Daniel McBride, a man he considered to be a complete tosser. He'd been three years into his second marriage with a child on the way. Since then, he'd split from Trudy, who'd moved back to Bristol with his two youngest. His other two, now teenagers, lived with his first wife Kerenza in St. Ives.

'Can I get you a tea or coffee?' She moved towards the units.

'No, I'm fine thanks. Claire I need to let you know this isn't purely social. I was glad to have an excuse to get away from the station to see you but it's about the death of a local dealer called Fergus Jennings; you may have seen it on the news?'

'Mind if I do, I'm parched?' she asked.

'No, no go ahead.'

She had her back to him as she reached up to pluck a teabag from the cupboard.

'Ah yes, but wasn't it an overdose? They didn't say anything about murder on the news?'

'No neither did I, it's early stages yet but we're checking it out because a few things don't add up.'

'But how can I help?' she said turning to face him.

'Well, your name has come up because your car was seen parked in the riverside carpark on the Wednesday and Thursday leading up to Jennings' death and I need to know what you were doing there?'

He noticed the hand holding her cup was shaking as she placed it down. He could tell her mind was working overtime. He'd seen enough lawyers in court, working on their feet to know what that looked like up close.

The fact she came back so quickly showed she was good at her job. Only a brief flutter of her left lid told him she was feeling the pressure.

'So, you know I wasn't there on the night he was killed?'

'Yes, and you're only one on a list of people we'll be interviewing, but it would be helpful if you could tell me why you were there two nights on the trot. Were you, or someone else in the car with you, waiting for someone? We know you didn't leave the vehicle.'

She paused, staring straight at him.

'Are you asking if I was there to buy drugs?'

'Well, were you?'

'No. Bloody hell Ross, you've known me years. I never took drugs when we were young, even when every other person I knew was popping e's like sweeties. Why would I be doing them now, when I'd risk my career? I'd be struck off if I was convicted of even a minor offence.'

'I know but you've had a lot on your plate over the last few years. Your job, your marriage breakdown and now your mum. We all need a bit of help now and again. I like a drink and I've lost count of the number of colleagues of mine on anti-depressants. It doesn't make you a bad person. Trust me, Claire, I'm not interested in pursuing you for some petty drug offence. You can tell me off the record. If that's why you were there it will go no further than this room, I promise.'

Her face hardened.

'Well, it wasn't why I was there. If you want to know I was with someone; a man.'

He felt disappointment jab at his ribs.

'And this man's name?'

'I'm not prepared to say. He's married and as we weren't buying drugs and adultery isn't a crime, it's none of your business.'

'Claire …'

'I'm not prepared to answer any more questions on this. If you want to question me further, you're going to have to do it under caution.'

He'd wound her up without meaning to.

'Claire, there's no need for this to get formal. This was just meant to be a friendly chat.'

Ross noticed her shoulders relax slightly.

'Right, well I suppose I can cross you off my list,' he said trying to make peace.

'Yes, I suppose you can,' then as an afterthought, 'I'm sorry I couldn't help you any further.'

She showed him to the door. He automatically bent to kiss her cheek. As he did so, a memory of warm summer-tanned skin against his and the smell of coconut oil in her hair flooded back to him and he was seventeen again, without a worry in the world. Then he remembered something else he wanted to ask.

'Claire, one more thing, your name cross-referenced with another matter on the database.'

'It did?' she said, a puzzled look crossing her face.

'Yes, you were the last person to see a Jane Donoghue alive.'

She hesitated and Ross noticed her face flushed slightly as she looked down at her bare toes.

'Yes, that's true. It was very sad, I was there that day for her will signing, tragic really, she was found by her niece.'

'Yes, I read your statement.'

He noticed the clenched fists, locked by her sides, and the flush he'd seen the second before darken a couple of shades.

'Don't be a stranger,' he said trying to lighten the tone before she got even more agitated.

'Thanks Ross, I won't. Sorry I couldn't be more helpful.'

'I didn't think for one moment you could tell me anything I didn't already know, but it was lovely to see you anyway.'

'You too,' she said closing the door.

Ross sat in his car and wondered why Claire had seemed so nervous; so on edge. Maybe it was seeing him again, maybe she was embarrassed at his pathetic excuse for turning up but didn't know how to tell him to sling his hook?

She'd seemed taken aback when he mentioned Jane Donoghue, but he could see how she might feel responsible there, her actions in buying the cake for the woman's niece, no matter how well-meaning, had been instrumental to her death.

He felt uneasy. Claire hadn't exactly lied to him, but she'd been cagey, and in his experience, people were only cagey when they had something to hide.

TWENTY-FOUR

The visit from Ross throws me. After he leaves, I sit on the floor, back against the front door, going over it in my mind. I'm certain I acted suspiciously. I'd sensed my odd behaviour but, taken off guard, was powerless to do anything about it. I've coached enough witnesses over the years; taught them how not to betray themselves, how not to appear shady or defensive, but all that expertise and experience went out the window as soon as I saw Ross on the doorstep.

Why did I make up the story about the married man? Why hadn't I just handed him the weed Fergus Jennings gave me. That surely would have been easier? I trusted Ross when he said he wasn't interested in pursuing me on it. I'd panicked, worried to admit to any contact with Fergie and when he'd let slip they didn't know whether there was someone else in the car with me or not I'd grabbed the chance of an alibi with both hands.

It should have been easier to talk to him than some plod sent to make routine enquiries, but it hadn't been. I'd been self-conscious with him, aware he'd pick up on every little slip, everything he perceived as out of character.

I'm not sure he was being truthful when he said I was just one name on a long list of interviewees or whether he knows or suspects more than he's letting on. I need to find out, but don't have much time left and first I have to talk to Sarah to make sure she's prepared. I've kept her in the dark for far too long.

***

I've booked our favourite restaurant. Years of office parties and licence applications on behalf of the owner guarantee a window seat even in the height of the tourist season and the cheery head waitress always takes good care of us. Sarah and I shop all morning for the perfect dress. I lied about the occasion of course; said I had an invite to a client's wedding but the sentiment is the same. I do have a date of sorts and it's important I look my best for it.

The restaurant is buzzing with lunchtime trade, the clatter of knives and forks lending percussion to the mellow Nina Simone ballad playing in the background.

A crowd of women gather at the bar, shopping bags piled around their feet, drinking flutes of prosecco; their loud conversation peppered with outbursts of raucous laughter.

Sarah nods towards the empty bottles on the bar.

'They started early.'

I laugh and make a gesture to the young barman trying to keep them in order.

'Can we go through, we've booked?'

'Yes, fine!' he shouts just about making himself heard above the uproar.

We settle in our seats; the smell of seafood and garlic waft from the next table as the lids lifted off a steaming bowl of mussels. Tempting as they look with their hunk of crusty warm bread on the side, I resist the urge to order the same. I need to have a serious conversation with Sarah and dipping sticky fingers in and out of a finger bowl will be too distracting. I settle on sea bass instead and Sarah joins me.

Once the waitress has brought over our usual bottle of Cloudy Bay, I begin.

'I've got something to tell you, but I don't want you to get upset. That's why I brought you here, so you can't get too emotional.'

Sarah's face drops

'Oh my god!' she says, 'Daniel's not leaving Louisa; you're not taking him back, are you?'

'No, no nothing as upsetting as that,' I laugh. 'I've made my will and I've appointed you my Executor. I've left a letter detailing my wishes for my funeral and a sum of money for a party afterwards. You can't be married to an Irishman for fifteen years and not know how to have a good death.'

Sarah looks baffled and I think she's about to interrupt me, but I'm determined to get it all out, afraid if I pause, even for a second, I might lose my nerve.

'There's another letter in my safety deposit box at the bank with Mum's jewellery. It contains confidential information that might never need to come to light but if you feel circumstances dictate it should, I want you to collect it and do what you think is best.'

'But why ...?'

'Don't ask me to tell you more now, because I can't. Hopefully you won't have to do anything with it.'

I exhale deeply, pleased I've finished that part at least.

Sarah scans my face for clues.

'Okay, but why are you telling me this now? You've had the all-clear. You'll probably outlive me.'

'I'm afraid I haven't been truthful with you. I know I should have been but I just couldn't face your disappointment ... my cancer is back, that's the upsetting news.'

Sarah's fork drops to her plate. I spot the tears welling.

'No, you're better, look at you, you look brilliant. I told you earlier you looked beautiful in that dress and you did, I wasn't just saying it.'

'I know, I know, and I feel really well and that's good because it means I'm in better shape to face the treatment, but it's back. I'll do my best to fight it like the last time, but I might not succeed and we have to face that possibility.'

I don't tell her I'm terminal and there's no point fighting this time because watching Sarah push her food around her plate, I know she isn't up to it and what point would it serve? It won't change my prognosis or my plans.

'I'm starting the treatment after the wedding; one last blowout; perhaps I'll get smashed, maybe I'll even get laid if I'm lucky, then I'll start the chemo. So, drink up and we'll get another bottle of wine before booze is off the menu for a while.'

Sarah's anxious frown relaxes a little. I have practiced this upbeat speech until it sounds convincing even to me. I deal with my true emotions alone; box them up and tie a ribbon around them.

After a couple of glasses of wine, the mood lifts and we're able to talk normally. I had to make up the wedding scenario to avoid Sarah dropping in at the weekend with the girls as she often does. I have plans for myself and Daniel on Saturday and can't risk interruptions. It's been hard thinking of an alibi that can't be checked. Sarah and I share a lot of friends so I've had to concoct the story. I hate lying to her, in fact, I can't remember ever doing so before.

'Will you be okay going to the treatments on your own?' Sarah asks. 'I mean do you want me to move in to look after you while you go through the chemo? I'd say move in with us but there's not much room.'

'No, it's not necessary,' I say knowing there won't be any chemo and the last thing I want is Sarah watching my every move. She means well. The last batch of chemo left me curled up in a ball on her sofa unable to keep anything down.

'It's kind of you but honestly, I think I can cope this time. Issy says I can monitor the medication myself as it's been tailored to my needs based upon the last time. Apparently, I won't be as sick as before and I know where you are if I need you. Let's plan to do something momentous when it's all over. That's when you'll be the most use to me, when I'm well again and I need some well-earned fun.'

Sarah beckons to our waitress.

'Another bottle?'

I smile. I know the effort it's taking my best friend not to bombard me with questions and I love her for it.

TWENTY-FIVE

Sarah abandoned her car in town and called Ben to pick up the kids from school. She hadn't intended to drink at lunch but Claire's bombshell put an end to her good intentions. The combination of alcohol and her friend's sunny resilience in the face of terrible news initially numbed the impact, but the effect was wearing off and a water wall was beginning to cloud her contacts, making it difficult to see. This would have been bad enough had she been at home, but she was negotiating the steep hill to the station to catch the train. She could see people staring as they passed her no doubt wondering what could induce a sensible-looking woman to cry in the street. She paused to blow her nose, only to find she didn't have any tissues. Out of desperation she grabbed a fabric sample from her bag, attracting further attention as she blew hard into a piece of gold brocade.

'What the hell's so bloody interesting?' she shouted through her sobs. 'This isn't even that fancy, you should see the ones in my drawer at home!'

The dread of what was ahead, made her head ache. She'd help but ultimately there was only so much she could do. It was Claire's determination to beat the disease as much as the chemo that led to her recovery the last time. Claire was a fighter; a force of nature, but when faced with a battle she couldn't win, like her mother's dementia or Daniel's adultery, she went to pieces like everyone else.

She could read when she was on the brink. Even though there had been no tears, no outbursts, she'd seen something in her eyes. She had plenty of friends who cried all the time; when their babies were keeping them up, when they didn't get that job they wanted, some even when they put on weight. Her kitchen had seen its fair share of tears over the years, but not many from Claire.

She hoped her friend was telling the truth and could manage

alone. She'd be watching her like a hawk for signs she couldn't cope and intended to warn Ben he might have to manage the girls on his own for a bit over the next few months. She knew she'd be going through the treatment step-by-step with Claire whether she wanted her help or not. It was what she did before, and what she'd do again and again for as many times as it took. She'd do anything to make sure Claire lived, because she couldn't imagine life without her.

TWENTY-SIX

No matter how many times he re-ran their meeting, Ross couldn't rationalise Claire's strange behaviour or the odd coincidence she'd been involved with two individuals who had died in suspicious circumstances within a few weeks of each other.

The old lady's death seemed to have been an unfortunate accident. Nevertheless, Claire was one of the last people to see her alive and her car had been in the vicinity on consecutive nights at a possible murder scene and Ross didn't believe in coincidences.

Back at the station, he'd called both case files up on the database. The facts were there for anyone to see. Claire hadn't denied being at Donoghue's house or in the carpark and her coyness in divulging her lover's identity because he was married seemed out of character. In fact, running around with a married man seemed out of character too. She knew first-hand what it was like to be on the receiving end of a husband's infidelity. He'd seen how she'd reacted back then; how worried her friends were about her. Claire wasn't a cruel person. She'd never inflict that kind of pain on someone else. Doubt hovered above the computer screen like a fly on shit.

Ross didn't believe in the instinct policemen claimed twisted their gut when faced with a crime scene. It was bollocks as far as he was concerned and coppers who relied on their instincts were either liars or idiots. Policemen's guts weren't any different to anyone else's. Criminals were caught because they cocked up or were grassed up and were convicted on hard evidence, usually supplied by forensics. Their job as policemen especially in a murder case, was to secure the crime scene and not lose the evidence; simple as that.

After hours of flicking through pages, not knowing what he was looking for, he printed off the background information on both incidents and went home. Once there, he cleared away at least three days' worth of dirty coffee cups and the discarded wrapper of the BLT bought the evening before. Then, after arranging the papers he'd brought home on the coffee table, he began to search for links.

The thin file containing Jane Donoghue's case notes held only a brief outline of the circumstances in which the woman's body had been found, her age and the details of the niece who'd discovered her.

There were four statements, each only a page long, testifying to the fact the deceased had signed her will on the day of her death. Cause of death was asphyxiation brought about as a result of choking on a cream cake.

Each statement supported the others. One was Claire's. She confirmed two neighbours had been there to witness the will she'd prepared for signature and had left afterwards with the niece.

In her statement one of those witnesses, Mrs Thompson, said she returned later having left her cardigan. She said a woman from the council let her in and Donoghue was alive then. They hadn't been able to trace the woman from the council but the old lady's niece said she had been expected to turn up some time because they'd put in a claim for Attendance Allowance. So the lack of information about the woman could just be down to bad record keeping.

Claire admitted buying the cake for the niece and said she'd told the old lady so. She said she hadn't thought she'd eat it, especially as she was diabetic.

Looking at this objectively, he wouldn't suspect anyone. If there was a possibility of foul play, the niece was the prime suspect as the one set to benefit from her aunt's death. She had a solid alibi. No, this was an unfortunate accident, thought Ross with some relief, although *Bake Off* would probably not be on Claire's to-watch list for a while.

Jennings was a different matter. His death was no accident. Maybe the woman with the dog was the key, but having seen the CCTV there was no way it was Claire. She looked nothing like her and Claire didn't have a dog. He'd looked for tell-tale dog hairs in her house and there were none. In any event her car wasn't in the carpark on the night of the murder and finally what was her motive? She'd never represented Fergie so there was no grudge material on either side; no history of bad feeling.

Ross took a long sip of his beer.

No, in all likelihood it was a professional hit. If Claire was up to something in that carpark it had nothing to do with Jennings. This had Jem Fielding's imprint all over it.

He was in the middle of watching the highlights from the test match he'd recorded when his mobile rang. It was Claire.

'Hi, I hope you don't mind me ringing, it's just I felt I might have been a bit off with you earlier, rushing you out of the door like that.'

Ross was not expecting her to call so soon; if at all.

'No need to apologise. I turned up unannounced, I should have rung beforehand.'

'Normally I wouldn't worry about an old friend calling in on the off chance but it was a bit of a shock seeing you, and then when it was official business, I was thrown. If you want to ask me anything else, I'd be happy to meet up.' She paused, then changed the subject.

'How are things with you anyway? I was sorry to hear you'd split up with Trudy. I half thought that's why you were calling, for a bit of free matrimonial advice, not that I'm great on divorce law.'

'No that's been sorted, she got all the money and the kids and I get access whenever she says so, which isn't often these days.'

'I'm sorry.'

'It is what it is.' He changed the subject not wanting to sound a self-absorbed loser. 'Sarah told me about your mum, I'm so sorry Claire.'

'Ah well, she seems happy enough, it's me who has the problem. It's harder outside looking in. I met Sarah for lunch today actually. We had a bit of a session. I mentioned you had called and she sends her love. Anyway, I won't keep you I just wanted to apologise and say perhaps we could catch up when you're not on duty?'

He could think of nothing he'd like more. He wondered if

maybe this thing with the married man wasn't serious and his spirits lifted. He tried desperately to think when his numerous commitments would allow him to meet up with her. He'd managed to get the coming Saturday off but had arranged to drive up to Bristol to see his kids. He couldn't cancel; he'd not seen them for weeks. He didn't like to let them down; he'd done enough of that already. Trudy would love an excuse to make it even more difficult for him to keep contact.

'Yes, that would be good,' he heard himself say lamely. 'I'll give you a call sometime.'

'Okay, I'll wait to hear from you then. Bye, Ross. It was really lovely to see you again, I mean it, really lovely.'

'Bye, Claire.'

He put the phone down, immediately regretting he hadn't stayed on the line longer; hadn't been chattier. She'd said, *really lovely* and he hadn't even had the gumption to return the compliment. Seeing her had been more than lovely. Despite the circumstances, it had been bloody fantastic.

He made his way back to the sitting room, where the crowd were cheering in the heat of the Barbados sun.

'And there we have it, Trenear once again, out for another duck,' he said aloud to the empty room.

TWENTY-SEVEN

I put the phone down, satisfied Ross knows nothing. Had he any real suspicions he'd have been all over me like a rash, wanting to come and interview me again on the pretext of a social call. I gave him every opportunity. He doesn't live far away and could have come there and then. I'm sure I sounded enticing enough and as a lawyer I know how useful an off the record interview can be, especially if you throw a couple of glasses of wine into the equation. I'd told him I'd had a few drinks that afternoon, which was true enough although of course I lied about telling Sarah he'd visited that morning. She would have talked of nothing else if I'd let that slip. She, like everyone else I knew, loved Ross Trenear. If I'm honest I feel vaguely insulted he'd seemed so matter-of-fact, reticent even. Had I misread the signals? I'm sure I felt some spark of what we'd once had; then again maybe his life was too complicated already for him to be interested in romance. That suits me, I'm dying after all. The last thing I need is complications.

In the kitchen I pour myself a glass of wine.

I've made my plan and intend to stick to it no matter what. The teenage girl who once swooned over Ross Trenear's tan line is long gone.

I'd shown willing. If I had anything to hide, he'd expect me to keep my head down. I only had to keep him off the scent for a little while longer, after that what good would his investigating do him? I'll be gone.

TWENTY-EIGHT

The next morning, I call Daniel. Louisa no longer monitors my calls in the way she once did. In the early days of the divorce, when I rang Daniel about selling the matrimonial home, it was rare Louisa didn't listen in to the conversation. The fact she no longer bothers first leads me to believe she should up her game, after all Daniel's got form, but then it dawns on me it's probably only my number she doesn't intercept because she no longer sees me as a threat? Even Louisa realises terminal illness dulls your allure.

I am business-like but friendly, when I say I have some important news to discuss with him and ask if he can pop over on Saturday morning.

At first he says Saturday is difficult because he has to take Connor to five-a-side football and drop the twins off at ballet-tots so Louisa can have a morning of 'me time'. I sympathise telling him I fully understand but that it's critical we talk soon; I need to discuss my will with him. For good measure, I add if he could manage to make it, he should bring along the paperwork for the Maserati as I'm sure we can work something out about the car loan and insurance premium. I say to talk it over with Louisa and get back to me later.

My mobile rings precisely six minutes after I hang up.

'Hi Claire?'

'Hi, Daniel, that was quick.'

'Louisa and I have talked it over and she'll look after the kids, so I can come over.'

'Good, make sure you leave plenty of time. We've got lots to discuss.'

'I've said to Louisa I'll be back early afternoon, and Claire?' he hesitates, 'I hope it's not too serious; that it's not … bad news.'

I'd like to think I'm hearing genuine concern, that Daniel's retrieved some of the feelings he once held for me; but all I hear is a man who can barely contain his excitement; a man who sees prospects looming on the horizon.

I imagine him shouting out the news to Louisa and them jumping around the room while in their heads a chorus of Mozart's *Requiem* plays.

TWENTY-NINE

That evening I sign the visitor's book at the nursing home knowing it will be the last time I see Mum. Making my way along the corridor I notice the staff laying out the tables for that evening's bingo session and wave to Matron.

Mum's asleep in her chair, a jigsaw on a padded tray balanced on her lap. She stays in her room a good deal these days and has taken up jigsaws. I peer over her shoulder and smile at the face of Darth Vader staring back at me. He's missing a piece of his grill-like mouth. The girl sent out to buy the puzzles is clearly a bit of a sci-fi freak. Mum has only recently completed one of Captain Kirk at the helm of the Starship Enterprise.

Mum looks so peaceful I let her sleep for a while. The last of the evening sun reflects amber light around the walls, streaking her sleepy head with gold. On the table there's a battered shortbread tin with a picture of two rosy-cheeked children in hand-knitted pullovers playing in the snow with a Scottie dog. I lift the lid the way I've done a hundred times before. I know every item. The order of service commemorating my nan's funeral; an old brown envelope containing family photographs; a couple of me and Daniel, some of me with my grinning cousins on the beach, one of me and Sarah and the one of my multiple dads with Mum decked out in her best seventies gear.

I remember how beautiful Mum had been with her long dark hair and tawny skin and how in the summer, at around six she'd finish work and join me and my family at the beach. Nan would always save her something to eat but she'd never sit down until she'd had a swim. She'd pull off her jeans and t-shirt and run down to the sea. She'd pause to hug me before plunging herself into the ocean and swimming far out, face down, her arms cutting through the water in steady rhythmic strokes. I glance across at her now dozing in the chair, her hands resting across Darth Vader's nose, and think how cruel time is. How it creeps like a thief stealing everything from us. I turn the photograph over, read the names and wonder if my father's still alive. Maybe, like Mum, he's in a home somewhere being visited by my half-brother or sister. I hope he hasn't lost himself, that he remembers his children's faces.

I wonder whether I should have tried harder to find out which of them he was but know it was not part of the deal. Mum made it clear it could cause untold harm to him and his family. No, Mum has been more than enough for me and at least now, whoever he is, he'll be spared the pain of losing me.

I put the photograph to one side and look through the rest of the stuff. My first school report, the one which referred to me as a 'bright girl with a lot to say for herself' which in teacher-speak meant I was lippy. Then a card; a wedding invitation. I don't recognise it. I assume Mum transferred it from her bureau before she moved. I open it. Inside it reads:

Mr and Mrs M. Wheatley invite you to the marriage of their daughter Karen.

I wonder why Mum has kept it? She must have received dozens of wedding invites in her time. I wonder why it's important enough to deserve a place in the 'special tin.'

I am about to put it back when I feel something inside the inner flap and pull it out. It's a handwritten letter folded several times. It reads:

Dear Eileen,

We were sorry you couldn't make it to the wedding. It was a beautiful day and David and I will remember it always. I fully understand why you couldn't come all the way from Cornwall so close to your delivery date, but you were missed. All the gang were there. Thank you for your lovely champagne flutes and make sure you write when the baby is born so we can toast you both.

All our love Karen and David.

I fold the note and return it to where I found it. I pick up the photograph again, turning it to look one last time at the names on the back, and am about to put it back when Mum begins to stir.

She looks up at me, squinting against the light glinting off her spectacles.

'Hello, dear.'

'Hello, Mum, you were sleeping.'

'Was I? I must have dropped off. I was doing my jigsaw, but I've lost the last piece somewhere?' She wriggled in her seat, putting her hand down between the cushion and the side of the chair. 'I think it's gone down the gap.'

I jump up to retrieve the tray before the whole lot falls to the floor and place it on the table next to the tin.

'I was looking at your photographs.'

'Ah, you're just like my Claire, she likes to look at the old photos, that's her in one of the photographs there with her friend, I can't remember her name I'm afraid; lovely girl.'

I guess she means the one of me and Sarah buried up to our necks in sand.

I pick up the photo and hand it to her.

'Yes, yes that's the one that's my Claire.'

My throat tightens.

'Pass me the tin, will you?' she says.

I do as she asks. The tin rests on her lap as she picks over the contents before putting them back, her arthritic fingers lingering over a face she seems to recognise now and then.

When she opens the wedding invitation, she says, 'Ah yes, such a lovely couple; so very happy but then she died quite young. So sad and no children; she couldn't have them and children are such a blessing.'

She pauses, contemplating the significance of the words, looking into nothingness for a second and then continues.

'I think he married again. I heard she was a much younger woman but we lost touch.'

I listen patiently to her reminiscence.

'You'd better be getting back to Matron. I'm sure she'll be wondering where you are. She's bound to have jobs for you, I'm sure.'

I'm used to her mistaking me for a member of staff. It no longer upsets me like it did at first when I tried to correct her. Now I just go along with it, that way Mum doesn't get too agitated.

'It's ok. she sent me in to help you with your jigsaw.'

Mum begins to put the lid back on the tin and then pauses. She shuffles through the contents again. 'There's one missing; a photograph,' she says.

'Yes, it's here, I was looking at it,' I reply.

I hand Mum the photograph of her and her friends.

'Ah, that's the one,' she says smiling, returning it to its rightful place.

'There they are, Karen and David, what a lovely couple; so happy. Look at all of us and there's me and the love of my life.'

'Which one?' I ask, craning to see which of the young doctors she's referring to, unable to help myself.

'Claire of course, there with me in the picture. I'm not showing yet. It was too soon for that, but I knew she was there; you can see it in my eyes.'

I walk over to her and taking the tin from her hands, kiss the top of her head, a sob catching the back of my throat.'

'Now, now; that's enough of that,' she says. 'Could you pass me back my puzzle dear before you go?'

Kneeling to her level, I carefully place the tray in a comfy secure position on her lap.

I search her face for a glimmer of recognition, but there is none. The kindly old lady who was once my mum smiles benignly without a clue who I am.

As I walk towards the door, I spot the missing jigsaw piece

under her chair. I bend to pick it up and place it on the tray.

'There you are.'

'Thank you, dear.' Mum says placing the missing piece into the gap to make the face of Darth Vader complete.

'Ugly beggar,' she says. 'There, finished, now I think it's nearly time for a cup of tea.'

Despite the pain tearing my heart in two, I'm pleased she doesn't know me. At least I know she won't miss me, won't watch the door or long for the sound of my voice. I need to know she's no longer here. If she was, I'd not be able to go through with it.

THIRTY
ISSY

Issy had made her mind up. She needed to meet with Claire and to tell her she knew all about her little box of names. That way Claire would finally see, after all these years they were the same. She was of course more skilled, although Claire's achievements weren't to be sneezed at. She was a novice after all. She envied her that.

Over the years the thrill had died a little for her; the faces blurred. It was a good job she'd had the presence of mind to keep meticulous records; without them she might have forgotten many of her achievements. She couldn't stand the thought of becoming like David; her brain turning to mush. She hoped her memories would see her through old age but how much better would it be to be able to share them with someone else?

Perhaps finally she'd get the recognition she deserved for all the work she'd done; all the money she'd saved the NHS. She had spent hours lately lying awake in bed wondering about Claire's motives; why she'd targeted particular people. What had they done? The people she killed hadn't done anything of course other than breathe when they had no business to, other than Karen, who was such a burden to David, and Mummy who was such a burden to her.

Once Claire and her had time to get to know each other they'd share their stories. She'd have to get rid of Sarah, of course, with her arty-farty ways. It was probably best not to involve Claire in that one. Maybe she'd get the place decorated after David went into care; ask Claire for Sarah's number for some advice. Accidents happen in the home; she'd seen the statistics. It was remarkable the damage you could do to yourself toppling from even a small ladder.

First, she had to break the good news to Claire she wasn't dying; then, when she'd got used to having her life back, they could get down to what they did best; ridding the world of its detritus. She'd ring her today and make arrangements to go around. This was the start of something big. She could feel it in her water.

THIRTY-ONE
CLAIRE

I rise early on Saturday morning; happy my preparations are complete. I brew coffee and sit back, content my affairs are in order. I am a lawyer, after all.

The other partners in the firm will get the 'key man' insurance payment on my death which will help pay out my partnership interest to my estate. I know amongst themselves they must have met to discuss the possibility of me dying when I was originally diagnosed and they've probably looked at how they will rearrange their schedules to cover my client obligations and court appointments. The money will be useful to entice some bright young thing into partnership to take my place. I'd have done the same had I been in their shoes.

Sarah will inherit all my personal belongings and my house. The rest; money and investments will go to pay for Mum's care and then afterwards be divided between various charities. Sarah has a list of small mementos I want friends to receive, along with my funeral wishes.

Sorting my stuff has been more problematic. The furniture can stay. I expect Sarah will let the property to holiday makers as a useful second income. The disposal of my clothes and shoes, particularly the shoes, has taken a ludicrous amount of time. I've put aside the vintage tour t-shirts from every concert Sarah and I have gone to together, for Sarah's girls. Sarah has the identical ones and it'll put a stop to any bickering between them as to who can lay claim.

It's taken weeks of trips to charity shops to get rid of two lifetime's worth of stuff. Mum's and mine. The volunteers on the desks looked as if all their Christmases had arrived at once. Now only two clothes hangers remain along with a drawer holding one set of expensive silk underwear. There's no going back. Daniel said he'll be here at eleven. At nine I run a bath. I've got out of the habit of luxuriating in a hot bath because it always ends with me surveying my body for the tell-tale signs of returning illness. Now I no longer care.

I watch the golden drops of bath oil bob and glisten on the surface of the water; the scent of Orange Blossom and Iris hovering in the steam. Letting my robe fall to the floor, I drop into the warm water, lie back and close my eyes.

I think about Daniel. Looking back, I should have read the signs better. I remembered clearly the first time I met his family in Cork. He was the youngest of four, the others all girls. His father had died from a heart attack when he was fifteen. As an only child, I'd been totally unprepared for the dynamic.

To say Daniel was the 'golden boy' was to grossly underestimate his status, it was like describing Elvis as a reasonably good cabaret act. He was the apple of every female eye in the room. His sisters ushered him through to the front with the hullabaloo reserved for boy bands and the Pope.

His brothers-in-laws were less enamoured.

Daniel held forth, dishing out advice and recounting triumphs.

I'd been gasping for a cup of tea. Given only a cursory once-over when I'd arrived, then left to fend for myself, I eventually wandered to the kitchen and there was joined by Daniel's mother.

'All fighting over their baby,' she said. 'That one will always have women to love him. From a wee man, he could wrap women around his little finger. His father was the same but unlike him, hopefully he'll stop the wandering eye now he's found you.'

I hadn't wanted to sound nosey and question the woman about her late husband's misdemeanours. In truth, back then Daniel seemed devoted to me and I didn't doubt it would stay that way.

Later, I came to realise it was impossible for anyone to provide the level of sustained adoration he received from his mother and sisters. Any criticism, no matter how constructive or well-meaning, was a slight.

When I told Mum we'd split up, she turned to me, and said: 'Do you know my darling girl how often a person can have their heart broken?'

'No, Mum, I don't,' I'd sobbed.

'Once, only once. After that, the pain is a little less each time, so by the end it doesn't hurt at all.'

She was right, of course. Daniel lost my love little by little through sheer perseverance, until he could no longer break what was already broken.

THIRTY-TWO

Leaving the warm comfort of the bath, I pull on my robe and head to the bedroom.

It was a good decision to shop with Sarah for a new dress. After searching for most of the morning I'd found a cornflower blue silk wraparound number in a little boutique off the main street. The dress is sexy but not obviously so.

I smooth my skin with moisturiser until it glistens and decide to let my hair fall in natural waves. I move to the drawer and lift out the underwear. The pale lilac silk trickles like water through my fingers and moulds itself effortlessly to my body.

I lift the dress from the bed and as I slip my arms through the sleeves, trace the scar where the melanoma was removed.

The skin grafts were successful in building out the deep gouge made around the mole. It no longer has the power to frighten me. Like the Bogie Man under the bed its power to terrify relied upon surprise. Now I have its measure there is nothing else it can do to me. It's done its worst.

I pull the dress around me, wrapping the tie belt twice around my waist. It fits perfectly and it's a pity it will have only one outing.

I wander down to the kitchen and pour myself a coffee, then move outside into the garden. The spring sunshine caresses my body like a lover's kiss. I raise my face towards it, closing my eyes, enjoying the bright orange glow nesting behind my eyelids.

'Hello there.'

Ross's voice startles me.

'I knocked on the door but didn't get an answer, so I came around the side gate. Look at you all *Homes and Gardens* in your floaty frock drinking coffee on the patio.'

'How long have you been standing there?' I ask, blinking away the red dots.

'Not long, I was enjoying the view. You looked so peaceful I didn't want to disturb you.'

His voice still had the power to take me back.

I glance down at my watch; ten fifteen. Even allowing for Daniel's terrible timekeeping he would be there within the hour, and if he finds Ross here my plan will be ruined.

'I tried to phone, but got no answer and I was passing, so I thought I'd call in on you on the off chance, I hope you don't mind?' he smiles.

'No of course not, I forgot you lot work on Saturdays too,' I say, trying not to appear as flustered as I feel.

'Oh, I'm not on duty. I'm on my way up to Bristol to see my kids. It's the first time I've seen them for weeks.'

'Oh I see.'

'I wanted to drop in to say sorry if I was a bit slow on the phone the other night. I'd fallen asleep in front of the telly and wasn't quite with it. I didn't want you to think I wasn't keen to meet up, because I am ... keen, I mean.'

I smile. Although he no longer has the boy band looks that made him every teenage girl's dream, he still has the mannerisms of someone much younger. He has no idea how attractive he is and it's endearing. I remind myself there can be no future for us. He's a policeman and I'm a felon, not to mention the fact I'm dying. Yet, despite everything I don't feel like letting go of the fantasy just yet.

'Do you want something to drink, a tea or coffee?'

'Coffee would be good, thanks.'

My mobile rings. Apprehension swells. I'm afraid it's Daniel saying he'll be early or worse still he isn't coming at all. I have to answer it.

'I'll just be a sec,' I say. As I brush past Ross, I feel a tingle run down my spine, that settles somewhere between my thighs. Lifting my mobile from the garden table I move inside.

THIRTY-THREE

The phone call is from Issy. She asks to see me saying we have a lot to discuss and am I available this afternoon? She sounds strangely excited at first but her tone changes when I tell her I'm in the middle of getting ready to go to a wedding. In an attempt to get her off the phone I promise to ring her when I get home later this evening, knowing I'll do no such thing.

'What time?' she demands, disgruntled.

'Well, I'm not sure. I really can't say with any certainty when I'll be back, but don't worry if I'm very late, I won't disturb you. I'll call you on Sunday morning instead.'

'I've told you before that you shouldn't be taking risks with your health,' she snaps. 'It seems to me you're determined to ignore my advice.'

I really don't want one of Issy's lectures. Ross is waiting in the garden and there is something about her spikey domineering tone that's beginning to grate.

'Look, I must go. Goodbye.'

'But I know ...' she stammers.

I cut her off before she can finish, thinking, yes, I'm sure you think you know what's best for me, but you don't, you *really* don't.

Back in the kitchen, I make Ross his coffee, avoiding the cup I've set aside for Daniel containing a sedative.

I'm surprised how easily I'm able to disassociate making coffee for an ex-lover and drugging my ex-husband.

I find Ross wandering in the garden.

'There you go,' I smile, handing him his coffee.

'Thanks. Your garden looks lovely, and so do you by the way,' he blushes. 'You do all this yourself?'

'Yes, it's my hobby I suppose; something I can lose myself in; not think about work or anything else for a few hours.'

'Like me and surfing.'

'Yes, I suppose so. Still chasing waves then?'

'Whenever I can get away, which is not often lately.' His face is boyishly animated as he speaks. Though still undoubtedly fit; he no longer has the soft suppleness of youth. His arms in his t-shirt are sinewy, the veins in his tensed bicep pulsing as he lifts the cup to his lips. I guess he works out but probably aches these days when he gets back from a day riding waves. Sun and wind have etched fine spidery lines across his tanned face. His lips are set, his profile stern, as if he hasn't had much to laugh about lately. That's fine, neither have I. Remembering his fair teenage curls, I want to cry, not because of his lost looks but because of our lost youth.

'I meant what I said Claire, you look lovely.'

I remember the lengths I've gone to to get ready for Daniel's seduction and feel it would be faintly ridiculous to say; 'Oh, this is something I just threw on,' and decide to go along with the story I've invented for Sarah's benefit.

'I've got a wedding to go to. I've been trying on different things; deciding what to wear.'

'Well, I'd go with that one, it's perfect on you; matches your eyes.'

'Thanks,' I say, feeling the flush of the compliment.

He finishes his coffee and hands me back the cup.

'I'd better go, you've got your wedding and I've got a long drive ahead of me. I do hope you didn't mind me dropping in?'

'Not at all, I told you, anytime.'

His hand rests on mine briefly as I trace the rim of the cup where his lips have been. I can't help imagining how those lips would feel against mine.

The heaviness hits me; the oppressive weight of missed opportunities.

Before we reach the gate, he stops and bends towards me, gently brushing a kiss near my lips. My heart aches with regret.

'Bye, Claire, I'll give you a ring next week and I'll bring you some plants from Mum's greenhouse, she'll be glad to share, especially with you. It's spring, after all. New season, new start.'

THIRTY-FOUR

Issy was furious. Claire had no right to shut her out like that. Friends didn't do that to each other. She'd planned her entire weekend around seeing her; it wasn't good enough. Well, she wouldn't stand for it. She'd go around anyway and see what she was up to.

She wondered whose wedding it was. She imagined Claire sipping champagne cocktails and eating canapés and hoped they choked her.

What she had to say was important; far more important than galivanting off somewhere with God knows who to watch two loved-up idiots say, 'I do'.

She'd watch the house; see whether she was going with anyone to this wedding. She'd follow her if need be. She had a right to, didn't she, after what they'd been through together?

Parking a little way up the street she opened the carrier bag of goodies she'd bought from the petrol station on the way; crisps, a large bar of Cadbury's Dairy Milk and some French Fancies. She could wait all day if necessary.

She was just about to open a can of diet coke when a man emerged from Claire's house. She supposed he was good-looking in a rugged, vulgar way. She waited to see if Claire followed him out. He looked very scruffy for a wedding. No, he looked more like someone delivering something or a workman in his t-shirt and jeans.

Once he'd driven off, she settled herself in her seat and put on the radio. She didn't watch television and was getting fed up with radio four as well, with its constant parade of guests whining about political correctness, but she'd been transfixed by the local news station's coverage of the Jennings murder. The thrill of knowing the truth when no one else did.

She'd felt the same when she'd read in the paper about Jane Donoghue. *Local Teacher and WI stalwart dies in tragic cake choking accident.*

Ha! The very thought of it gave her goose bumps. She bit the top off a lemon French Fancy. No sooner had she begun to lick at the cream than a bright red car pulled up out of which jumped another man who was now heading down Claire's path.

This one was better dressed, but still not in a suit and he could do with a haircut.

She watched as Claire opened the door and let him in. She never saw him come out.

THIRTY-FIVE

Daniel knocks on the door only minutes after Ross leaves, giving me no time to process his visit. I find myself floundering between my routinely suspicious lawyer self and a woman who wants to believe Ross's motive had nothing to do with his investigation. After all he hadn't once mentioned Jennings or Jane Donoghue.

Daniel beams as I open the door.

Once inside, he falls back into the arms of the leather sofa we bought together.

'Do you want a coffee?'

'Yeah that would be grand and ... do you have anything to eat? I know we're having lunch later, but I'm starving. I had to get the kids' breakfast and then take the dog for a walk and I didn't have time for anything myself.'

Selfless as ever.

I pour the hot coffee from the pot over the sedative, making sure I stir it carefully, knowing the dark Columbian blend Daniel prefers will disguise any residuary taste.

'You've got a dog; I thought you didn't like dogs?'

'Louisa says it's good for the children to get used to them, so they're not frightened if they meet them in the park, and they learn to care about something other than themselves.'

Maybe you and Louisa should have got a dog earlier, if it can do that for you, I think to myself.

He looks older and tired. His dark wavy hair, now grey at the temples, needs a cut. As I bring his coffee, he looks me up and down.

'You look good, Claire, sort of summery.'

'Thanks.' Putting the cup on the table, I bend forward, flashing my silk underwear as my dress gapes slightly. I've dabbed his favourite perfume into my cleavage and he inhales deeply.

'You've let your hair dry curly,' he says exhaling.

'Only for today,' I reply truthfully.

'I like it. It's the way it was when I first met you.'

I need to change the subject. We're in danger of taking a turn down memory lane earlier than I anticipated. I've underestimated the effect of the dress.

'What do you want to eat? I've got a couple of croissants, but no jam.'

'Have you got any bacon? I'd love a bacon sandwich. Louisa's vegetarian these days and doesn't like meat in the house.'

I wish he'd shut up about Louisa. I begin to wish I hadn't taken her name out of the box.

'Probably, I'll have a look.'

I've cleared the fridge of practically everything but kept a few things for my own breakfast, including a couple of rashers of bacon and a few eggs.

After his coffee, bacon sandwich and second croissant, he settles back in his seat, tapping his belly in a *I'm full and ready for business* way.

'Have you brought the paperwork for the car?'

'Yeah,' he perks up, 'I left it in the glove compartment.'

'Well, if you go and get it, I'll clear the plates away and we can look it over.'

By the time Daniel returns I'm sitting at the kitchen table. He plonks the papers on the table. There is a loan agreement and an insurance policy.

'So how much is the balloon payment?' I ask.

'30k or thereabouts.'

'And the insurance?'

'Well, technically that ran out last week, when the premium was due, so I was hoping you'd be able to settle that online for me today?' Then as a bit of an afterthought, 'I really appreciate this Claire, I was dreading having to lose her after all we've been through together.'

He means him and The Beast; give me strength, I think.

'So, you drove it here today uninsured?'

'I know it looks bad, but I haven't driven it since it ran out, it's just that Louisa had the other car today and it was either drive it or get an Uber and I would've had to ask you to give me a lift home, so I just thought I'd bring it with me so if you paid online I could drive it back and everything would be okay.'

I know Daniel thinks there is no way I'll let him drive without insurance and so this way I am guaranteed to settle the premium.

Picking up his insurance details, I begin typing the information into my laptop as he peers over my shoulder. I go through all the required fields ticking boxes and asking him for details when required. Then it comes to the final payment stage.

'Oh damn, I've forgotten my security code, can you go to my desk and get the card? It's on the top somewhere.'

I wait until he's inside the study, rustling papers, before shouting, 'It's okay, don't bother, I've remembered it!'

Daniel comes back, card in hand just in case.

'All done,' I lie, closing the lid of the laptop.

'My printer is on the blink, so I requested they post the policy schedule to you, hope that's okay?'

'Yeah, fine by me,' grins a grateful Daniel.

'Now for the cheque.' I grab the cheque book lying on the kitchen counter and, turning my back to Daniel, write out a cheque to him for thirty thousand pounds.

Had I not obscured his view he might have noticed the cheque book isn't mine, but my mother's, retrieved from her house before she went into the nursing home. I sign my name with a flourish above the typed E.M Penrose knowing it can never be cashed, then seal the cheque in an envelope and hand it to Daniel.

I know even he won't be crass enough to open it.

'Oh my god Claire, I don't know what to say, you don't know what this means to me. I thought I would lose her. I haven't told Louisa; she thinks I own her outright already. I haven't slept a wink for weeks worrying about someone knocking at the door and driving her off and me having to explain everything. You're a life-saver.'

If only you knew how wrong you are, I think.

'How about a glass of fizz to celebrate' I ask.

'That would be perfect.' Daniel can barely settle he's so excited by the whole thing. Having chilled a bottle of Moët in the fridge, I carry it to the table and pour two glasses.

'Cheers,' I say, kicking off my shoes; settling myself down next to him.

'Slainte! You know what I said earlier, about you looking lovely, I meant it Claire, you really look well and I'm glad, and so grateful for what you've just done for me, I know I really don't deserve it.' He actually looks remorseful for one moment and I think I might have been too harsh on him, but then he follows the compliment with;

'Well I suppose as you're on your own now you don't really need the money. It's not like you have a partner or kids to spend it on … all this is paid for,' he gestures around the room.

'Well, yes,' I retort, not being able to bite my tongue, 'that's because whilst you were buying a Maserati and taking trips to swanky hotels for extramarital shags with your girlfriends I was saving for a rainy day.'

'Look Claire, I know you've always thought me a waster, and you've always been sensible with money, but really you must understand, a man needs to reward himself for his efforts to keep the momentum going. All work and no play, makes Jack a very boring boy and sends him looking elsewhere for comfort. Men need rewards, we're not like women, strong and stoical, able to put up with things.'

Only Daniel could make an admission of his failings sound like an accusation.

'What rewards do you get now?' I smile, desperately trying to keep the mood light.

'What do you mean … oh, other women? No, no, all that's behind me. I've got the children and commitments.'

'So, you're never tempted?' I ask, turning towards him and placing my hand on his chest. 'Say, for example, you could get away with it; say you could have your cake and eat it knowing you'd never be found out?'

'But I always would be found out. You found out, and so would Louisa.'

I know detection is Daniel's real concern. He's not averse to lying, he was happy to do so for a couple of rashers of bacon. I lean back and he leans in towards me, resting his head on my shoulder. He closes his eyes like a little boy.

'It's so nice just sitting here,' he whispers. 'It's so peaceful without the kids. Don't get me wrong, I love them, It's just they're always there with their mess and their noise.'

I fight the instincts to knock his lights out; instead, I reach over and pat his leg. 'Well Louisa ought to realise you need some 'me time' too. Perhaps you could look at this time with me, as your 'me time'.

Daniel opens his eyes at this revelation. 'Yeah, I could come here when things get a bit fraught at home and we could just, you know, chill.'

In your dreams, I think. I imagine Daniel turning up randomly expecting me to drop everything and feed him or mop his furrowed brow or worse still become his 'friend with benefits'. I can see his brain mulling over the endless possibilities.

Tilting his head, he moves forward tentatively to kiss me. As his lips touch mine, I no longer feel the tingle I used to feel every time we kissed. I need to control this and get him upstairs and undressed.

'Daniel?'

'Yes,' he mumbles, as his hand hovers over my breasts.

'Do you think you could make love to me? You know, properly in our bed, as if we were still together. It's just I haven't … since you and I split, with my treatment and everything, I just haven't had the time for relationships and I miss it … I miss you.'

He looks at me earnestly as if I'm a toddler being given a toy reserved for older children. 'I understand,' he says solemnly, clearly barely able to contain himself.

'Rest assured it'll stay between us. I wouldn't want to do anything to jeopardize your life with Louisa and the children, it's just I trust you and you've been a hard act to follow.'

He resembles one of those plumped-up birds of paradise in full mating regalia from the wildlife programmes. In my head, David Attenborough's voice whispers;

'And now the cock known as the Egotistical McBride moves in on the female knowing that she's chosen him above all other suitors to be her mate.'

I take the hand of my smug ex-husband and lead him upstairs.

'Bring the champagne.'

THIRTY-SIX

Ross set the sat-nav to his ex-wife's address. It would take him at least two and a half hours to get to Bristol if the traffic wasn't too bad and there weren't any roadworks or diversions. It meant he'd get three hours at most with the kids before he'd have to take them back to Trudy, that was, if they didn't cry or complain to go home earlier to play some computer game Trudy's new bloke had bought them.

Lately the visits had become awkward. It took at least an hour for them to feel comfortable with him. He could tell from their body language as they wriggled in their seats, avoiding eye contact that might betray their mistrust. On those occasions he wished his police training hadn't taught him to read so much into things. It would have been less painful. He had to cajole them into giving anything beyond monosyllabic grunts in response to his questions about school or what they were up to. They'd cling to each other in a way he knew they never usually did. He knew it because by the end of his visits they started to behave normally, teasing and arguing, just like siblings did when left to their own devices. If he was lucky and managed to get to that point early in the visit, he might even get a hug when he left.

Each time he saw them he hoped it would get easier, but each time was disappointed.

His mind returned to Claire and their conversation earlier. She had taken his breath away when he'd walked around to the back of the house and seen her sitting in her garden. He didn't think of himself as romantic, or at least if he ever had been, he was pretty damn sure it had been knocked out of him one way or another, but when he'd seen Claire today, he felt alive.

He had, he supposed, felt a raw, youthful kind of love for her once, when they were kids, a sloppy sentimental love copied from films and TV. He'd fancied her and they'd got on. They had the same friends and liked the same things and that was all it took back then. It worked for a while, maybe it wasn't love but it was something and a damn sight more than he'd felt for anyone lately.

When he'd brushed his lips against hers, he'd had to stop himself telling her how he felt. He winced with embarrassment just thinking about it as he twisted his hands on the steering wheel, as if it were his own neck he was wringing.

The traffic was terrible. It had been stop-start ever since Bodmin and the sat-nav was now saying his arrival time was at least an hour later than he'd planned.

He wouldn't reach Bristol until at least two thirty and that meant he'd have to ring Trudy and say he'd be late. He knew she'd still want the kids back at the same time no matter what, giving him just two hours if he was lucky.

He sat as the minutes ticked away, edging slowly forward, changing lanes occasionally, although it made no difference as the traffic halted again.

He'd left it as long as he dared. He tapped in Trudy's number.

'Hi it's me, look I'm stuck in traffic and I'm going to be late. I won't be there until two thirty at the earliest. Do you think I could keep the kids a bit longer, maybe take them for a pizza or something, I could even book into a Travelodge?'

'No Ross, it's out of the question, they have their routine, and I'm sorry, I'm not prepared to change it for you. You can come as planned, but I've arranged to take them to the cinema this evening and they're looking forward to it.'

'Maybe I could take them instead and you could have a break?'

There was silence on the other end of the phone for a moment, and then, 'No, I don't think so. I appreciate the thought, but no.'

Ross wanted to shout, why the fuck not? but didn't, instead he kept his cool.

'Okay, I understand, but really Trudy, with this traffic it's hardly going to give me any time with them at all.'

The traffic was still not moving and the chap in the car in front had turned his engine off altogether. Ross did the same.

Trudy's voice took on a frosty, indignant tone, 'Well, that's not my problem, is it? Don't come at all if you can't be bothered,' she sniped.

'I didn't say that; I was just saying—'

'I know what you're saying Ross, that your children are not important enough to you, that they're not high on your list of priorities!'

'Trudy that's just not true and you know it.' He knew he was raising his voice but the traffic and his frustration at her predictable response to his request had rattled him.

'Don't shout at me,' she screamed. 'In fact, I'm putting the phone down and don't bother to come today because we won't be in when you finally get here!'

She slammed the phone down and when he rang back the line was engaged. He tried three times more only to hear the same beep beep beep.

When the traffic began to move, he took the next exit and began the drive back to Cornwall, but he wouldn't be going home; he was heading back to Claire's. He had something to ask her, something that couldn't wait.

THIRTY-SEVEN

I sit Daniel down on the bed. I'm not nervous, you can't be married to someone for fifteen years without knowing what buttons to press. I slowly untie the belt around my waist, letting the blue dress fall to the floor to reveal the lilac silk underwear.

'Oh my god Claire, you look incredible, Louise hasn't been able to lose the baby weight yet,' Daniel said. 'She's trying but it's quite difficult you know.'

Could he be any more of a knob if he tried, I thought, ruffling his hair?

'Why don't you make yourself comfortable?'

Daniel needs no encouragement. He pulls off his shoes and throws them across the room; his trousers, shirt and boxers follow swiftly behind. He launches himself back on the bed, arms behind his head staring at his manhood with smug satisfaction.

I move towards the dressing table to pour the drinks, slipping the second of the sedatives Issy gave me for my insomnia into Daniel's glass. I hand it to him and he knocks it back in one.

Noticing how exhausted he looked when he first walked in, I thought I'd only need one more sleeping tablet in addition to the one I'd given him in his coffee. I'd thought two, along with the booze, should do the trick. I know Daniel can fall asleep just about anywhere. I'd seen him do it on long-haul journeys the moment the plane took off, only to wake just before landing, or at the cinema, and even in mid-sentence at parties when he'd had too much to drink and had lost the thread of the conversation.

Whilst I've pulled off the seduction easily enough, I'm having difficulty dealing with the prospect of actual sex if he doesn't fall asleep soon. I thought I'd be okay with it; it wouldn't be the first time I'd slept with Daniel after all, but now the moment has arrived I find myself desperately trying to think of a viable alternative without ruining my plan. The aim is to orchestrate a situation which will lead to Daniel being tied up as part of some erotic roleplay. I thought it would be easy to set the whole thing up; the fluffy handcuffs, the blindfold and all the other paraphernalia I've tucked under the pillow but I hadn't reckoned on him being quite so perky. I need to think; and quickly.

'I'll go and get another,' I say tipping the empty champagne bottle upside down into the ice bucket. 'I'll be back in just a second.'

Downstairs I decide I've no choice but to slip him another tablet. I retrieve the new bottle of champagne from the fridge along with another pill from the pack, take a deep breath and walk upstairs.

To my relief Daniel is fast asleep. I prod him; dead to the world.

'Thank God,' I whisper, carefully placing the champagne bottle on the bedside table with the two glasses.

I go to the other side of the bed and pull the fluffy handcuffs and blindfold from beneath the pillow. I fasten Daniels wrists together locking him to the wrought iron headboard. Next the stockings. I'd had the sense to buy extra-large but nevertheless hadn't factored in the effort it takes to get them over his huge feet or the fact they stick to his hairy legs. Eventually I have them both sort of on with a few ladders.

Picking up my phone, I select the camera function.

I carefully choose my angles so the champagne and the glasses are in shot. I e-mail one of the obscenest to his surgery. When he arrives at work on Monday morning, he'll be aware that something's not quite right. He'll clock the tittering and sideways glances; notice the abrupt end to a conversation as he enters the room. There will be a niggling sensation he can't locate, then slowly, as if a bug has crawled from his ear, it will dawn on him I've e-mailed the photo to everyone.

He'll face the biting sting of humiliation, just like the countless, toe-curling humiliations I suffered when I visited him there and was forced to squirm through the pitiful red-faced excuses his receptionist gave for his absence.

I send a second photo of Daniel by text to Louisa's phone.

I pick up Daniel's clothes from the floor, carefully removing his mobile and the envelope from his trouser pocket. I take the envelope and write upon it; *For services rendered. Love Claire xx*

Propping it up against the champagne bottle beside the empty glasses, I make my way downstairs. I put on my dress, put my phone in the pocket and carry Daniel's clothes and mobile to the utility room. I open the door of the tumble dryer and retrieve the plastic bag containing the clothes I hid there the night Fergus Jennings died. To these I add Daniel's clothes and his mobile. I tie a knot in the bag and carry it back into the kitchen, retrieving Daniel's keys from the top of the kitchen table where he set them down.

Finally, I open the cupboard door beneath the sink and lift out the box. I open it, take out Donoghue, Jennings and Daniel's name, carry them to the cloakroom and flush them away.

I leave the house carrying the box and don't look back.

Pressing the keypad to open the Maserati I feel a surge of relief as I place the plastic bag and the box on the back seat.

'Afternoon, Beast,' I say as I turn the key in the ignition.

Driving away from the house, out of town along the quiet back roads, I'm glad I exercised restraint. I'm pleased with myself for showing compassion in Daniel's case. I hope when this is over, he'll count himself lucky. I hope he'll change and come to value what he has; his wife, his children; his life.

Whether he's capable of stepping up to the mark, I don't know. He's old enough to battle his own demons and deal with the fallout. My part in his sorry soap opera is over. I've got my own drama to star in. I need to focus on my own journey.

This is my 'Me Time.'

THIRTY-EIGHT

Issy was jolted awake by the sound of a car engine revving. Wiping the chocolatey dribble from her chin, she shuffled down into her seat as she spotted Claire in the flashy red car, she'd seen the dark-haired man arrive in earlier. She had no idea where he was. Claire was alone and sitting in the driver's seat. Perhaps he'd left earlier, whilst she was asleep?

She didn't have long to ponder as the car pulled away.

Issy swept the empty crisp packets and wrappers into the well beneath her passenger seat. She couldn't lose her.

She followed Claire as she took the second exit on the roundabout. She managed to time her own exit so there was another vehicle between them and felt pleased with herself.

It was quite exciting now she came to think of it; stalking someone; hunting them down.

THIRTY-NINE
CLAIRE

Daniel's right about one thing, The Beast handles beautifully. It sticks to the coastal road like glue as I swing it left and right, snaking my way around the sharp, unforgiving bends. I slow down, and open the window, pulling the vanilla-scented air into my lungs, letting it wash through me like a spring clean.

I'm dazzled by a shard of sunlight piercing the blossomy branches arching the road and feel in the glove compartment for my sunglasses, before remembering firstly, this isn't my car and secondly they've gone to the charity shop with everything else. I hadn't thought I'd need them; hadn't thought I'd see another summer. Putting my foot down, I leave the canopy's strobing light for open sky and catch my first glimpse of the sea blindingly blue against a cloudless sky, truth and redemption, meeting at the horizon. The noose lifts.

I've purposely picked a beach off the beaten track; used by locals rather than tourists put off by the steep access which is a challenge even to the best of drivers and a nonstarter to anyone who worries about their lipstick red paintwork. I am certain it's The Beast's first visit to Penmorvah.

This time of year, a gusting south westerly sandblasts everything in its path. Wild and remote, this was always Mum's favourite.

Pulling onto the uneven patch of hardcore above the beach I check I'm alone. I sit to take stock for a moment before reaching behind me and heaving the plastic carrier bag onto the passenger seat. It seems comically ordinary; just another supermarket bag for life.

I smile at the irony. Untying the knot, I tip out the creased remnants of my disguise. Lifting the cheap eBay parka, I delve into the pocket for the disposable lighter I know is there. Rummaging again, I shake free the yellow tartan scarf that proved the perfect decoy and place it with the lighter on my lap. Holding the scarf and the lighter in one hand, I pick up the box and, kicking the car door shut behind me, lay it on the bonnet and walk to the back of the Maserati.

My dress billows around my legs and I shiver as the icy breeze whips my bare arms. Mum would chastise me for not wearing a coat. 'You'll catch your death,' she'd say if she saw me, and she'd be right.

Unscrewing the petrol cap, I drop one end of the scarf into the tank. Keeping tightly hold of the other end, I pause, feeling the weight of the fuel suck up through its fibres, then, controlling the shake in my fingers, light it and watch with deep satisfaction the yellow cloth disintegrate like old film.

I compose one last text;

Thanks for re-lighting my fire, Darling Daniel.
Happy to return the favour! Claire xx

Two thunderous BOOMS echo in quick succession.

Although by now metres away, a surge of sizzling heat propels me forward, almost toppling me to the ground. I turn and watch the billowing plumes of acrid smoke scar the perfect blue sky. The car is alight.

I lift my mobile, snap a photo, attach it to the text and press send before tossing my phone back towards the flames.

FORTY

Louisa had just settled the twins at the kitchen table when her mobile pinged. She'd been racing around all morning, running Connor to football, then taking the girls to ballet-tots. She'd sat watching the toe pointing and listening to the dink, dink of the tinny piano whilst Madam Shirley put the little mites through their paces. Daniel usually looked after the children on Saturday mornings. She didn't know any of the mothers and as she watched their besotted faces thought; what the hell am I doing here?

When they were finally finished, she quickly ushered the girls out and rushed to the park to pick up her sweaty son.

The children fought in the car, the two girls overtired, bursting into tears when Connor told them that they looked like sissys in their pink leotards. Neither of them knew what a sissy was but the put-down by their brother was enough to set them off. She'd shouted at them to shut up and the response from Connor had been; 'Daddy doesn't shout at us when he picks us up.'

'No, of course not,' she shouted back, 'he's perfect; funny easy-going Daddy.'

Daniel would have chatted up the mums at the ballet class, asking them to cast an eye over the girls, and then driven Connor to football and watched the match, cheering him on, beaming every time the little boy touched the ball. She knew she was a crap mother; she'd always known she would be, but she'd wanted to keep Daniel once she'd netted him. She'd devoted too much time and effort to the relationship to lose him to someone else or, worse still, for him to go back to Claire.

Claire, the very thought of her made her anxious. Claire who Daniel talked about constantly:

'Claire and I went there on our fifth wedding anniversary,' or 'Claire always understood that sometimes I had to work late.'

There she was looming over their relationship like the Ghost of Christmas Past, Claire the capable clever, understanding ex-wife. Then, when she'd been diagnosed with cancer, she'd had to put up with her beatification to Saint Claire. Daniel went on endlessly about how she didn't complain, despite everything and spent what seemed like hours on the phone talking to his mother or his annoying sisters about how brave good old Claire was.

When she heard him talking about her, the mother of his children it was a different story; the tone less affectionate and the conversation less complimentary, 'Oh well you know how she is, she does her best, but she finds things difficult and she's so particular.'

Louisa knew she was fussy and the birth of the children had made her anxieties worse. She worried about what they ate, whether they watched too much TV, whether they'd get into a good school and whether they were developing adequate social skills. There was no relief from the drudgery of her motherly paranoia.

That Daniel was at that very moment with Claire, albeit to discuss her death, filled her with panic. She'd allowed him to go because he'd said Claire wanted to discuss her will and he was certain being such a 'good egg' she'd be generous and make sure they were financially secure.

Money was tight now she no longer worked and despite her protestations, Daniel hadn't curbed his spending habits.

As she prepared the children's vegetarian pizzas, she felt abandoned and put upon by the pair of them. She imagined them, heads locked together like a scene from *Love Story*, tears in their eyes as Saint Claire planned her funeral.

When the mobile pinged, she picked it up. There was a text from Claire.

She wondered if her husband had forgotten the children's middle names and they might be needed for the will. She read the text and cursed him.

Claire was asking her to come and collect him. She was furious, firstly because it was Claire texting her and not Daniel himself, and secondly that he'd driven there, obviously become maudlin, had too much to drink and now expected her to drop everything and go pick him up. Then she saw there was an attachment. She opened it and, as she watched the photograph gradually reveal itself, felt the viper coil around her throat.

Her husband lay naked on a bed; mouth open, an empty bottle of champagne and two glasses on the bedside table next to him. He was tied up, wearing a pink satin blindfold and black, laddered stockings.

'Bastard!'

She pulled the children from their seats, ignoring their protests as she shoved a triangle of pizza into each of their hungry little hands. Grabbing three cartons of juice from the fridge she hurried them out the door.

She settled them in their booster seats and drove, head pounding, to Claire's house.

As she pulled up outside, she wondered if her husband had left already. The Maserati wasn't there. Daniel hadn't driven it for days but for some reason had made a huge point of taking it that morning. For a moment, she didn't know what to do, but then thought she'd have it out with Claire anyway. She'd tell her to stuff her money and that she hoped she died an agonising, messy death.

She got out of the car.

'Connor, you look after your sisters, Mummy won't be long. You be a big boy, you're in charge. I'll put your CD on so you can listen while Mummy's gone.'

Passing them each a carton of orange, she pushed the bendy straw attached to each box through the tiny hole in the top. Her hands were shaking as the sticky juice overflowed onto her fingers. Opening the car window, a couple of inches, she switched on the CD and got out, locking the doors behind her.

She walked slowly up the path, looking back to check that the children were okay, pleased they seemed as worn out as her from the morning's activities. The front door was ajar. Gently pushing it open she paused for a second on the threshold before walking inside, leaving it open behind her so the children wouldn't worry.

She listened for voices but could hear none. Downstairs seemed empty but there was a smell of cooking, although she couldn't quite put her finger on what it was. She remembered Daniel said he was staying for lunch and thought, as it was a nice day, they might be eating outside, but on checking the patio, they weren't there.

She made her way to the bottom of the stairs, stomach roiling; the smell not helping. Part of her wanted to shout out Daniel's name in the hope he would run to the top of the stairs and tell her it was all some elaborate sick joke, but another part of her wanted to creep into the bedroom and catch them together, so she could for once take the moral high ground.

On the landing, she gently tried the handle of the first room she came to. It was the bathroom and was empty. The door opposite was open and she gave it a gentle push.

Daniel lay on the bed in the same position as in the photograph. He was fast asleep, and Claire was nowhere to be seen.

She checked the en-suite, half expecting her to be there smiling triumphantly, ready to scream: 'I've got him back. He's mine again,' but she wasn't there either.

She walked back into the bedroom.

'Daniel …'

Nothing, no reaction at all, Daniel didn't move.

'Daniel!' she bellowed.

Daniel stirred clearly bemused and bewildered to hear her voice.

Louisa felt physically sick and that smell; seemed to be everywhere?

'What the hell's going on, Daniel?'

Then suddenly as if from nowhere, it came to her; she recognised the all-pervading aroma.

'Daniel … have you been eating bacon?' she screamed, incensed.

Daniel tried to move but couldn't. His hands were tied and he couldn't see a thing.

Louisa tore the blindfold from his face. She stood over him frothing at the mouth as she flicked the switch on the handcuffs and freed him.

He slid from the duvet cover, ripping the stockings from his legs; throwing them under the bed in a pathetic attempt to hide them from her, not knowing about the family snap Claire had sent.

She could tell he was racking his brain for a halfway plausible excuse for his state of undress and why he was in his ex-wife's bedroom. Louisa watched him flounder as he scrambled to find his clothes.

She looked around the room. Everywhere was remarkably tidy for the scene of an orgy, even the bed covers seemed undisturbed.

Her eyes drifted to the envelope propped up for all to read the disgusting words written on it. Ripping it open, she pulled free a cheque made out to her husband for thirty thousand pounds. Claire had paid him for this; this sordid, unspeakable liaison? She'd had sex with Daniel and while he was no slouch, he wasn't 30k's worth even to his sad, dying ex-wife. No, it had to be something more? Maybe he'd told Claire he would go back to her, stay with her for the rest of her pathetic life. That he would, for the right sum, abandon her and their children. Was that the service he was rendering?

She wanted to rip the cheque up and shove it down his treacherous throat. Then, she noticed whilst it had been signed by Claire, she was not the account holder detailed in the bottom right-hand corner: E.M. Penrose. Claire's mother. It was one thing for your husband to be someone's whore, at least she and the children could be compensated through the money changing hands. It was quite another for him to be duped into selling his body without reward.

She finally lost it.

'Daniel, what the hell is this?' she ranted, waving the cheque in his face. 'Didn't the lovely Claire get her money's worth? Is that why she gave you a dud cheque, and by the way where's your car?'

'What do you mean?' asked Daniel, pausing from his search.

He took the cheque and looked at it for the first time.

'Shit,' he said, his face dropping to his bare knees. 'Shit, shit … shit.'

His clothes were nowhere to be found and out of sheer desperation, he stumbled into the bathroom and grabbed a towel from the rail for the sake of his modesty before padding downstairs. He rushed to the front door to see if his car really was missing like Louisa said. He was hoping upon hope he'd forgotten he'd parked further down the road, but he knew it wasn't the case as soon as he saw the empty Beast-shaped space.

He backtracked to the kitchen where he'd left his keys. They were gone.

Louisa joined him downstairs and seeing the children fighting in the back of the car, insisted they leave. Daniel reluctantly followed her, bare footed, still draped in the towel.

As he opened the passenger door the girls chorused their greeting;

'Daddy!!! Daddy. Daddy.'

'Have you been swimming, Daddy?' squealed Connor spotting the towel.

Just as a furious Louisa was about to drive off, her phone pinged again with a new text from Claire; something about Daniel lighting her fire and her returning the favour.

If Claire thought there would be a repeat performance of today's filth she could think again. Louisa clicked the attachment half thinking it would be another pic of Daniel naked or worse still, one of Claire, but it was a photo of the Beast on fire.

She lifted the phone pointedly in front of Daniel's face.

His scream, like that of a tormented banshee, could be heard halfway down the street.

***

Ross pulled up outside Claire's front door just as Daniel emerged wearing only a small towel. There was a woman with him with a face like thunder, who Ross assumed was Daniel's second wife. It could mean only one thing: Claire had been with her ex-husband. That's who the blue dress was for and why she'd been so coy about who she'd been with in the carpark the two nights before Jennings' death.

She'd lied to him. She hadn't been trying on outfits for some wedding, she'd been getting ready for that waste of space, Daniel McBride, and they'd been caught in the act.

You fool, he thought to himself, starting the engine and doing a U-turn to get out of there as fast as he could without being seen, you stupid, deluded fool.

FORTY-ONE

ISSY

Issy pulled up in the lane leading to the beach carpark. She'd managed to follow Claire without her realising but if she parked any closer, she was bound to spot her. What was she doing here? She'd watched men come and go from Claire's house all morning. First the scruffy looking one in the t-shirt, then the one whose shiny red car Claire sped off in and she'd followed. Perhaps this was another rendezvous with yet another man?

'Slut,' she muttered under her breath. Without starting the engine, she released the handbrake, letting the car silently roll down the MC, keeping close to the hedge to avoid being noticed. She had a good view of the car now and watched Claire get out, look around and kick the door shut behind her. She was carrying something but she couldn't see what.

She watched Claire scan the carpark before walking first to the back of the car, then around to the far side where she loitered for a minute before heading off towards the beach having picked up what she could now see was a box with a ribbon, just like the one in her bedroom containing the names.

What came next shook Issy's car back and forth like a fairground ride sending a rumble up her spine. Two enormous blasts sent huge plumes of black smoke high into the sky as the red car was engulfed in flames.

'What the ...?' she screamed, ears ringing with the vibration from the blast.

Instinctively she opened her car door and ran, half expecting her own car to explode too. She stumbled, and felt a sharp pain as a piece of grit pierced the palm of her hand.

Clambouring to her feet she leaned over the hedge just in time to see Claire take a photograph of the burning car with her phone.

FORTY-TWO
CLAIRE

Tasting burning rubber in the back of my throat and the heat on my shoulders from the explosion, I start down the sandy path leading to the beach. Every step is familiar, every batch of sea thrift, a precious pink memory. I kick off my shoes.

I feel grounded again, the fine sand sifting between my toes.

I'm not afraid to die, not in the least, nor of being dead, but don't intend to wait for death to call. Instead, I plan to knock on death's door and when he opens it, grab him by his scrawny neck and shout; 'This is my moment! Don't fuck with me; you don't know who you're dealing with!'

If I was a different person, I might have bought a ticket to Switzerland, but the whole concept seems over civilised. The prospect of death with dignity conjuring up a vision of piped music and white walled sterility; all a little too tidy for my taste.

I want my death to mirror the wonderful, messy life I've led.

My cancer temporarily unnerved me, turning me firstly into a petrified, puking mess then later, when it returned, flooding me with the compulsion to right wrongs and punish those who abused their chance to lead a decent life, those whose names I placed in the box. Now they've been dealt with; I can finally concentrate on myself.

Looking out to sea I feel as if I've come home.

The saltwater spray and iridescent light is as much part of me as my cancer. As I look out across the blue water, thoughts of my childhood, dominated by the tides and the weather, flood my memory.

I think of my gran and Mum's three sisters who had charge of me during school holidays when Mum was on duty. I visualise them walking with me now, armed with windbreaks, blankets and

Tupperware, my younger cousins in tow. I imagine my uncles, heaving the small dinghy up onto the beach, their mood lifted by beer, carrying the dozen or so mackerel they've caught; telling stories of the ones that got away. When dusk falls we'll throw sand on the fire and make our way home.

Glancing down at my bare feet and the footprints they leave; I think of all the times I've made the same prints before. I remember seeing on the news how during an extreme low tide, the footprints of a prehistoric family had been found on a beach near Southport. Plaster casts and photographs had been taken to preserve a snapshot of their outing seven thousand years ago, before the tide returned and reclaimed the memory.

I think of all the footprints that have made up my own chequered history.

FORTY-THREE

ISSY

Choking and spluttering Issy pulled her rollneck up to cover her nose. Making sure she kept several metres behind, skirting the bottom of the cliff, she shadowed Claire as she made her way down the beach. The tide was on the turn and it was a long hike to the water but it was clearly where she was heading.

Issy shivered. Although she wore a jumper and her favourite fleece, she felt cold. Claire seemed to be wearing a ridiculously flimsy dress. She'd said she was off to a wedding when she'd called, maybe that explained the fancy blue frock? Perhaps the box contained a wedding present and wasn't the box from her bedroom? It suddenly crossed Issy's mind this might be some kind of bizarre wedding stunt. Maybe someone was being *pranked* or whatever they called it and the thing with the car was part of it? She suddenly felt vulnerable.

What if people were watching or worse still, filming this? She'd watched ridiculous things like this on television. She'd seen Jeremy Clarkson blow up cars on TV. David thought it hilarious; she thought it juvenile nonsense and a waste of a good car.

She looked around. She couldn't see anyone filming; no overhead drones or revellers lurking in the sand dunes ready to pounce on the unsuspecting couple shouting, 'SURPRISE!'

Claire's back was to her; walking purposefully towards the shoreline. Surely if she was expecting someone to arrive on the scene, she'd be looking around for them by now? No, she was alone, Issy was sure of it. She seemed transfixed; pulled by an invisible chord towards the water. Issy ventured from the shelter of the cliffs to follow her not knowing what she'd say to her if she did turn around.

164

She could hardly believe her eyes when Claire began to wade into the water. She watched as she walked deeper and deeper into the surf until the waves lapped at her waist.

Issy stopped walking. Her rage held her rigid, rooting her to the spot.

FORTY-FOUR
CLAIRE

The icy water bites my toes but is nothing to the aching numbness as it hits my thighs. When the water reaches my waist, I set the box down, letting it float away. It bobs up and down; the pink ribbon darkening as the surf bats it back and forth. It drifts away on the next wave and with it all the anger, pain and sadness of the last two years. It contains only one name now; my own.

I glance back at Daniel's car still burning on the clifftop, like the beacons burning long ago, warning of Spanish invasion; alerting the populace they would need to fight for their lives. I've done with fighting for mine, I've had the best of it and now, I'm ready to let go.

As I look back, I think I glimpse Mum, in her favourite yellow bikini, beckoning to me to come in. I hear her calling my name.

'Claire … Claire.'

Once I would have reluctantly left the water to be wrapped in a towel and have the chill rubbed away. Now I just wave back, tears blurring my vision.

I begin to swim towards the horizon. As the waves wash over me, I let my body fall under them. I feel peace; safe in the element I understand and trust the most.

FORTY-FIVE

ISSY

Issy watched as Claire released the box she was holding out in front of her like a compass then followed her gaze towards the clifftop and the burning car. In the seconds it took for her to look back out to sea, Claire had disappeared and there was only one place she could have gone; under.

Suddenly it was clear as day, Claire was there to kill herself. The cowardly bitch was going to end it all, like some soppy heroine in a gothic romance. Well not on her watch she wasn't.

She'd decide when Claire McBride got to die. She'd decide when this finished. She'd have to go in after her. She looked down at her clothes, they'd be ruined. She slipped off her fleece and trousers and began to run.

It was years since she'd moved that fast. The relentless thumping in her ears, must be her heart, she thought, as her pendulous breasts swung back and forth. Her legs solid and heavy thundered along the sand, thighs rubbing together as she gathered speed. The shock of the cold as she entered the water made her pee and she felt disgust and anger at herself for not doing the pelvic floor exercises they endlessly harped on about in woman's magazines.

Catching her breath, she shouted, 'Claire!'

Issy could feel the pull of the rip tide on her ankles as she tried to keep her balance in the choppy water.

'Claire,' she shouted again as loud as she could.

Claire's body surfaced for one second before dipping under the waves again.

Issy made a final effort to wade towards her, fighting the current. Closing the gap, she managed to get within an arm's length.

A huge wave tossed her off her feet. Salt burned her eyes and made her nostrils raw as they streamed with water and snot. As the swirling surf tumbled her, she struggled to find her bearings. She used all her strength to fight her way towards the light. Air filled her aching lungs as she spun around looking for Claire, gasping in horrified disbelief as she spotted her out of reach beyond the waves floating face down. With one last effort she launched herself forward and grabbed a handful of wet black curls only to watch them slip through her fingers.

'No… no … she can't do this. She can't do this to me!'

She reached out again. This time she managed to grab Claire's skirt. Reeling her in she flung herself onto her back, pulling Claire on top of her so her limp body rested on her chest. With every muscle aching, she let the next wave propel them back to where she was within her depth and she could get a foothold on the rocks beneath them. She did the same again, dragging Claire through the water back to the shore.

Issy felt like the life had been punched out of her as she lay next to Claire on the wet sand. With an almighty effort she heaved herself onto her knees and leant over Claire to clear her airways, and begin CPR.

She shivered as she tried to breathe life back into her patient, trying desperately to fend off a strange hollow feeling she was unused to and didn't like.

She'd felt like it only once before when Mummy told her Daddy had died.

'You can't die. I won't let you die,' she shouted.

Claire coughed, salt water spewing from her blue lips.

Issy rolled her onto her side. She felt a lump rise in her throat and a feeling she couldn't diagnose as she watched Claire shivering, the blue dress clinging to her body like a shroud. Issy immediately took control. She needed to get her further up the beach in case the tide was coming in.

'Claire I want you to slowly try and sit up. We need to move further up the beach.'

Claire let out a moan, turning her head away.

'Look at me you're going to do as I say,' ordered Issy, grabbing her face so she would have no alternative but to meet her eye. 'I'll help you.'

Issy put her arm around Claire's shoulders, lifting her into a sitting position.

Claire immediately vomited again.

Issy made an effort to hide her disgust.

'Good that's good; better out than in. Now we're going to try and get you up.'

Claire nodded.

Issy, squatting behind her, reached under Claire's armpits heaving her to her feet. She was surprised how light she seemed now without the drag of the water. She slipped her arm around Claire's waist, lifting Claire's arm over her shoulder so she took her weight.

'Okay good, now lean into me, we're going to walk slowly up the beach onto the dry sand.'

Claire nodded again, wet curls falling over her face.

Issy steered her slowly up the beach to the spot where she'd discarded her trousers and fleece.

She sat Claire down, her back against the rocks.

'I'm going to take off that wet dress, and put this on you.'

Claire looked at her blankly.

Issy tugged at the dress's belt. The tight wet knot was impossible to undo and in the end she had to rip the silky material to get it off. She paused for a second when she revealed the lilac silk underwear, wondering whether she should remove that too but decided it wasn't necessary. She rubbed Claire vigorously, bringing some colour back to her arms before slipping the fleece over her head and pulling up the hood. Claire immediately curled her knees up under the fluffy garment so only her feet poked out. Issy thought how huge it looked on her considering how snug the fit on her was when she wore it.

Issy then pulled off her own wet jumper and wrung it out before pulling on her trousers. She was surprised how warm she felt. Adrenaline, she guessed.

'Okay now we're going to walk to my car . It's not far.'

She helped Claire to her feet and slowly walked her up the beach to the slope where her car was parked.

The driver's door was open, just as she'd left it. She opened the rear door and manoeuvred Claire into the back seat.

Issy left her there to retrieve a tartan picnic blanket from the boot and an old Barbour of David's which must have been in there for months. She slipped it on.

'Lie down,' she said tucking the blanket over Claire. 'I'll turn the heater on as soon as we get going.'

Once in the driver's seat, she lifted her phone from the charger where she'd left it. She'd call the hospital and tell them they were on the way and to get a foil wrap ready for Claire.

She was about to tap in the number when the thought came to her.

If she took her into A&E they would want to know her connection to Claire and when she told them she was her consultant they'd ask difficult questions about the medication she was taking and her prognosis. She could control her own department but if other disciplines got involved discrepancies in Claire's medical records would come to light and she might be found out. She couldn't risk that. They might take the view Claire was likely to attempt this again and section her. Then she'd be at the mercy of the psychologists. They were the ones who landed her here in the first place. They were the ones who suggested that stupid box. She wouldn't leave her patient to the mercy of charlatans and shrinks.

She could care for Claire as well as any hospital. She'd have the chance to talk with her about Donoghue and Jennings; to reassure her there was nothing to feel guilty about; nothing to warrant taking her own life. She'd take her home and care for her there. They had a spare room. She and Claire would have the chance to get to know each other better and if things worked out she could stay permanently when David was gone. She'd have to sack Rita of course. It wouldn't do for her to be nosing around but that was no real loss and once David was out of the picture there wouldn't be a job for her anyway, she'd be bringing forward the inevitable, that was all.

She called home.

'Rita it's me. I need you to make up the bed in the room opposite mine … yes the yellow room. I have a patient,' she corrected herself; 'a personal friend coming to stay for a while. When you've done that give David his pills and put him to bed. He had a restless night and needs to catch up. Once he's settled you can leave. I'll be home in about forty-five minutes and can take over … yes, I'm sure.'

Issy started the engine; pleased things had taken this unexpected turn. Every cloud had a silver lining.

FORTY-SIX

David watched Issy come up the drive from his bedroom window. He knew something was up. She was home early and he had been rushed off to bed by Rita who'd told him she was under orders to prepare the spare bedroom opposite Issy's room.

He asked who for, thinking for one awful moment Issy intended to put him in there so she could keep a closer eye on him. The room was canary yellow; it gave him a headache every time he went in there. Rita had reassured him they had a guest arriving, a friend of his wife's who would be staying for a while but that she had not been given a name.

As far as he was aware Issy had no friends in fact her lack of friends was something she took pride in. She once told him, 'friends hold you back. I haven't got the time for socialising and all the bigging up and kowtowing that goes with it.'

When they'd first come to Cornwall he joined the golf club but she couldn't be persuaded despite admitting she'd had lessons as a child. In the end he had given up asking.

He was intrigued and when Rita brought his tablets he'd hidden them under his tongue and spat them out when she left the room. Not that Rita ever really monitored his medication. She didn't need to, he was usually only too willing to take the pills and go to bed early if it meant spending less time with Issy. Lately however he'd needed to keep his wits about him at all times and had quite a collection of little white pills lined up on the window ledge outside.

Instead of parking on the drive Issy opened the garage door and drove in, pulling the door down behind her. Several minutes later he heard her and someone else coming up the old servants' staircase off the utility room. He couldn't hear what they were saying. His hearing wasn't what it used to be but Issy seemed to be doing most of the talking and he could tell from the mumblings the second person was a woman.

He crept to his door, opening it a fraction enough to be able to see to the end of the corridor where the staircase joined the landing. As the two women reached the top he could see Issy was wearing one of his old coats. The brown oil skin duster swept the floor. The young woman with her wore one of Issy's favourite fleeces, which brushed her knees and nothing else as far as he could tell. Both had wet hair despite it having been a fine day and neither wore shoes.

The young woman seemed listless as Issy, red-faced and puffing like a traction engine held her up. He was getting used to daily revelations about his wife, but who the mystery guest was and what Issy intended to do with her was beyond his powers of deduction.

He was in bed feigning deep sleep when Issy came into his room. She hovered by his bedside for a minute before leaving. Every time she did that these days, and she did it often, he found himself waiting for the pillow to land on his face.

FORTY-SEVEN

Ross drove home to his dingy flat where he drowned his sorrows with a bottle of red wine. He wasn't sure why he was so upset. In the end he'd put it down to the fact for one blissful second there had been a chance, no matter how small, his shitty life was about to change for the good and he'd got ahead of himself.

He had no right to feel aggrieved about Claire's liaison, it was nothing to do with him what she did, but it had shaken him, nonetheless. It was the last thing he'd expected, even if it did explain a lot.

To make matters worse, on waking in the early hours, still groggy from drink, he'd rung Trudy meaning to apologise for whatever misdemeanour she had him down for this time, but ended up giving her a mouthful, telling her what he thought of her and her petty point scoring at the kids' expense. By the time he got dressed on Sunday morning, despite his thick head and no prospect of another day off on the horizon, he decided to go into work because he'd had enough of his own company.

On arrival at the station matters took an unexpected turn. The desk sergeant told him there had been a call for him, from a Daniel McBride reporting his car and his ex-wife missing.

Ross remembered having seen Claire's car in her drive and had assumed she was inside the house having been caught in flagrante, so this development was surprising to say the least. He'd returned the call immediately.

Daniel told him that Claire had taken his car and set it alight. He said he also believed she'd duped him into going to her house on some pretext, drugged him and got him naked with the aim of having sex. Ross thought that unlikely. Why would anyone need to be persuaded to have sex with a woman like Claire, especially the way she'd looked that morning, and from what little he knew about McBride, he was no saint.

Daniel said that Claire had sent a compromising photograph of him on her bed to his wife, although he'd stressed, he was asleep and had definitely not had sex with Claire.

Not like you hadn't wanted to, Ross thought.

Daniel was hyper, but it was only when telling him she'd also sent a photo of his burning Maserati, Ross heard a quiver in his voice.

'Could you ping me a copy of both photos?' asked Ross, remaining on the line.

They arrived as attachments a few seconds later. The one of the Maserati was a spectacular shot, like something out of a Bond film. The other had him struggling to keep his composure. He was sure when he spoke next his voice was an octave higher as he tried to suppress a fit of giggles.

'Do you have any idea why Clare would do this now? Has something been going on between you, something that has blown up recently, perhaps financial issues relating to the divorce, that might have brought this on?'

'No, nothing. All that stuff was settled long ago, I've no idea what she was thinking. She knows that I'm happily married and wouldn't do anything to put my marriage at risk.'

Ross guessed Daniel's wife was listening in. He wasn't convinced by his act and thought the woman must be a fool if she was.

Daniel continued. 'She's always been so sensible, even during the split she was level-headed and very understanding.' Ross thought he heard a woman groan in the background. Daniel said he wouldn't be pressing charges but his wife insisted he ring because she felt threatened by the whole experience and was worried Claire might do something else, and next time it might involve her or their children.

Daniel made it clear he personally didn't think Claire was any further threat but Louisa's response was 'understandable, if a little emotional'.

Ross didn't know what to think. This was totally out of character. Listening to Daniel's slippery side-stepping, he couldn't help but feel a sort of reluctant respect for what Claire had done, albeit that it was a bit extreme. It had all the hallmarks of a domestic. He wasn't sure if he believed Daniel's assertions that there was nothing going on between them and complicated on-off relationships could be volatile. With this stuff going on in the background as well as her job and her mother's illness, something was almost bound to give.

He had first-hand knowledge of how corrosive divorce and the aftermath could be. Look at him and Trudy. Although he'd never done anything to Trudy, he'd often thought about payback for all the grief she'd given him over access to the kids.

He wanted to find Claire and get to the bottom of all this.

He wasn't ruling out a relationship with her quite yet, after all if Daniel had been in the picture recently, Claire had now made it abundantly clear through her actions it was over between them. He still had to tie up a few loose ends on his enquiry but the girl he knew and the way she'd been on Saturday in her garden was nothing like the loose cannon being described.

He would take it slowly. He had no intention of leaping from the frying pan into the fire. Trudy provided more than enough drama to be going on with, but a woman like Claire was worth a second chance. In fact, several second chances.

The behaviour he'd worried about, that had aroused his suspicions, had an explanation and the rest was pure coincidence. After all it was one thing to blow up your ex-husband's car, it was quite another to commit murder.

BOOK TWO

A friend is one to whom one may pour out the contents of one's heart, chaff and grain together knowing that gentle hands will take and sift it, keep what is worth keeping, and with a breath of kindness, blow the rest away.

George Eliot

FORTY-EIGHT
SARAH

Daniel called Sarah on Sunday morning to say the police were looking for Claire. He said she'd taken his car and it had been found burnt out on the cliffs above Penmorvah Beach, but there was no sign of her. Sarah immediately thought the worst, until he reassured her, she'd not been in it when it had gone up because she'd sent a text with a photo of it on fire.

Sarah spent the rest of the day calling Claire's mobile, then had driven to her house only to realise she'd forgotten the spare key Claire had given her and could only search the garden and peer in through the downstairs windows for signs of life.

Reluctantly, she'd driven home but had not been able to settle to anything; Ben's questions only adding to the strain.

'Was she alright when you saw her last? Did she say anything unusual?'

The illness was back, she knew that much, but Claire had looked well. She'd fought it once and she'd do it again. They'd discussed her will, of course, but they'd also talked about the wedding she'd been invited to and she'd bought that lovely blue dress to wear.

It was early Sunday evening when she got the call from Daniel to say they still hadn't found Claire but had found her melted phone by his burnt-out car along with her shoes and her blue dress further down the beach. He'd identified it as the one she'd been wearing the last time he saw her.

Sarah fell to her knees, letting out the tortured wail of a wounded animal. Ben ran from the living room to see what on earth was the matter. Taking the phone from her, he struggled to lift her to her feet. It was as if every fibre and ligament had melted away. When the girls ran in, he told them to go to their bedrooms not wanting them to see their mother like that. Sarah was beyond all consolation. Unable to speak, the only noises emanating choking, body-wrenching sobs. That night when he finally managed to get her to bed, he held her in his arms as her body quivered with the afterpains of shock and grief and when he kissed her in the morning her cheeks were wet with tears.

Ben rang Daniel later that morning.

'You know I really loved her.'

'I know mate, I know you did,' Ben replied, thinking, *not enough though, not enough.*

That afternoon Daniel turned up at Sarah's and the pair sat holding each other on the sofa while Ben kept them supplied with whiskey.

Daniel told them about the events of Saturday afternoon and how The Beast hadn't been insured and how he still owed money on it. He didn't relay the information in any way suggesting anger and by the end of the evening, he and Sarah were joined by their loss, both clinging to the memory of Claire in a cornflower blue silk dress.

FORTY-NINE
ISSY

Watching Claire sleep in her new bedroom, Issy marvelled at her accomplishment. It had been hard going getting her there but it had been worth the effort.

Rita, as instructed, had left by the time they arrived having put David to bed.

She'd parked in the garage and walked Claire through the utility room up the narrow back staircase to the bedroom. They'd taken it slowly, a step at a time. Claire was quiet but that was to be expected. There would be time enough for her to thank her for saving her life later. At the moment having her here was reward enough.

As soon as she'd got her into bed she had given her a sedative to help her sleep but she had managed to retrieve her fleece and dress her in one of her favourite brushed cotton nighties before she'd nodded off. She'd inserted a catheter so she didn't have to worry about the sheets. She'd locked the door, checked on David, then made her way to her own room not expecting to sleep at all with all the excitement, but had dropped off almost instantly. Clearly the day's events had taken their toll.

She'd kept Claire sedated all day on Sunday so she would be starving by now. She'd let her sleep for a little longer while she slipped the catheter out and made her breakfast. Then once she'd eaten they'd have a good chat about things.

She told Rita when she'd arrived that morning her friend was suffering from a mental breakdown after her treatment for cancer and that she had offered her a place to recuperate. She would be seeing to her personally. She'd prepare a meal chart for Rita to refer to but the food would be delivered by her.

She told Rita the situation was extremely sensitive and she must not discuss the matter or her friend's presence with anybody, least of all David who couldn't keep his mouth shut these days. No one was to disturb their guest who would receive no visitors. She was her patient as well as her friend and as part of her recovery she needed complete rest.

Rita had nodded along to her instructions and she was pleased she'd managed to find someone in this world who did what they were told without question. She'd be sad to let her go.

Once back downstairs she paused for a second in the hallway by the kitchen door.

David was finishing a bowl of cornflakes while Rita was buttering toast.

Issy was struck by the easy domesticity of the scene. The radio was on and they were chatting away as if they had something interesting to say, which of course she knew neither did.

They stopped as she walked in and she felt a spike of annoyance.

'Is the tray ready?'

'Yes,' replied Rita, 'the toast just popped up.'

Rita arranged the triangles of buttered toast on a plate which she added to the tray sitting on the worktop.

Izzy scanned it for mistakes but there were none. Her order had been filled correctly. Porridge to line Claire's stomach, orange juice to combat low blood sugar, buttered toast and black coffee. She'd noticed when around at Claire's she drank her coffee black.

'Good,' she said disappointed there was nothing to criticise.

Balancing the tray, she made her way back upstairs.

Claire had kicked off her covers but was still asleep.

Issy put down the tray, walked towards the bed and gave her a prod.

'Claire.'

Claire stirred, groaned, licked her lips and turned over.

This time Issy shook her.

'Claire, wake up.'

Claire sat bolt upright.

'Issy?'

'It's okay, you're safe.'

'But?'

'Don't you remember I brought you here after I rescued you from the water?'

Recognition swept Claire's face.

'Oh.' Her eyes filled with tears.

'Enough of that nonsense.'

'But you don't understand.'

'What don't I understand, why you felt you had to take your own life?'

Claire began to cry.

'I want you to stop that right now. You need to get some food inside you and then we'll talk.'

Claire dabbed her eyes with the edge of the duvet cover.

Issy reached behind her, plumping her pillows before settling the tray down on her lap.

She pulled a hardback chair up next to the bed and waited for Claire to begin to eat before she spoke again.

'A miserable, painful death from terminal illness is a frightening prospect, exacerbated by your unwillingness to take the prescribed medication, which would have dulled these feelings, making it easier to cope.'

Claire had taken a couple of mouthfuls of porridge and then put the spoon down.

Issy nodded at the orange juice, which Claire then dutifully began to sip.

'And then there's all that other stuff you've had to deal with,' Issy continued, 'the death of the Donoghue woman and that dreadful man Jennings. I understand the need to lash out, but you're not alone in this. You have me. I promise I will stand by you and no one will be the wiser. Your friends, your mother, everyone, including the police, will believe you've drowned as long as you do as I say. I'll see to it.'

Issy was no longer talking directly to Claire. A piece of wallpaper on the opposite wall had caught her attention. The join had begun to unstick. She'd never noticed it before but now she had she was finding it impossible to draw her eyes away. *It would have to be done again. The whole wall. There was nothing else for it. It was all wrong; all wrong.*

She walked over to it and pulled at the small gape in the overlap, ripping a large, jagged shred of paper away.

Claire gasped.

Issy turned to face her, a strip of limp yellow chrysanthemums dangling from one hand.

Claire had stopped crying. Issy could tell she was finding it difficult to put into words the gratitude she felt.

'Aren't you hungry?' Issy said, walking across and snatching up the tray. 'Never mind just drink the rest of the juice get some rest and we'll try again later. I'm going out for a little while. I'll pop into the hospital to get some medication and to the shops for some clothes for you to wear. Size eight that's right, isn't it?' she said remembering the clothes hanging in Claire's wardrobe.

Claire nodded.

'I thought so, now don't you worry about a thing. I've got your back, girlfriend. Isn't that what they say these days? Why don't you have a shower while I'm gone then we can go downstairs; maybe sit in the conservatory. You'd like that I'm sure.'

Issy left the room satisfied they had finally begun their adventure.

She needed to go into work to tidy up a few loose ends. She'd tell them David had taken a turn for the worse and she needed some leave. She was long overdue a break and frankly if they complained they could stuff their job. She might need to make alternative arrangements in any case if she and Claire needed to move away.

She'd put a smaller dose of lorazepam in Claire's juice as a bit of a top-up so she'd stay awake but be listless for a couple of hours. The door was locked and she'd be fine there with David and Rita until she got back. Until then she wouldn't be going anywhere.

FIFTY
CLAIRE

I'm unable to process what just happened. Everything is sluggish, my body, my mind. It's as if none of my synapses are sparking.

Issy saved my life and is offering me a refuge. Why aren't I thankful?

Issy said the food would help but my stomach's cramping and I think I'm going to be sick. I push the tray from my lap and run to the bathroom. I lean over the sink. trying desperately to fend off the urge to throw up in someone else's house. The orange juice has left my mouth sour and sore. I pull back my top lip and see in the mirror, the inside is ripped. I trace the tear with my tongue. I notice a new toothbrush in its packet and a tube of toothpaste by the sink. I brush slowly feeling every stroke through my aching jaw. I gulp water from the tap to ease my throat which is sore too.

A terrible pain between my legs urges me to pee. When I sit on the loo nothing comes. I close my eyes trying to stay calm despite the heat rising through me, making my top lip sweat. I reach up to push my hair from my forehead. It's crisp to the touch; a mass of salt-crusted curls.

Heaving myself from the loo I pull the huge pink nightie I'm wearing down over my body so it falls like the head of a dead rose to the floor. As I step out of it I notice the cuts on my feet and the bruises on my shins where I guess I was tumbled against the rocks..

I turn on the shower, letting the water run only as hot as I think my tender skin will bear. Steadying myself with one arm against the tiles I let the spray beat down on the back of my neck. Pink tinged water travels down between my legs to the drain and I feel light headed. I let myself slip to the floor pulling my knees up to my chest as the deluge washes over me and the cubicle steams up.

The fire ignited by my diagnosis, the drive to right wrongs, has been extinguished leaving a ruin. I have nothing and no one to live for. Why did Issy save me; why was she even there and how does she know about Donoghue and Jennings? The police are looking for me and there is no comfort in knowing those who love me think I'm dead; no comfort in having been rescued. I'm trapped. I'm still dying but it won't be a death on my terms anymore. It's not what I wanted. All I have is pain and fear. My only hope is death will come quickly or better still Issy will take pity on me and help me finish what I started. If not I know this terrible dread hollowing my chest will stay with me until my last breath.

FIFTY-ONE

When Issy returned, Claire was sitting up in bed. She was pleased to see she had showered. She dropped the shopping bags containing clothes for Claire on the floor. She'd had a surprisingly enjoyable time buying them. It had been a relief not having to try things on and suffer the indignity of the stick-thin changing room attendants as she handed back the garments asking, 'no good, not for you?' when she knew they were thinking, *too small for the likes of you, heifer.*

She knew how those types saw her but didn't care. Her waist measurement was bigger than their IQ.

She told the sales assistants she was buying a whole new wardrobe for her best friend who'd recently moved to the UK from Australia after her entire life's possessions had been consumed by a rampant forest fire. She'd enjoyed their admiration at her generosity especially when she added, for good measure, that her friend had been horribly disfigured by the flames.

They ran around after her picking out this and that until she virtually had to do nothing but sit there watching them flitter about like demented budgerigars. They'd waved her off when she left with good luck wishes for her friend's recovery.

'There you go,' Issy said pointing to the bags, 'there's plenty of choice in there for you. Perhaps after a few days we'll go downstairs for a bit of exercise in the garden. It's completely secluded. We're miles from anyone here. '

'I'm not sure I'll be up to it.'

'Nonsense, you can't stay cooped up in here all the time. There's only David, my husband, and Rita, our housekeeper. She comes in most days but she'll be busy. I should also warn you not to listen to David. I'm sorry to say he has dementia and is prone to telling lies. In fact I think it's best you don't talk to him if you can help it. Now for a name. We can't call you Claire, do you have a middle name we could use?'

'Ruth,' Claire mumbled, 'but—'

'But nothing, you have to wave goodbye to Claire McBride if you don't want to spend your last days in jail. Ruth, yes I remember now from your patient record. Ruth it is then.'

'Okay.'

'Now chop, chop,' Issy said reaching into the bag and pulling out a t-shirt with a kitten on it along with a pair of cropped trousers. She knew they weren't exactly Claire's style but the aim was to make her look different. She would be starting a new life and she'd read actors often began with the costume when getting into character.

'There are trainers and some sensible underwear in there too, along with the usual necessities. Right, I'll leave you to it. We'll skip lunch as you didn't eat your breakfast. I'll bring you up some tea later this afternoon.'

Issy felt quite excited at the prospect of showing her friend off to David and Rita.

She walked into the kitchen where David sat slurping some homemade soup Rita had left for their lunch.

He shot up as she entered.

'I want to tell you about Ruth,' Issy said, 'she's a very good friend of mine who is staying with us for the foreseeable future. You're not to bother her. She is not well and needs plenty of rest. Do you understand?'

'Not to bother her,' repeated David. 'Fair enough, Captain.'

FIFTY-TWO

The helicopter rescue team from St Mawgan continued their search for Claire's body until the following Tuesday evening. Three weeks later on the Friday afternoon, Sarah got a call from the coroner's office explaining there would have to be an inquest.

'Usually, we would correspond directly with Mrs McBride's family at this stage of an investigation but given her divorce and the fact her mother has dementia we will liaise throughout with you as her executor and the person named next of kin in her GP's records.'

'I don't understand,' said Sarah, 'how can there be an inquest without a body?'

'Where there is no body but evidence to suggest an unnatural death has occurred within the coroner's jurisdiction he can at his discretion call for an investigation. It allows there to be a certain amount of closure. It will greatly assist Mrs McBride's partners in the firm for example. They will be able to take certain long-term steps in respect of her clients and her business interests.'

She wondered if Claire's partners had pulled strings for this to be happening so soon after her disappearance. She put the question to Ben that evening.

As always he was kind but honest.

'I don't know, maybe, but does it really matter if they did? Either way we have to face it's been three weeks since she went missing and by the time they open the investigation it will have been almost a month. You and I know she would never stay out of touch for that long. She's gone love and the sooner we face it the sooner we can concentrate on remembering all the good stuff.'

Sarah knew he was right of course. It was clear Claire's death hadn't been an accident. She was a good swimmer but would never have gone in at this time of year.

Her shoes and dress had been found on the beach. The forensics on the car had concluded arson and it seemed to everyone she had planned a dramatic finale before ending her life. Ben was right she had to come to terms with the reality she would never see her best friend again.

***

The next day she visited Claire's mum.

Eileen didn't know who she was but smiled and chatted about her day. Sarah talked generally about Claire but saw no hint of recollection and saw no point in telling her the daughter, once so loved, was dead.

Daniel telephoned to say the police had questioned him because he'd been the last one to see Claire alive but the text message sent from Claire's phone to Louisa, and a nosey neighbour's recollection of seeing him in a skimpy towel getting into a car with a woman and two children, ruled out any foul play on his part.

Sarah decided not to tell anyone about the letter Claire had deposited at the bank until she'd read it. After all, Claire entrusted her to reveal its contents only if she thought it necessary. Sarah assumed it would divulge her reasons for taking her own life. If it did she'd let the coroner know when the inquest opened officially.

The following week she collected it from the bank. She decided to read it at Claire's house, partly because she didn't want to take it home and run the risk of the girls walking in on her in yet another state, but mostly because she needed to feel her friend's presence when she opened it.

She'd only been there once since Claire's death, when the police had rung to ask for her to accompany them there and lock up afterwards.

She'd been shocked to see Claire had stripped the place. It was one of the reasons the police believed she'd killed herself even though no suicide note was found. Their investigation revealed she had for some weeks beforehand, been getting her affairs in order and offloading clothes and bits and pieces to charity shops. She wondered what the police had made of the scene in the bedroom. It was certainly evidence Claire had a dark sense of humour. She was pretty sure Daniel hadn't been as forthcoming with them as he'd been with her and Ben about the events of that Saturday morning. Had he divulged the full details, she was sure there wouldn't have been a straight face down at the station amongst the officers who knew Claire.

Today Sarah was struck by the silence as she opened the door. Usually, Claire's music would be playing or there would be the sound of her bustling in the garden. but now there was just emptiness. The house was stuffy and she opened the French doors.

The garden looked magical in the morning light, everything racing towards summer. The heady scent of Wisteria around the door was overpowering. The beauty served as a reminder of how, despite everything, it was good to be alive.

She lay the envelope on the garden table. She sat for several minutes; her fingers locked together in her lap staring at it. She knew Claire well enough to understand why if faced with the prospect of more chemo she would do this, but even so she couldn't bear the thought of her struggling with the decision alone. The very idea she'd had to write this down; that she hadn't felt she could talk to her in person made her angry.

Part of her hoped the letter was about something completely different.

Perhaps it was information about her firm. Or maybe it was something to do with Claire's father. Claire always said she'd never asked Eileen about his identity but Sarah had always wondered if she ever got curious. Maybe she'd traced him and had wanted her to let him know she was dead?

There was nothing for it. She'd never know unless she opened it.

Her fingers were shaking as she peeled open the envelope and lifted out the letter:

Dear Sarah

I'm going to get the cliché over and done with, so here goes. If you are reading this letter it is because I am dead! I have either succumbed to the terrible disease my consultant has told me is incurable or I have taken charge and ended my life. If it's the former and my final weeks were filled with pain and drug-induced gibberish you've been forced to witness then I apologise. I never wanted that to happen and if it did, I must have relented and taken the morphine Issy prescribed. If so, feel free to lock those memories away like bad dreams and think of me as I was before. I know that's possible because it's how I remember Mum; before the dementia took her somewhere else and I became a stranger to her.

Sarah's throat tightened and she wondered whether she was up to reading this just yet. Taking a deep breath to galvanise herself, she carried on.

If you haven't been forced to face my gradual disintegration, then I can confirm I've taken my own life. If my body has been found I hope it was early on and the sea was kind to me but, if you haven't found me, rest assured that's where I am and don't feel bad about it. My life! My choice!

That was all very well, Sarah thought, but what about the rest of us?

This letter should reassure you I was not sad when I did it and there was absolutely nothing you or anyone else could've done to stop me. I made up my mind the day Issy told me the cancer had returned and I wouldn't survive it.

You will by now no doubt have heard about Daniel and my revenge upon 'The Beast.' If he hasn't told you the full story make sure he does. It will give you some much-needed light relief during a grim time. SORRY.

Coming to terms with your own mortality is strangely liberating. It makes you realise you're not that important in the scheme of things. I know you'll miss me. I know you'll never forget me (unless you become like Mum and then you most definitely will) but trust me like they say, 'this too will pass.'

The difficult part is over for me. Now for the difficult part for you, the part that might change how you feel about me, forever. If it does, I hope in time you'll come to understand and won't think too badly of me for what I've done.

You see I've broken the law and more than once. Yes me! Miss Goody Two Shoes. You probably know what I've done to The Beast if everything has gone to plan but at the time of writing this I've forged a will and have I believe been instrumental in the death of a man. I don't say an innocent man. That's because I don't believe he was innocent or anything close to it. I'm relying on you to use the information at your discretion and trust you implicitly to do the right thing, whatever that turns out to be.

The victims, and I use those terms loosely, were our old form mistress, Jane Donoghue, whose will I forged so her niece Maureen would inherit, and a drug dealer and all-round evil bastard called Fergus Jennings, who I believe caused or at the very least contributed to Mum's dementia. If I'm honest the will was done on a whim and the result satisfying after all these years but I didn't kill her, that was a lucky coincidence. Jennings was different I had a plan for him. My terminal diagnosis gave me the strength to realise not everyone deserves a second chance. You don't need to know the lurid details, in fact the less you know the better, but you do need to know I did not mean to kill him and to believe what I say and not think I've gone completely loopy.

So, upstairs in my wardrobe on the top shelf I've left a bag containing band tour t-shirts I would like the girls to have. Tucked inside one of them is an envelope containing a photograph. It is all you need to prove I am telling the truth both for the police and yourself. I'm confiding in you, not because I need to confess or want your approval but because I don't want anyone else punished for my actions. If that looks likely I insist you show this letter to the police no matter what. If you hear nothing more about these crimes, then it is up to you. If the burden of knowing is too much then I fully understand. I'm only able to place it upon you because you're the strongest person I know and had the tables been turned I'd hope you could have relied on me. I don't think myself wicked and hope that you won't either. I just scattered a little justice in a world with precious little in it, to balance the scales.

I hope nothing has to be divulged until Mum's gone. I wouldn't want her care home bombarded with telephone calls from the tabloids asking for her comments about her outlaw daughter. Please try and visit Mum once in a while for me. She'd love to see the girls and may even recognise you occasionally. I've left enough money for her to be able to stay where she seems settled. I know you'll take care of matters after she's gone in the same way you'll deal with all of that for me.

As for you, my lovely kind friend carry on being the mad wonderful person you've always been. Hug Ben and those two gorgeous girls of yours for me. Walk on the beach barefooted at least once a month, breathe the sweet Cornish air and think of me now and again. I'll be there with you. If you look hard enough, you'll find me.

I love you.
Claire x

It was surreal: like reading the script to a whodunnit, something on Sunday evening telly, where the detective finally reveals the culprit before the credits roll.

Sarah had read about the deaths of both Miss Donoghue and Fergus Jennings in the paper. In fact, Jennings' death had made the local TV news. She wouldn't have thought much about the death of the drug dealer if not for the fact the police announced they were looking for a woman with a Golden Retriever wearing a Cornish tartan yellow scarf. Her girls had laughed when Ben joked the police should only interview dogs barking with a Cornish accent. She would never have suspected Claire, her kind gentle friend, of being the woman in the CCTV footage with the dog. She looked nothing like her. It was ridiculous!

She remembered the photograph Claire mentioned. Clasping the letter, she ran upstairs to the bedroom. There, sure enough on the top shelf of the wardrobe was a bag. She tipped four t-shirts out onto the floor. Lifting them one by one, memories of her teenage self flooded back. Dancing around her bedroom with Claire waving the gig tickets above their heads.

The envelope was pinned to the inside of a Glastonbury '95 t-shirt. She opened it. Inside was a photograph. Claire's garden and a

Golden Retriever looking directly at the camera, a yellow scarf tied around its neck. On the back was written the word. 'Jennings'.

Sarah held the photograph to her chest.

It was true; it was all true.

FIFTY-THREE

Sarah decided to keep the letter to herself. How could she show it to anyone now she knew what it contained? What did it matter if the coroner was unable to reach a conclusion without it? She knew the truth; Claire had drowned. She didn't need a report to tell her that. Her friend was dead, wasn't that enough? She wouldn't be the one to denigrate her memory unless she absolutely had to because someone else looked like they might be held accountable for her crimes.

A fortnight later, the coroner's office rang to confirm the investigation into Claire's death had been opened and closed and she'd receive a copy of the report later that week. As expected when it arrived it concluded that in all likelihood Claire committed suicide and her body had been lost at sea. It arrived with an interim death certificate.

Sarah scoured both for references to Claire's terminal illness but there were none. She appreciated Claire had not actually died of cancer but she'd expected it to be detailed somewhere. She telephoned the office and spoke to the coroner's assistant. He told her the medical reports from Claire's GP revealed the removal of a malignant melanoma two years previously and successful chemotherapy treatment subsequently. There was nothing in them about a reoccurrence of the disease. Claire was a healthy middle-aged woman.

Sarah was confused. None of this made any sense if Claire hadn't been dying. Why did she say in the letter she had a terminal diagnosis? She knew she wouldn't have intentionally misled her and Claire wasn't stupid, she must have known if her body was found there would be a post-mortem and the truth would come out, so why lie? Why had she told her the cancer was back when it wasn't?

Perhaps she'd had some kind of breakdown following what she'd done with Donoghue's will and to Jennings?

She immediately headed for Claire's house.

There must be something there. Something amongst her paperwork from the hospital. She'd had a check-up recently. There must be a record of the appointment or a copy of the test results somewhere?

Her first stop was Claire's study. She rifled through the desk searching for anything with a hospital reference. Whilst there were diagnostic reports and treatment plans along with letters confirming chemo appointments and a couple with a psychologist, dating back two years, there was nothing more recent.

She headed upstairs to Claire's bedroom. There was nothing in the bedside drawers or on the dressing table.

What about her tablets; her medication must be somewhere? She'd said this time she would be able to self-administer? Sarah rushed to the bathroom. There they were in the cabinet, several unopened packets of Oral Morphine. On the label Claire's name, the date, which was recent so they weren't an old batch from previous treatments. The name of the doctor who had prescribed them was Elizabeth Moran. Not Claire's GP; her consultant oncologist.

It was a relief Claire hadn't lied to her but surely Claire's GP should have been kept in the loop. She needed to speak to Elizabeth Moran before she took this further but she was concerned. Daniel had been given a sedative. If her GP prescribed it but didn't know about the consultant's prescription it was possible Claire was adversely affected. Perhaps there were contra indicators for the two drugs that impacted on Claire's mental health. How come her doctors got it so wrong?

FIFTY-FOUR
ISSY

Issy originally had high hopes for Claire. The first week had gone relatively well. Claire had been understandably shaken for the first few days but her appetite had improved and she'd even sat in the garden one afternoon. Issy had fleshed out Claire's story to Rita telling her their guest had no relatives and was in the last throes of her illness. The hospital had been unable to place her in a hospice and she as her consultant had volunteered an alternative to her spending her final weeks on a crowded hospital ward. Rita had been impressed with her kindness but expressed surprise she would go to so much trouble for a patient until she explained Claire was special, that she had treated her for several years and they had become close friends.

She'd been annoyed at the need to justify her actions to the help but it had made her realise she couldn't maintain the myth of terminal illness for much longer if she and Claire were to move on to the next stage of their relationship. The problem was she wasn't sure how Claire would react to another remission or indeed a cure? At present she was willing to accept she had already said goodbye to her family and friends. There was no point interrupting their grief just to tell them she'd soon be dead but once she told her she was well, she was bound to feel differently. Would she forget everything she had done for her and crawl back to Sarah and the life she'd left behind? Would the threat of a police investigation be enough to keep her in check? She was a lawyer after all and everyone knew what conniving individuals they could be when cornered. She wasn't prepared to lose her to anyone else after all she had invested.

She'd feigned surprise when the coroner's office phoned for Claire's medical records. They'd been advised by Sarah, who was Claire's Executor, that Mrs McBride was suffering from a terminal illness. She'd wrongly assumed there wouldn't be an inquest because there was no body. She'd had to think on her feet and it had felt odd talking about Claire as if she were dead when she'd only left her minutes before.

She knew the GP's records would say Claire was in remission and if there were discrepancies there would be questions asked. She'd told the coroner her patient was indeed in remission, although she'd had some problems accepting it. She'd explained when Claire had been first diagnosed, she'd been concerned about her mental stability and had referred her to a psychologist for therapy. She believed she'd benefited from the treatment, but maybe things had once again got on top of her. She'd made all the right noises about how tragic it was a young woman should be so troubled as to end her own life. The coroner revealed that on the day of her death Claire had taken her ex-husband's car and set fire to it on top of a cliff. Issy agreed that such behaviour was totally out of character and whilst she was no expert in this field it would seem another indication that Claire had suffered some kind of breakdown. She'd ended the conversation saying she'd send a written report but it would provide little other than the woman was physically well.

She had received no further requests from the coroner for information. She'd forwarded her reports supported by her doctored medical records. She'd included a link to Claire's therapists for good measure knowing it would lend support to Claire having mental health issues. It all seemed to be taking shape.

When she'd heard the inquest had been closed she'd heaved a sigh of relief. Claire was officially dead. She'd received an invite to her memorial billed as a celebration of her life.

Issy had half wondered whether she should tell Claire about the memorial; ask her if she wanted her to record it on her phone so they could listen to it together later but she thought better of it. She didn't think Claire would want to hear it in her present state of mind. In fact Claire's attitude as the weeks passed had left a lot to be desired. It seemed to her she wasn't as grateful as she should be. She had saved her life after all. The circumstances dictated there could be no public recognition but nevertheless the fact she showed no gratitude was disappointing.

In fact if she was truthful Claire was generally disappointing. Most of the time she was more than happy to stay in her room. Even when not sedated she spent hours in bed. She'd hardly worn any of the clothes she'd bought for her and she'd had to remind her more than once to shower and wash her hair. When she did venture out of her bedroom she was listless and unresponsive. How many people would love the chance to wipe the slate clean and begin again? It had taken a huge effort for her to do that a number of times when circumstances indicated she move to a new hospital in a new area in order to avoid uncomfortable questions. Claire had been handed the opportunity on a plate. She'd hoped she'd buck up but as the weeks passed it became very clear Claire was stuck in the past. She'd saved her so they could become close companions but instead Claire was behaving more like Mummy every day. On top of that, the frisson of excitement she'd felt at the prospect of attending the memorial knowing Claire was still alive was tempered by her knowledge she would need to use the opportunity to tie up loose ends.

She had to cover her tracks. The coroner would be satisfied with the information given and her own hospital records would give no indication of any treatment, only the check-ups. The drugs were the only issue; the morphine Claire had chosen not to take. There would be no record of them at the hospital as they'd been taken from her own personal stash, the pharmacy she kept locked away at home, full of the drugs she'd prescribed but never given to those she chose not to treat. The problem was the unused tablets at Claire's house. Her name would be on the label along with the excessive dosage and the date. She'd been very particular to make sure Claire was not suspicious about them in any way. Anyone who found them would see they'd been prescribed by her and would inevitably question why she'd done so when her patient clearly wasn't sick. She had to get them back.

She was angry at Claire for putting her in this position and for proving such a massive disappointment after she'd begun to show such promise. She'd thought maybe she'd discovered a fire in Claire McBride she recognised in herself, but her protégé was turning out to be another run of the mill, self-pitying nobody.

FIFTY-FIVE

Claire had left her wishes with her will. She'd already paid for a funeral package and left instructions she was to be cremated, her ashes kept and then scattered with those of her mother when she died. Only there wasn't a body to cremate. Sarah couldn't even begin to get her head around the letter and the questions stemming from it until Claire's memorial service was over. It would be one of the worst days of her life and what she'd learnt in Claire's letter wouldn't make it any easier.

The lady at the village hall where the memorial was to be held was very helpful and with a few adjustments they were able to come up with a suitable compromise. Claire had wanted the service to take place in the morning so as to get it over and done with and everyone moved on to an early lunch at the pub. She'd picked the music and a piece of poetry. She hadn't wanted a religious ceremony and no one was to wear black. There were to be no flowers, only donations to a cancer charity. The way Sarah saw it, most didn't get the chance to plan their own funerals, let alone their own deaths. Claire had managed to do both. She just hadn't reckoned on how everyone else would feel about it, that was something she couldn't plan for.

Sarah met with Daniel to talk about the arrangements. He looked drawn and slightly bewildered. When she told him there would be no flowers, he said he wanted to send them anyway; he couldn't let her go without them. He seemed to deflate and she relented, saying they could maybe pick some from Claire's garden; she would like that better than a formal arrangement.

The memorial was scheduled for the following Friday at eleven o'clock. Lerryn was to read a poem chosen by Claire and the evening before was taken up with her practicing. She'd wanted to do it justice and so had learnt it by heart. By the time the girls got to bed, Sarah had still not looked through the notes she'd prepared for Claire's farewell.

FIFTY-SIX
DAVID

David knew Issy to be meticulous and as such she was bound to have made a record of the drug allocation somewhere. Without one, it would be difficult for even her to keep track. Like a dodgy businessman she'd need two sets of books. The official patient records he'd seen and the ones she kept for herself, that told the true story. Issy didn't trust computers, they could be hacked.

First he'd revisited the attic but not only was there no sign of any record, but the drugs had also been moved and he'd began to worry Issy might think Rita had been sniffing around. He'd searched the house with a greater sense of urgency since, even looking behind the books on the top shelf in his study. He'd decided last night if it was in the house at all it must be in Issy's bedroom and today was the day he'd end this. Either way he'd call the police. He'd picked today because he knew he'd have the house to himself without interruption because Issy had said she'd be out for most of the day and had given Rita the job of cleaning out the chest freezer in the garage.

He hadn't seen Ruth for two days now. She had taken all her meals in her room. The poor girl seemed to get frailer by the minute. He'd heard Issy telling Rita she was not to be disturbed for food; that the drugs were making her nauseous and she'd given her something to knock her out. as the pain was particularly bad today. He wished he could help.

'Well, I must get on, that freezer won't clean itself. What are you doing with yourself this afternoon?' Rita asked as she cleared away the lunchtime dishes.

'I have Sherlock Holmes on audio; I thought I might listen to it upstairs; catch forty winks in-between chapters.'

'Good idea. I'll bring you up a cuppa at about three, before I go.'

Upstairs he listened to Rita close the utility room door leading to the garage.

Once he was certain she'd settled to the task, he found the audio book on his iPad.

He enjoyed a good detective story and he'd get back to dear old Sherlock later, but now he had his own detective work to do.

He knew if Rita came up she'd listen at the door, hear the book and let him rest. Unlike Issy, Rita respected others' privacy. She'd not go into Issy's room because it wasn't her day to clean it. Rita knew enough not to deviate from her boss's task list.

Satisfied he'd bought himself enough time for a thorough search, he walked the little distance down the hall towards Issy's bedroom.

He knocked at Ruth's door. There was no reply. He tried the handle. The door was locked, the way it always was when Issy was out. He listened but guessed the young woman was still sleeping off Issy's sedative. At least she'd get a few hours relief from her sickness. Rita had filled him in on the story and said she'd spoken to the girl in the garden about it. He hated the disease that could turn a young life to tragedy so quickly.

He entered Issy's room.

It was gashed in two by sunshine slanting through the large bay window. Around the ledge sat Issy's stuffed toys from her childhood. He never understood her need to hold on to them but guessed maybe they were her means of rewriting her tattered past.

He'd once suggested a Springer Spaniel or a Retriever but she'd said she couldn't think of anything worse than some filthy animal bringing dirt and disease into the house so it clearly wasn't something to cuddle she was after.

Scrutinising the room he thought the stuffed toys seemed in keeping. It wasn't like the room of a grown woman, with its ditsy wallpaper and ornate white bedroom furniture and there was too much stuff. It was decorated like the room of a little girl who still had dreams of becoming a fairy princess. *Not much chance of that.*

He thought of the bedroom he'd shared with Karen before she'd had to move downstairs; the wardrobe filled with clothes she could no longer wear. She'd inhabited them so perfectly, swished her way through life with such cheerful grace. He remembered pressing his face into her dresses after she died in the hope she lingered there.

He started with the dressing table. The surface was completely covered with pots of face cream, some with their lids on, others off, their contents gouged with the marks of thick shovelling fingers. There was an open eye shadow box with a brush sitting on top, the powdery rainbow colours blended together into a muddy mix. Balls of cotton wool smeared with mascara were scattered like grubby snowballs. Six or seven different brands of perfume all in various states of use were pushed into one corner along with a knotted spaghetti of necklaces.

David remembered Karen's dressing table with its few carefully chosen items. The crystal ring tree with her necklaces hanging from it and the bottle of Jean Patou's 'Joy' bought by him once a year on her birthday.

He'd been worried about disturbing Issy's things but looking at all the detritus, she clearly wouldn't have a clue. The double bed was littered with clothes as if a child had been playing dress up and been caught mid-play with a string of pearls around her neck and lipstick smeared across her face. It struck him the chaos reflected the mind of its owner.

Returning his attention to the dressing table he opened the deep drawers either side of the crowded table top. Both were stuffed to the brim with underwear. He rummaged through with a tinge of embarrassment, feeling like a peeping tom, except he wasn't remotely aroused. He felt no erotic stiffening in his trousers at the prospect of running his fingers through Issy's smalls and that's what they were, smalls; all impossibly tiny, like they belonged to a woman half Issy's size and age. He picked the pieces up one by one. Bras with pale blue bows and small padded cups and cerise cheese wire thongs with nothing to them. None of them would ever have fitted his wife even when they'd first met and yet there were dozens of them, all the same mini-me size. He felt to the bottom of both drawers but there was nothing of interest there. Closing them carefully he walked towards his last hope, the large wardrobe along the end wall.

The adjoining bathroom sported the same disarray of toiletries as the dressing table along with several pink fluffy towels tossed into one corner. If you didn't know better, you'd think they'd been burgled, he thought. Poor Rita having to deal with this every week.

Sliding back the wardrobe door, he was struck by the difference between its regimented tidiness and the rest of the room.

Formal suits, blue, black and grey, hung along the rails along with white and cream blouses all practically identical. There were a couple of beige raincoats and nothing else. Carefully folded jumpers in neutral colours were stacked on shelving to the side. Above was a storage box which, he discovered when he lifted it down to peek at its contents, was filled with unopened packets of American Tan tights. On the floor was a tidy row of black and blue court shoes and a pair of trainers that he'd never seen Issy wear.

He knelt to see if there was anything towards the rear, a box maybe he couldn't see, but there was nothing. Reaching further back he recognised the feel of the velvety cover of Issy's jewellery box. He pulled it out and opened it. It held the various pieces he'd bought her over the years going back to when they were having the affair. He was glad he'd given Karen's jewellery to her sister when she died. He couldn't now bear the thought of Issy wearing Karen's things. He returned it to its place and closed the wardrobe doors, completely at a loss.

Perhaps he'd been wrong and she kept the records in the surgery or perhaps she had somewhere else altogether, somewhere he didn't know about?

He wandered to the window. Rita was loading up her car with the freezer bags piled up outside the garage door. He had no idea why Issy was passing on the freezer's contents to Rita. It was most unlike her to be so generous. Perhaps some of it was out of date?

He looked down at the glassy-eyed teddy bears, their stupid stitched-on smiles grinning, and felt something very close to despair. He punched one of them in the face and it toppled slightly. As it did, David noticed the rabbit sitting behind it wasn't a stuffed animal at all but a nightdress case; its body a pocket of pink flowered material with a lop-eared rabbit head attached.

He moved to straighten it before putting the bear back and noticed it had something inside its pocket. His mouth was suddenly dry, the pulse in his neck sounding in his ears as he unzipped the case to reveal a bubble-gum pink leather book, like a teenage girl's diary.

Moving some of the clothes cluttering the duvet cover he sat and tried to make sense of the contents. Page after page of names.

The first was headed up '2000 the Millennium' and underlined. Had this been going on since then, two years after they'd been married when they were still in London and Issy was all but newly qualified?

The page had been divided with a ruler into a schedule of sorts, the four headings of which read: Date of Death-Name-Duration of Illness:-Age and Other Factors.

Mostly the 'Other Factors' section was blank other than the age of the patient, but occasionally something more was noted, like in 2003 against Roger McKenzie there was an entry; 'diabetic/overdose of insulin'.

On each page were listed about five names and there were between one and two pages for each year. The schedule went on year by year in the same way over the period. There were twenty pages in total. Page after page of names; a macabre list of poor unfortunates Issy had decided had no right to live; her very own Book of the Dead.

He scanned the current year which held one name only; Claire McBride. There was no date of death. He took a deep breath and looked at his watch, three o'clock, he had to get a move on.

If the police checked the official patient records against the names in the diary, there would be enough discrepancies to show what she'd done; he was sure of it and it would stop; at last, it would stop. Yet despite the relief, he felt oddly deflated. The contents of the book would build a criminal case against his monster of a wife, but it wouldn't give him closure.

He still didn't know whether Issy's murderous tendencies had been utilised nearer to home. He had no confirmation of any kind she'd killed her mother or Karen.

He positioned the rabbit and the bear exactly as they had been and was about to reach for his mobile from his pocket when something caught his eye.

On the bed, her head resting against the headboard, a large rag doll with yellow plaits and button blue eyes. Something on her dress was glistening. David thought it might be a little gold buckle around the waist of her gingham frock, but it sparkled too much for that. It cast colour wheels around the room like a crystal on a chandelier and despite his wish to get out of the room and phone the authorities he moved towards the doll, bent down to her level to see what was causing the light show.

It was a tiny diamond bumble bee brooch with dainty gold wings and ruby eyes. It was a piece he knew well because he'd seen it many times before, not as a brooch but on a chain around Karen's neck. She'd worn it every day since he gave it to her on their tenth wedding anniversary. She'd been wearing it on the last day he saw her alive; the morning he'd kissed her goodbye, before leaving for a conference in Manchester where he'd met up with Issy later in the evening.

He'd been surprised when the undertaker told him she'd not been wearing any jewellery other than her wedding ring when they'd taken her body to the mortuary, and afterwards he'd searched the place high and low for the bumble bee necklace so it could be buried with her. Now he'd found it, he knew why it was here; as a trophy. Issy didn't need a written record of killing Karen, because she had this physical reminder with her every day.

He'd read somewhere all murders were born of rage. Whether it took the form of a blinding red mist behind the eyes or the kind he felt now; the buttoned-up variety in a Marks and Spencer's cardigan kept under wraps until one by one the buttons came loose and the sleeves unravelled. Rage coursed through his sad sack body, fermenting in his mouth and he knew he wouldn't be calling the police today or any other day.

He made it back to his room just before Rita rounded the corner with the tea tray and in time to hear Sherlock say; 'And that my dear fellow is elementary'.

FIFTY-SEVEN

The village hall was packed. They'd set out all the chairs they'd found stacked in the back room and Ben had gone home to fetch some more just in case. Even with the addition, there still weren't enough and many had to stand at the back. Sarah had expected Claire's family, friends, and colleagues to turn out in numbers but hadn't expected so many of her clients. Claire never discussed her work with her to any great extent, being a lawyer was just something she did for a living, it was not who she was. Her clients' presence was testimony to the help she'd given them and the respect they felt for her. Sarah knew Claire would have been touched.

It was strange having the service in the room where she and Claire took Pilates once a week, where they'd attended planning meetings to object to the development of the greenfield site behind the hall and where once a year they reluctantly dragged themselves to the village Bring-and-Buy sale. Children's paintings hung on the walls, cheerful hand prints from the mother toddler group and behind the stage a mural by the kids holiday club depicting the effects of global warming. As the sun streamed through the skylight the room crammed with people in their colourful clothes looked more like a festival about to burst into life than a final goodbye to a dear friend.

Ben had positioned a blown-up photo of Claire at the front on an easel, smiling, the wind in her hair. Next to it a microphone had been wired up to the temperamental sound system.

Sarah stood at the entrance to welcome people. In the absence of Claire's mum and as none of her relatives felt up to it, she thought it a role she should take. She knew many of those who had come to say goodbye.

She was pleased Ross had turned up. He was talking to one of Claire's lawyer friends, Eden Gray. They were both avid surfers although Eden didn't fit the flip flop and boardie mould, tall and elegant in a sea-green silk dress. Ross looked pale and she'd noticed he was particularly off with Daniel when they met in the foyer.

Elizabeth Moran was there too. Sarah only had time to speak to her briefly but managed to get her mobile number so she could call to arrange a meeting. She was careful not to divulge why.

Sarah noticed she'd chosen to wear a dark formal suit whilst everyone else had taken note of Claire's wishes not to wear black and come regaled in their brightest outfits. Pam, one of Eileen's friends, was wearing a marvellously flamboyant straw hat trimmed with an array of bows and ribbons. She told Sarah she'd miss Claire terribly because she used to look after her Golden Retriever when she went away to visit family in Bristol. She said she was moving there permanently to live with her daughter but unfortunately she'd have to re-home her dog. Had Claire been alive, she was sure she'd have taken him because she and Barney got on so well. Sarah knew why Claire hadn't mentioned the dog. She remembered the Golden Retriever on the CCTV with its yellow tartan scarf and only just resisted asking Pam if her dog was as snappy a dresser as she was?

Claire had requested Kiri Te Kanawa singing 'Chi il bel sogno di Doretta', for when her coffin arrived. The song had sent their teenage hearts soaring with the promise of unbridled romance when they'd watched *that* kiss in *A Room with a View*. There was no coffin but the ripple of chatter turned to silence as the aria began and Sarah's chest tightened.

Lerryn made her way to the front. Sarah assumed her overwhelming wish for her nervous daughter to get through it without a hitch would curb her emotions. She was wrong.

'This was Auntie Claire's favourite poem and she wanted me to read it to you. My mum said it's about Shropshire, which is a county in the middle of England, but Auntie Claire always said it was about the place you call home, and the memories in your heart. It is by Alfred Edward Housman and it's called "The Land of Lost Content".

'Into my heart an air that kills
From yon far country blows:
What are those blue remembered hills,
What spires, what farms are those?
That is the land of lost content,
I see it shining plain,
The happy highways where I went
And cannot come again.'

Ben began to clap, starting the rest of the congregation off. Lerryn blushed all the way back to her place next to Sarah who sat with tears rolling down her cheeks.

Eden Gray gave her tribute. She thanked Claire for giving her a piece of advice which she firmly believed had made her a better lawyer.

'People aren't cartoon characters, all good or bad. Any one of us could cross that line in the right circumstances. Always look for your reflection when you stare a defendant in the eye.'

Finally it was Sarah's turn to speak.

She found it easy to talk about her friendship with Claire; to tell tall tales of their various exploits, the boys, the bands, the holiday romances, all those things were easy. It was the elephant in the room, Claire's suicide, that had kept her tossing and turning all night thinking what to say and the letter of course. She couldn't forget the contents of Claire's letter.

Had she been certain Claire was dying she could have told everyone she'd merely circumvented the inevitable but it wasn't true and she didn't feel able to perpetuate the lie. She definitely couldn't say Claire killed herself because she'd forged an old lady's will and thought she might have killed a man. In the end she decided to relay the only truth she knew; Claire took her life because it was hers to take.

As she finished she felt enormous relief at managing to get through it without totally disintegrating, but no sense of closure. She knew she wouldn't find that until she knew the truth. She could dress it up any way she needed in order to make it palatable for everyone sitting there but there were questions she needed answered no matter how terrible those answers turned out to be.

As they filtered out to the sound of 'True Colours', she knew she'd love Claire forever, no matter what she had or hadn't done but she couldn't rest until she knew everything there was to know.

FIFTY-EIGHT

Issy sat at the very back of the hall so she could get away easily. She'd had trouble parking, having to drive around twice to find a space. She hadn't expected so many people to turn up to Claire's memorial. It wasn't like it was a real funeral with a coffin and a proper church service and as far as they were concerned, she'd taken her own life. It wasn't as if she'd died in a terrible accident. That would have been a tragedy. If she'd been in charge and things had gone as she'd originally planned, then it would have been a more traditional affair, just like all those other patients' funerals she'd attended over the years. She'd have been central to proceedings not relegated to a minor role. No, this was typical Claire; self-indulgent and attention-seeking. She shouldn't complain. She could take satisfaction from the fact all these people were here under false pretences. Claire was alive and well, for the moment at least. Whether she stayed that way would depend on how things turned out today.

She imagined the look on their stupid faces if she stood up and told them how she'd saved Claire from drowning and she was at that very moment sleeping off a dose of sedatives in her spare bedroom. Not to mention how they'd react to the revelation Claire was responsible for the deaths of a helpless old lady and an addict down on his luck. They wouldn't be so solemn and teary-eyed then, she thought.

She watched the gathering of colourful clothes, the men in their bright shirts and the women in their floral dresses, with growing annoyance. The announcement had said 'no black'. She'd worn a smart black suit. If Claire thought she could dictate to her, she was mistaken. She'd wear what she damn well liked.

At first, the memorial had been her route to contacting whoever was in charge of Claire's affairs in the hope she could arrange to go to the house and collect the tablets. It was routine for all unused medication to be returned when someone died, but then she'd started to think doing so would draw undue attention to the medication, which was probably languishing unnoticed in a drawer somewhere. She wished she'd not been distracted by that wretched box weeks before. It was then she'd decided to go to the memorial but to leave during the service. It was the one time she could be relatively certain no one would be at Claire's house. While everyone was otherwise engaged, she'd go there, break in and collect the tablets. She'd been to the house before and hadn't noticed any burglar alarm. There was a side gate leading to the back garden. She would park her car away from the house and try and get in and out quickly.

She'd introduced herself to as many people as possible when she'd arrived to ensure her alibi. She'd been greeted by Sarah. Issy saw no recognition in her eyes as she shook her hand, but the woman had asked for her number so she could call her to discuss a few things about Claire. Issy assumed, as the order of service announced donations were to be given to the oncology department, she'd wished to discuss some sort of memorial or recognition of Claire's generosity. They could forget that, she thought.

She'd played the caring physician and said how sorry she was and how they'd gone through so much over the last few years together to make her well. She'd made a point of saying how much she'd come to like Claire and how she'd been so brave during her previous treatment. Sarah had thanked her for her kind words and it seemed as if she was going to finally acknowledge how important she was in Claire's life when they were interrupted by some woman in a ridiculous straw hat.

She wondered how long she'd need to wait until she could leave unnoticed. She sat through the dreary operatic, and the poetry recital from a girl she assumed was Sarah's daughter and the sycophantic nonsense from Claire's red-headed lawyer friend then, as Sarah walked to the microphone, slipped away unnoticed.

She knew everyone had been invited for refreshments at Claire's local around the corner from her house. She guessed from the number of people there'd be a good deal of hanging around chatting after the service as everyone waited for the backlog of cars to move off.

She drove the short distance to Claire's, parking a little way down the road. She didn't anticipate anyone challenging her but just in case, she'd armed herself with a card expressing her condolences in case she was accosted by a nosey neighbour and needed an excuse for calling.

As she thought, no one answered when she knocked. She crept through the side gate around to the back garden. It would be easier to get in there unnoticed. She thought she would break the kitchen window but couldn't believe her luck when peering through the patio doors she spotted some idiot had left the key in the lock. She took off her suit jacket, wrapped it around her hand and punched through one of the panes. She knew it was unlikely anyone would hear the glass break, but just in case she waited a minute before reaching through and turning the key. She thought how overgrown everything looked in the garden, how unkempt. The abundance of greenery made her uncomfortable and the perfume from the purple flowers above the door was suffocating. She never understood why people didn't stick to gravel and a bit of grass? She looked at her watch, estimating she had roughly twenty minutes to get in and out of the house and make her way to the pub.

She retrieved her jacket from the floor and shook the tiny shards of glass onto the patio before heading upstairs to the bathroom where she pulled open the cabinet door above the sink. To her relief, the tablets were there. She gathered up the packets making sure she took every last one. She could see one pack was empty; the one Claire had given Fergus Jennings. She put the rest of the packets in her jacket pocket.

She left satisfied she'd dodged a bullet.

FIFTY-NINE

Ross left the service early to miss the jam in the carpark. He was meant to be on duty but he needed to talk to Sarah.

If anyone knew what was going on in Claire's mind, it was her. The two had been inseparable since they were teenagers.

Sarah had held up well at the service, especially as she'd had to take the brunt of the organisation, although he'd noticed Daniel hanging around, acting more like a husband than an ex. His mind drifted back to the image of him leaving Claire's house, a towel wrapped around him, and he bristled at the thought of it. He wasn't sure why it mattered to him now Claire was dead, but it did.

Having arrived at the pub before Sarah, he made sure he grabbed her almost as soon as she got through the door.

'Sarah, do you think I could have a quick word?'

'Yeah, sure,' she smiled, hesitating just long enough for him to note the apprehension in her eyes.

'Somewhere private, if we could?'

'I'm a bit pressed. I need to meet and greet.'

Ross smiled at Lerryn standing beside her, the image of her mother at that age.

'Could you do that, for your mum?' he asked. 'And by the way you spoke beautifully today.'

The girl blushed. 'Yeah, I could do it for you, Mum,' she said.

'If you're sure?' said Sarah. 'Dad will help you. He'll be here in a minute; he's just parking the car. Tell the guests to help themselves to the buffet and there's a free bar.'

'It's okay, I've got this, seriously!' she rolled her eyes.

'Right, I'm all yours,' said Sarah looking around, 'where shall we go?'

'There's a small bar through there,' replied Ross, gesturing to a door marked 'SNUG'.

Sarah led the way into the empty room. It was cosy with a low beamed ceiling and a blackened inglenook fireplace. Ross ushered her to a threadbare velvet armchair by the window. She seemed glad to take the weight off her feet and Ross thought she probably hadn't stopped all day.

He remained standing. He didn't want this to feel too comfortable for her.

'So, what did you want to talk about?' she asked rather too quickly.

'It was a lovely service. Well done, it couldn't have been easy,' he said.

'No ... no, it wasn't but I owed it to Claire.'

'Yeah, I get that, but difficult nevertheless, especially in the circumstances.'

Sarah looked at him quizzically.

'The suicide I mean, and it not being a funeral; no set format.'

'Yeah ... it was but Claire left her wishes.'

Once again, the hesitation.

He circled her seat.

'There's nothing, you want to tell me? No other reason other than depression or whatever you want to call it, why Claire would kill herself?'

'What do you mean?' said Sarah, diverting her eyes as she picked at a loose thread on the arm of her seat.

'I mean, was there something else bothering her other than the usual stuff?'

'No!' she practically shouted. 'Wasn't that enough for anyone, with her mother's dementia and everything else she had on her plate?'

'Yeah, of course,' he said touching her shoulder, as he paused to look out of the window into the carpark. 'It's just her behaviour, taking Daniel's car, and setting it alight?'

Sarah's eyes brimmed with tears; her cheeks flushed.

'Well, she wasn't herself. She wouldn't have killed herself if she was. We wouldn't be here if she'd been thinking straight!' she blurted.

She got up and moved towards him, both palms up to her eyes, rubbing away her tears like a little girl with the cuffs of her jumper. Ross couldn't bear it. Policeman or no policeman this woman was his friend and she was grieving. He walked towards her and pulled her to him to comfort her.

'Sarah. You know you can trust me. You know how I felt about Claire?'

She nodded, unable to speak.

'I want you to know I would never have hurt Claire when she was alive and I would never do anything to harm her now she's dead.'

'I know.' Sarah sniffed.

Ross held her at arm's length. 'Are you okay to carry on with this?'

'Yes,' she said walking to the back of the chair.

'I think Claire might have been involved in a serious crime,' Ross continued.

For the first time he saw deceit in her eyes.

'I know,' she mumbled, 'taking Daniel's car and setting fire to it.'

'No, not Daniel's car, something much worse.'

Her eyes darted between his face and the door. Had he been questioning anyone else he would have readied himself to give chase. She'd betrayed herself.

'I'm going to ask you some questions Sarah and I want a simple yes or no to each of them.'

She didn't reply.

'Sarah?'

'Yeah,' she said, reluctantly meeting his eye.

Ross could see her chest heaving, could hear little bursts of breath escaping into the silence. He'd seen that reaction many times in his career. The weight of a secret.

'Did Claire murder Fergus Jennings?'

Sarah steadied herself, gripping the back of the armchair with both hands, her nails digging into the scarlet fabric, head bent.

'I'm not sure,' she said exhaling loudly.

Ross's heart began to beat faster.

'When you say you're not sure, are you saying you have suspicions or there was someone else involved?'

'I don't know.'

She slumped back down into the chair, leaning forward, her head in her hands.

'All I know is that she was the woman in the CCTV; the one with the Retriever.'

She looked deflated but as she looked up he saw relief too.

'When did you know?'

'I only knew afterwards. After her death.'

'Don't tell me anything else.'

'But ... I need to tell you about ...'

'Seriously Sarah. I mean it, shut up right now, before you incriminate yourself.'

Ross gave a long hard stare to show he meant business.

Ben walked in. 'Everything okay in here?' he asked, scanning the two of them for clues of what was going on.

'Yep,' said Ross looking at Sarah, 'everything is fine here, we were just reminiscing, weren't we Sarah?'

'Yes,' she replied.

'Bye you two, I can't stay for the shindig; stuff to do. It was good to see you both, even though I wish it had been in different circumstances.'

'Bye, Ross, take care,' said Ben.

Walking from the pub towards his car, Ross's phone rang. It was his fourteen-year-old daughter, Livvy.

'Hi, Dad.'

'Hi, sweetheart, to what do I owe this pleasure?'

He was pleased to hear her voice.

'Mum asked me to ring. She said you've had a difficult day.'

'I'm alright love,' he lied.

'She said to ask if you want to come for your tea tonight?'

He felt his throat tighten. In sharp contrast to Trudy, he'd remained good friends with his first wife Karenza. She'd known Claire and that he was cut up about her death.

221

'Tell her thanks, but I'm fine, really I am.'

'Mum said not to take no for an answer,' she persisted.

'Okay. I give in, who am I to argue with your mother?' he said.

'She said six o'clock sharp.'

He looked at his watch, two thirty. He'd pop into the station to show willing, do a couple of hours and then head off for St. Ives.

'Alright, I'll be there.'

'Love you,' she said cheerily.

'Love you too,' he replied hanging up.

Tears welled and he looked around, embarrassed. The stragglers from the funeral were wandering in twos and threes into the pub. He opened the car door and got in. The pressure of the past few weeks had taken their toll and now the realisation Claire had been involved in the killing of Jennings and his suspicions had been justified, was too much for him.

He realised now he hadn't wanted to know the truth. Now he did, it served no purpose other than to make him feel even more desolate.

He wasn't sure of anything anymore. The sound of his daughter's voice and his ex-wife's kindness had tipped him over the edge.

SIXTY

Issy arrived at the pub just as the stragglers from the memorial were arriving.

She'd known she'd have to show her face so everyone would assume she'd come straight from the village hall.

As she walked through the swing doors, she saw Sarah with a few others standing at the bar. She went over, stood beside her and asked the barman for an orange juice. Sarah was talking to someone but Issy could see she was looking at her out of the corner of her eye. She took a sip of the juice. She was satisfied things had gone to plan but couldn't shake a niggling feeling she'd forgotten something. She'd run through everything she'd done that morning. She didn't think she'd been missed, that wasn't it. It was something else she couldn't put her finger on.

One of the guests she'd walked in with had engaged her in banal conversation about the wonderful eulogy Sarah had given. How moving it had been, so personal, so evocative of Claire. When Sarah walked over to speak to her, Issy repeated almost verbatim what the woman had said, giving the impression she too had sat through the emotional tribute. Sarah thanked her for being so kind and said it had been difficult but she'd needed to do it for Claire.

Blah, blah, blah, Issy thought. When is everyone going to stop rattling on about that non-entity?

She was about to say something else out loud, rather more complimentary, when she noticed there was blood on her glass. She turned her hand and saw she was bleeding and realised she must have, without noticing, cut her hand on a sliver of glass left in the pocket of her coat when she'd slipped the tablets into it.

'Excuse me,' she said hurriedly to Sarah. 'I need to go to the loo for a second I seem to have cut my hand on something.'

'Oh, my goodness, is there anything I can do, shall I fetch you a plaster? They're bound to have a first aid box in the kitchen.'

'No, no I'll be fine, I just need to wash it under the tap,' Issy said turning her back and making her way to the ladies, leaving Sarah at the bar.

'I'll come with you,' Sarah shouted after her

'No, I said I'll be fine. I'm a doctor, I'm perfectly capable of dealing with a simple cut thank you very much!' She wanted to say, *I saved your beloved Claire from drowning I think I can manage this.*

SIXTY-ONE

When he'd finally pulled himself together Ross made his way from the carpark back to the pub.

As he entered, he spotted Sarah standing by the bar. He lifted his hand to her.

She looked worried for a second, but as he pointed towards the door to the gent's loo and smiled, she seemed to relax.

Looking at his face in the grimy mirror, Ross felt old. Who the hell was he anyway? He was damned if he knew. He looked for the policeman in the mottled reflection but that guy was clearly AWOL. He had no intention of telling anyone about Claire's involvement in the Jennings case. He had no idea why she was involved but he was pretty damn sure she had no connection with that scumbag or his boss Jem Fielding. She was no bloody assassin that's for sure. If Fielding had needed a hit man he wouldn't have had the imagination to pick one with a golden retriever in tow.

He had no idea where his life was heading. Twice a husband and four times an absent father. On both fronts he'd cocked up big time and lost sight of what mattered. He'd been better than that once. He'd thought he'd caught a glimpse of the man he could have been in Claire McBride's eyes but he'd been wrong. She'd had other things and other people on her mind.

He walked out of the gents in a daze, losing his balance as he was jostled by the suited woman he'd noticed earlier at Claire's memorial service. 'Sorry,' he said automatically.

'Watch where you're going,' she snarled back at him.

He guessed grief affected people in different ways.

SIXTY-TWO

Sarah scrutinised the woman's glass for cracks, but it seemed intact. She ran her hand over the bar but couldn't see or feel any glass there either. She shrugged, assuming Issy must have injured herself elsewhere. Hesitating for a moment she wondered whether she should wait for her return and ask her about Claire's treatment and in particular why she'd prescribed morphine to a perfectly healthy woman? Claire had always described her consultant as kind. Sarah didn't see it herself. She saw no warmth. The woman said all the right things and there was the sympathetic smile, but behind it, her eyes were dead and when she'd taken her hand at the memorial she'd felt an inexplicable urge to pull away from her.

She waited for five minutes before being whisked off by the landlady who needed to talk about whether she should cut some more sandwiches. It'll wait, Sarah thought. Given her tetchy reaction earlier she was better off confronting her with the tablets in her hand to back up the accusation, not here, not at Claire's wake. She decided to call into the house on the way home and pick them up; that way she'd have them with her on Monday morning when she rang to make an appointment to see her.

SIXTY-THREE

It wouldn't have been any use Sarah waiting. Issy exited the back way past the gents' toilets. She'd no intention of spending another minute with the Claire McBride fan club, especially as she had exclusive access to the object of all their misplaced affection at home.

It wasn't until she sat down for a cup of tea with David, she realised what had been bothering her. She'd left the condolence card at Claire's house.

Panic sliced through her like a scalpel. She slammed her cup down on the table.

She'd sensed there was something, she'd felt it when she'd arrived at the wake. The card; the stupid bloody condolence card. She had to get back to Claire's house and retrieve it before someone found it and she'd have to take David with her.

She ran upstairs to check on Claire. She was still fast asleep; that was something at least. Looking at her now with her hair pulled back, scrawny and uninteresting she wondered how on earth such a loser could accumulate the sycophantic fan club that had turned out for her today. Mediocre idiots everywhere she looked. If religion had once been the opium of the masses it had been replaced by mediocracy.

SIXTY-FOUR

David spotted the order of service poking out of Issy's suit pocket just before she banged her cup down and ran upstairs. Had she ended another patient's life? If so, something had obviously gone terribly wrong. For the first time ever, he'd seen real alarm in her eyes. He pulled the sheet free.

A Celebration of the Life of Claire Ruth McBride.

He recognised the name from the chart he'd found tucked away in Issy's bedroom. There was a photograph of a pretty, dark-haired young woman with bright blue eyes. Ruth, it was Ruth's face staring back at him. Ruth was Claire McBride.

He slipped it back into Issy's pocket just as she walked into the kitchen with his loafers in her hand.

'Here take those slippers off and put these on. We've got to go out.'

He couldn't contain himself. There were certain advantages to her thinking he wasn't all there.

'Who died?' he asked.

'What are you talking about?' snapped Issy.

'The patient. Who was the patient that died?'

'Be quiet ... senile old fool!' she shrieked, 'nobody died.'

He smiled vacantly.

There's only one of us being fooled here, he thought, and despite what you think my love, it's not me. I have no idea where we're going or what you've got planned for that sweet girl upstairs but I know what you are and your time is nearly up.

SIXTY-FIVE

After the guests drifted away, Sarah bundled the girls into the car to go and retrieve the tablets from Claire's house. Ben took his own car and went to get fish and chips for tea. She was starving. She'd been too busy to eat the evening before and too nervous for breakfast. At the wake, she'd grabbed a sausage roll but nothing more. She didn't intend to be long at Claire's, and was looking forward to opening a bottle of wine and finally sitting down.

A rush of air funnelled through the hallway from the back of the house as she entered. It caught the door, slamming it behind her. She walked through to the kitchen. One of the French doors was open and there was glass on the floor. She scanned the room, worried someone was inside. She could see one of the small window panes near the door handle, was broken but otherwise the room seemed undisturbed. She lifted her mobile to share the news with Ben.

'I think I stupidly left the keys in the French doors so whoever they were, managed to smash a window and open the door with the key. I'm such an idiot.'

'Seriously love, don't beat yourself up. You've had a lot on your plate. They would have got in anyway. There's no alarm. It's probably just kids,' he said, 'They've seen the house is empty, if not you'd expect something to be missing. Don't worry, I'll call the police but it may not be high on their list if they think it's vandals. I'll be there in ten minutes, if nothing else we can secure the place.'

Sarah told the girls to stay in the car until their dad arrived. She went back inside, filled with dread that the break-in as Ben had suggested might be the work of children and they might have taken the meds.

SIXTY-SIX
ISSY

Issy eventually managed to bundle David into the car.

He whistled the theme to 'The Great Escape' all the way to the first set of traffic lights. When she told him to shut up, he complained about her not letting him drive and how he always used to drive and had some very nice leather driving gloves. She tried to pacify him, promising he could have a whiskey when they got home and could drive another day if he was good.

She hadn't worked out what she was going to do with him when she got to Claire's. She would just have to turn on the radio, and activate the child locks.

She need not have worried.

She spotted the car parked in Claire's driveway as soon as she rounded the corner; two young girls sitting in the back seat, one of whom she recognised as Sarah's daughter; who'd read at the memorial service. She couldn't see Sarah and guessed she must already be inside.

That didn't mean she'd found the card. She might be able to distract her. She could say she was passing.

'There might still be time, there might still be time,' she muttered under her breath.

The notion vanished the minute Sarah ran from the house, looking worried as she lifted her mobile to her ear.

Issy pressed her foot down on the accelerator and drove past.

'Damn, damn, damn!'

'Tick tock, tick tock,' shouted David, rolling his head like a pendulum from side to side.

SIXTY-SEVEN
SARAH

The tablets had gone from the cabinet. Why hadn't she handed them into Claire's GP surgery? She'd never forgive herself if some kid took those pills, because of her stupidity.

She'd have to tell Ben and he'd think she'd been reckless, but he didn't know the circumstances. He didn't know she'd left them, because she didn't know why they were there in the first place and wanted to talk to Issy before handing them over to anyone. If she was honest, she'd felt compromised by Claire's confession, and didn't want to be implicated further. She hadn't wanted to take the deceit home with her, naively hoping if the evidence stayed in Claire's house, she could close the door on it and forget she'd ever read the coroner's report or Claire's letter. Now she was paying the price for her cowardice. Turning her back to the cabinet she leant against the basin, wondering how on earth she was going to tell Ben about all this. They usually told each other everything but this was Claire's secret and she and Claire had kept each other's secrets long before she'd met Ben and it felt right to do so now, even though her friend was dead.

She heard a car in the drive. Ben.

She was about to go downstairs to face the music when she noticed something on the floor, wedged by the door. It was a small envelope. She bent to pick it up. She could tell there was a card inside. The envelope was blank and hadn't been stuck down. She knew it wasn't there previously, she wouldn't have missed it when she tidied the house. She'd spent time in the bathroom looking at the pills and since the police finished their search she was the only one with a key. It was obvious, whoever broke in, dropped the card. It might give a name at least. She could give it to the police and they might know them and could trace their fingerprints and find the drugs before they got into the wrong hands.

Her fingers were shaking as she slipped it from the envelope.

'With Sympathy' and a picture of a dove. Not what she'd expected.

She'd seen many like it over the past few weeks, the flowers, the butterflies and sunsets.

She opened it. Beneath the predictable four-line verse about loss and memories, a signature.

Elizabeth Moran ...

She read it again, Issy!

She remembered the cut on her hand. She must have been in the house that day; she must have slipped away from the service, broken in and taken the tablets. Turning up at the pub was an attempt to cover her tracks but why did she leave a card? Was this some kind of threat?

What kind of person would do that, she wondered? The kind who prescribed tablets to a perfectly healthy woman and now wanted to get rid of the evidence. Her instincts had been right. There was something deeply wrong and Issy Moran was right at the centre of it.

She decided not to tell Ben about the card or the missing tablets or the police if they bothered to turn up to investigate the break-in. She needed to speak to Ross.

She slipped the card carefully back into its envelope and into her bag.

Ben was downstairs inspecting the damage. She watched him as he measured the broken window and thanked God for him; this kind uncomplicated man.

'Hi love, what did the police say?'

'They took a record of the incident but said there's not a cat in hell's chance of finding the people who did it. They said sometimes they scour the obituaries for the details of someone who's died then search for their address on the electoral roll. Apparently they break in, watch to see if anything is done about it and if not, return later, either to steal stuff or sometimes to squat in the property. They gave me a case number to give to the insurance company and recommended we get a burglar alarm fitted as soon as possible.

She tried not to show her relief.

Ben temporarily secured the place by boarding up the door and arranged for a mate to mend the glass early the following week. Sarah knew there was no rush; this wasn't random. She knew who the culprit was and she'd already got what she wanted. The only thing she couldn't work out was whether Issy was already on to her. She'd have to be on her guard when she met her. The woman was not to be underestimated.

She told Ben to go on ahead, she'd stay behind to clean up the mess. He offered to leave her fish and chips but she was no longer hungry and told him to take them home and she'd warm them up later.

As soon as he had left with the girls, Sarah called the number she'd tapped into her mobile at the memorial. The pickup was immediate and curt.

'Hello Doctor Issy Moran speaking.'

'It's Sarah, Claire's friend; we met at her memorial service. We need to talk. I've found the card.'

The woman on the end of the phone was silent for a second. When she did speak she didn't deny the card was hers. 'Where and when?'

'At Claire's this evening; six o'clock.'

Sarah didn't know Issy and she certainly didn't trust her. She called Ross.

'Ross, it's me. I think something really bad may have happened to Claire.'

SIXTY-EIGHT

She told Ross everything. She told him about Claire's letter, about Donoghue and Jennings and Claire's wrongful belief she was terminally ill.

'Have you still got the letter?'

'No,' she lied, I burnt it.

'Look I'm on the road on the way to St. Ives. I'll turn around but the traffic will be bad this time of the evening with everyone leaving work. I won't get there until close to six.'

The plan was for him to hide in Claire's study as a witness to the women's conversation and only intervene if things got out of hand or if Issy confessed.

'It's best we keep this informal to begin with. She's more likely to open up to you,' he said. 'You have to realise this might not be a crime it might be negligence. I can't get too involved until we know for sure.'

At half past five he still hadn't arrived and Sarah's anxiety level bubbled from a simmer to a boil. She tried calling him but the call went straight to answerphone.

'Ross, where the hell are you?'

Without him, she felt out of her depth.

She was beginning to think this wasn't such a good idea after all. Every muscle in her body was telling her to get out of there but then nothing would be resolved. She needed answers only Issy Moran could give. She had to do this, Ross or no Ross.

She called him again, still no response.

She waited, Issy's condolence card propped up in front of her on the kitchen table like a call to action.

At exactly eleven the bell rang. Hands sweating she opened the door.

Claire's doctor gave a tight-lipped nod as she stepped uninvited over the threshold.

The makeshift boarding cobbled together by Ben from bits of wood he'd found in the garage, made it unusually dark in the kitchen. There was a chink of light cutting through a side window above the sink but without the sunlight streaming through the patio door there was a distinct police interrogation room feel to the place, made more so once Issy took a seat at the opposite side of the table from Sarah.

Looking at the plump woman in her 'Theresa May' casuals, cross-armed and expressionless, Sarah was struck by an overwhelming sense of the ridiculous. What on earth was she doing? How exactly did she go about something like this? Issy didn't look like she was up for chit-chat. Nevertheless, like loose teeth words fell from Sarah's mouth.

'Did you have far to come?'

'Let's not pretend this is a social visit just say what you have to say,' Issy replied brusquely.

'Fine by me,' Sarah said, hackles rising as she slipped the card out of its envelope and slid it towards Issy. 'How do you explain this?'

She sounded like an extra from *The Bill*. There was meant to be a trained policeman the other side of that wall. Where the hell was Ross?

Issy stared at her with the blatant defiance of a stroppy teenager; a look Sarah knew only too well. 'It's a condolence card. A patient of mine has died and it seemed a perfectly natural and respectful thing to do to send a card. Or, isn't that the answer you're looking for? Then again maybe you're not asking the right question. Maybe you should be asking why I broke into this house and took Claire's tablets from her medicine cabinet?'

Sarah didn't know what to say. Was that a confession? She hadn't needed to force it out of her at all. She'd just come out and said it. If Ross was here he'd know what to do. She coughed, trying to gather enough saliva to speak.

'Well, why did you?'

'I didn't want them to get into the wrong hands. I know you have a copy of the coroner's report, so I know you're aware Claire wasn't ill, so there's no point in my pretending any different.'

Sarah felt a persistent pulsing behind her left eye as she tried to decipher each new revelation.

'But Claire thought she was dying. Are you saying you played into that; went along with it? She was clearly mentally unwell. I can't believe you fed into her paranoia and prescribed tablets knowing she didn't need them. Are you saying they weren't the real thing?'

'Of course, they were the real thing. You really aren't very bright, are you? Claire thought she was dying because I told her she was.'

Sarah was struggling now.

'But why would you do that?' she asked incredulous at the woman's bare-faced candour.

'Do you really want to know, or are you asking because you think you owe it to *poor old Claire?'*

The woman bent her fingers in a quotation sign around Claire's name.

Sarah felt a surge of hatred for her.

'Of course I want to know.'

'Because I felt like it; because I'd had enough of her, because I was bored with her. It was vaguely interesting to watch her go through the needless hours of chemotherapy the first time around. I enjoyed her dependency and of course ... watching her suffer, but once she was in remission, she soon forgot everything I'd done for her. She needed to be reminded; brought down a peg or two and told she was sick again and this time it was hopeless.'

Sarah simply couldn't comprehend what the doctor was saying.

She'd taken Claire's word she was ill but looking back, she'd appeared so well the day they'd gone shopping. Then when she'd received the coroner's report it cast doubt on everything. At first, she'd thought maybe she'd misread the results of the investigation, or the coroner hadn't received all of Claire's medical records. Then, when the tablets were stolen, she'd considered the possibility Issy may have made a wrongful diagnosis and was now trying to cover up her negligence by stealing the evidence. This would have been horrendous enough, considering it had led to Claire becoming unhinged and her suicide, but at least it would have stemmed from a mistake; a terrible mistake but a mistake, nonetheless. She hadn't in her wildest imaginings thought for one moment this so-called doctor had misdiagnosed Claire on purpose, putting her through the agony and trauma of the chemo on a spiteful cruel whim. Sarah felt light-headed, as if all the oxygen was being slowly sucked out of the room. She was angry but her rage was drenched with a churning sweaty fear, as it dawned on her what this woman was truly capable of.

Looking at Issy's flabby, expressionless face she was scared; her thoughts whispering; *what are we going to do, what are we going to do?*

Issy paced the room. There was a lumbering awkwardness about her, like a prowling bear. A large sweat patch stained the back of her blouse where her flesh bulged around her bra strap and in that moment, just as if someone had turned on a lightbulb, Sarah recognised her.

It was immediate, and visceral, the vision of a girl in a PE lesson with that same sweat mark, the same excess flesh and the same ungainly gait.

Sarah couldn't contain herself; 'Elizabeth? You're Elizabeth Major!'

Issy spun around, her face screwed into a tight red ball.

'What if I am? What are you going to do about it, you haven't got your little friend anymore to get me thrown out, to send me off packing? What are you going to do, pin this on my back and parade me through the town?' She picked the card up from the table, waving it in front of Sarah's face, before slamming it back down.

'I don't understand?' Sarah said.

'That's your usual style isn't it, you and Claire, doing things behind people's backs?' spat Issy.

'I honestly don't know what you're talking about.'

Sarah was beginning to wonder whether she ought to be planning an escape route. The woman was mad.

'Don't lie to me you cowardly bitch, Claire McBride ruined my life. She pinned that vicious note to my back and it was reported to the Board of Governors and then everyone knew, everybody knew about daddy and they had to get rid of me.'

Sarah remembered her conversation with Claire on the afternoon she'd taken Chloe to the beach, how they'd talked about Elizabeth leaving school. Then she remembered her own mother's staffroom gossip at the time. How she'd said it was a shame because it wasn't the girl's fault, but there had been an incident. The word LIAR had been pinned to her back in class. It had been the work of one of her friends, a girl whose parents had lost money in the fraud engineered by her father. The same parents, who were regular contributors to school funds, had also insisted the girl leave even though the headmistress had already put in hand an application to the governors for a bursary to enable her to stay.

'But Claire didn't do it,' Sarah said quietly.

'What?'

'She didn't do it. It was one of your friends. One of the girls whose parents invested money with your father. It was one of them who pinned that note to your back, not Claire. She'd never have done something like that ... never.'

It felt good to defend her friend. Her recent actions seemed indefensible, but they were discussing the old Claire now; the kind generous girl who Sarah knew and loved.

Issy stood motionless as the tension seemed to fall away from her body like a discarded coat. She looked completely without cover.

Sarah decided to attack whilst her defences were down.

'Besides, even if she had done it how could it ever warrant what you've done?' she said.

Issy's eyes widened.

'I don't know why you think that so strange, your friend Claire did the same thing. I'm not the only one who feels the need to punish past misdemeanours. She killed a man ... and you dare judge my motives?'

'I don't know what you're talking about,' Sarah lied.

'Then let me educate you.'

Opening her handbag Issy pulled out an envelope with a flourish, slamming it down on the table.

'Look for yourself. It's all there, dates, times, places. She planned it all and killed him in cold blood and if you tell the world about me, if you ruin my life, my career, everything I've worked for, I'll tell everyone the truth about your precious friend. I'll take her and you and her demented mother with me. So, think really hard about what you're going to do next.'

She was pacing again, back and forth, back and forth, her arms flaying around like a frenzied flight controller. 'Yes, I gave her drugs. I treated her when she wasn't ill and told her she was dying, but she murdered someone.'

Sarah sensed any control she'd had over this woman slipping through her fingers like sand.

'I watched her the night she killed Jennings. I saw her leave with the Golden Retriever in the tartan scarf. Of course, I didn't know what I was witnessing until I saw the news bulletin. Then I suspected her alright.'

Sarah wanted to defend Claire, to divulge her motives and deliver a plea of mitigation but deep down knew there was no valid excuse for Claire's behaviour. She thought she was dying, yes … but that wasn't an excuse to take others with her, even if those others were vile despicable shits.

'Your friend killed herself because she couldn't face what she'd done, not because she thought she was dying.'

Sarah didn't know how to answer her.

'What good do you think will come of exposing me. I'll just admit I made a wrong diagnosis; that the stresses of work and of having a sick husband conspired to make me drop the ball. One incident in an exemplary twenty-year career, but Claire … well she was different, she was a killer and all of you, your husband, your children and Claire's frail old mother will be killers by association.'

At the threat of harm to her family, Sarah's self-control tumbled like a kite in a storm. The string snapped. She lunged at Issy, shoving her to the floor.

'Don't you dare talk about my family and if you think I'm going to let this go; let you get away with torturing my friend and threatening me, you're wrong. You're meant to be a doctor; you're meant to care for people. Claire thought you were caring for her, but you weren't, were you? You were slowly killing her?'

Sarah straddled Issy; fists full of wispy hair.

'Get off me; get off me.'

Issy rolled, heaving her heavy frame from side to side like a rodeo bull, trying to throw Sarah off; sweaty cheeks puffing; eyes bulging.

'You're like her, just like your precious Claire. You want to kill me, don't you? You want to kill me just like she killed that junkie. Go on then do it,' she screamed, 'do it! We're all killers. It just takes someone to press the right buttons to get us started.'

The words hit Sarah straight between the eyes. Claire hadn't been like this vile woman and she wouldn't let herself become like her. She let go of Issy's hair and rolled away.

She tried to get up but her legs felt heavy. Out of the clouded corner of her eye she saw Issy grab the table, pull herself to her feet and stumble away.

Sarah tried to get up again but her head began to swim as the edges of the room darkened.

***

When she came around, she was flat on her back with Ross kneeling beside her.

Issy had gone.

'Can you get up?'

'Elizabeth ... Issy, Claire's doctor, she's a liar. She's dangerous.'

Ross lifted her to a seat.

'Okay, calm down, calm down.'

'I'm fine ... you need to get after her.'

'I know who she is, she won't get far. I'll call it in and they'll trace her address. I'm more concerned about you for the moment. Come on let's get you some air.'

Ross lifted her to her feet. Outside, he sat her down in a garden chair.

'Are you alright here for a second while I ring this in. I'll call Ben too?'

She started to cry imagining all the explaining she had to do.

SIXTY-NINE

By the time Issy got home she'd made her decision. She needed to finish Claire off and get away as soon as possible. How dare Sarah attack her? She was clearly unbalanced and if the authorities turned up, she'd tell them as much. She'd grabbed the card from the table on the way out and already had the tablets. Sarah had no evidence. Sarah was as bad as Claire. They were as bad as each other. Goodness knows what might have happened had she not run for her life.

At least she'd turned a page; finally put her ghosts to rest. The conversation with Sarah had been difficult, but it needed to be had. If Sarah was sensible there wouldn't be any need for either of them to trouble themselves about Claire McBride ever again. She'd done Sarah a favour letting her know the real Claire. Granted, she'd had to admit her own part in the saga. She'd deceived Claire, it was true, but ultimately, Claire hadn't taken the morphine and so everything she'd done; the killing; the suicide attempt had been of her own volition. She had no one to blame but herself.

It had come as a surprise that Claire wasn't the one to pin the notice on her back all those years ago. The realisation it had been one of her so-called friends all along, and it had been their parents who'd forced her out of the school, had shocked her. She hated them all; those hypocritical two-faced bitches.

She'd had enough of people, and she'd had enough of Cornwall. She'd made up her mind at Claire's memorial. All those people wallowing in their pain; living in each other's pockets, it made her want to be sick. She hated the incestuous nature of the place and the suffocating closeness of the community. She couldn't bear to stay a second longer than she had to.

There were always jobs to be had for highly qualified hard-working professionals like her. She'd cast her net wider this time, perhaps abroad. Australia, she thought, she'd always liked the idea of Australia or New Zealand, a person could lose themselves in New Zealand.

She wondered about David. She wouldn't be taking him, it wouldn't be fair, how could he possibly manage somewhere new? She'd ring around some care homes later that day, there was bound to be a vacancy somewhere in the country. Then she thought again. Care was expensive and who knew how long he'd last, maybe she'd need all the money they'd saved between them to start her new life. She wouldn't want to leave herself short. She might want to set up in private practice, as a consultant. David would love her to do that, he wouldn't want to stand in the way of her career. Perhaps it would be better for everyone if he were to fall, maybe on the way to the loo, in the middle of the night? Landings were treacherous, especially in the dark if the surroundings were unfamiliar and he'd had a couple of glasses of wine or a mild sedative to help with the pain of his arthritis.

As for Claire. Well that was simple. To the rest of the world she was already dead and there was an empty freezer sitting in the garage that needed to be dumped.

Opening the front door, she could see David in the kitchen. He was stark naked but for Rita's apron tied around his waist, covering his unmentionables and a pair of tan leather driving gloves. She'd told him to stay in his bedroom until she got back.

'Eggs?' he asked, holding up the frying pan.

'No David,' she said, 'I don't want eggs; in fact, it's too late for breakfast, and take off those ridiculous gloves.'

David looked bemused and she relented a little, thinking, not long now before I'm free.

'They look very nice,' she cajoled, 'but you won't be driving again so I think we'll throw them away.'

SEVENTY

David spotted that look Issy got when she had a plan.

He didn't know where they'd been that morning or where she'd come from now but the panic he'd witnessed earlier had evaporated and had been replaced with a self-satisfied smugness that meant only one thing. She thought she was home and dry. She knew there would be no comeback. It was time to end this now before he and Claire McBride, the girl he knew as Ruth, crept to the top of her 'to-do' list if they weren't already there.

He didn't care about the consequences; they couldn't be worse than doing nothing. He'd played it over and over in his head and knew what he had to do. If he was caught, what could the authorities do? He wasn't *compos mentis*: he couldn't be held accountable. They'd keep him under supervision for a while, until they were sure that he wasn't a danger to anyone and then he'd be able to book himself into some top-notch care facility where he could live out the rest of his life in relative peace. He fancied somewhere with a nice view and grounds where he could have a wander when the mood took him, and where Rita could visit, maybe with her grandchildren.

He'd have plenty of money to pay for it and, unbeknown to Issy, he'd contacted his solicitor and appointed Rita as his Attorney. He trusted Rita to look after his best interests, after all she knew what he'd been through, he'd shown her the marks, the welts on his wrists and ankles and the bruise on his cheek; all those little signs of abuse Rita had seen and logged.

Then there was Issy's book. Once everyone knew the truth about Doctor Elizabeth Moran no one would really blame him. They might even see him as a hero.

He had once taken the Hippocratic oath; 'Do No Harm' but what were you meant to do when you see someone day after day, year after year, harming others?

He had to do this for the patients, for Karen and for the pretty blue-eyed young woman upstairs and all those sad vulnerable others who would die if he did nothing.

SEVENTY-ONE

'I'm going to check in on Ruth,' said Issy, 'she was looking much worse today. I have to say I don't think it'll be long now. When I come down, David, I expect to see you in your dressing gown and those gloves in the bin.'

As she walked towards the hall cupboard to hang up her jacket, she felt a heavy blow to the back of her head. The sickening thud sent her to her knees. Lights flashed before her eyes and a shooting pain seared through her temples. She lifted her hand to the back of her head and felt a warm stickiness. She turned just in time to see David swing the frying pan again landing a lethal blow. As blood filled her nostrils she thought she caught a glimpse of Daddy.

***

David arranged his wife's lifeless body into a contorted sprawling heap between the wall and the bottom step. He laid her face up, the back of her battered head resting on the hard floor. Pulling her navy-blue court shoe from her right foot, he held it for a second, then snapped the kitten heel clean off. Carrying the two halves of the shoe he made his way up to the second stair down from the landing and placed the heel there, on its side. He threw the rest of the shoe down the stairs, watching it tumble and land by Issy's misshapen, swollen head.

Back downstairs, he took a deep breath, then reaching across pulled his wife's skirt askew, revealing a dimpled white thigh beneath her torn stockings. Leaning over he ripped open her straining suit jacket, sending a button spinning across the patterned floor tiles, until it came to rest against the skirting board.

Grabbing her left arm, he pulled it up behind her back. The crack of the bone breaking, made him wince, but he'd heard worse during his time as a surgeon. He noticed a deep pink trickle of blood running from Issy's floppy mouth had stained the collar of her blouse. Her glassy rag-doll eyes fixed on him in a stare of stunned surprise.

Running his finger across her forehead, he pushed a strand of hair from her face. Leaning in, he whispered one word into her ear, 'Monster.'

He took one last look at her; her limbs lolling haphazardly around her overstuffed body. She reminded him of a puppet with its strings cut.

Stepping over her, he removed his gloves and walked back to the kitchen. Remarkably, there wasn't a mark on them. He was pleased, he would have been sad to see them go. He placed them in the drawer of the dresser. He carefully washed the frying pan in the sink, returning it to its usual place in the kitchen cupboard.

After he'd showered and put on his pyjamas and dressing gown he made his way to the yellow bedroom to check Claire McBride was still safely asleep. He felt her pulse then bent and gently kissed her cheek.

'You're safe, dear girl,' he whispered. 'Everything will be alright now.'

Back downstairs he called the police to report the terrible accident before retreating to his study where he carefully placed an LP onto the turntable then settled into his favourite chair.

It was there, ten minutes later, Ross and his team found him after breaking down the front door. He was fast asleep snoring to Bob Dylan singing 'The times they are a-changin' ...'

On his lap was a pink notebook full of names, including Claire McBride.

SEVENTY-TWO
Ten months later

I've waited for a fine day to scatter Mum's ashes; nothing too wild; nothing to make me feel sadder than I already feel.

Mum deteriorated fast after my forced absence. She seemed to sense the cord snap and the futility of carrying on. I've collected her few possessions from the home, a box of trinkets and the old shortbread tin. I've brought the little brown envelope containing the photos with me. Somehow it seemed the right thing to do.

It's a beautiful morning. I've not been to Penmorvah beach since I attempted to take my own life. I look around for signs of Daniel's burnt-out car, some scorched gravel, or wreckage, but there's nothing. It's as if none of it ever happened.

Daniel's visited a couple of times over the past few months. He's changed, as if what happened made him realise you shouldn't be careless with the things you love. He seems to take pleasure in talking about his kids and what they're doing, every bit the proud father and happily married man. I have to give credit where credit's due, Louisa, presumably through sheer force of will, and with a little help from me, has managed to change the leopard's spots.

He told me during his first affair he'd found the need to look elsewhere 'because life had become so fucking ordinary.'

I bet ordinary looks pretty good to him these days. Ordinary looks pretty good to me too.

Sarah offered to come with me today but I knew I had to do this alone. I called on Sarah and Ben on the way here and was almost licked to death by Barney.

After Pam told her she was going to have to re-home him, Ben and the girls persuaded Sarah it would be a good idea for them to have him. It led to a bigger conversation about the possibility of moving. In the end, they chose an old farmhouse with a large garden and outbuildings they hope to turn into a studio. Barney is in his element. He's got a new lease of life now he's not cooped up all day in Pam's maisonette. I think of the role he played in the death of Fergus Jennings. Ben and the girls don't know he's wanted by the police and it doesn't seem to bother Barney he's a fugitive.

Sarah was her usual cheerful self and it was great to see her and the family have settled so well in their new home. Sarah's forgiven me and I'd like to think in time we'll be as close as we ever were.

As for me, I've come to terms with what I did.

There is no excuse for my actions but I honestly believe I would not have done any of it had Issy not told me I was dying. When I heard about her death and what she put me through I couldn't help but think it was poetic justice.

The news broke the day after I was rescued from the house by Ross. The body of a woman, a consultant at the local hospital, had fallen down the stairs, hit her head and died from a massive bleed to the brain, whilst her elderly husband slept unaware. I wrote to David with my condolences when I heard. I understand he was instrumental in exposing his wife's crimes but nevertheless you can't be with someone for that many years and not feel some loss.

He's in sheltered accommodation now; a really swanky place with a warden and a tennis court.

The police found a diary at the scene detailing a catalogue of murders going back years. Elizabeth Moran had taken the lives of dozens of her patients and it could take months if not years to unravel the full extent of her crimes. There is an ongoing inquiry into how she managed to avoid the detection of numerous hospital authorities.

Instead of taking the familiar path to the beach I take the coastal track along the clifftop to where it forks. The old coffin path leads straight on. I take the other route across the rocks, gingerly tracing their slippery backbone down to the sea. In a matter of hours, the rocks will disappear as if never there, hiding beneath the surface, waiting to crush those who venture too close to their barnacled shoulders. Those who live near the sea are always wary of it. For me to have walked into it knowing I'd never walk out again showed a certain surrender to its authority.

I had felt the point of no return, when the choice was no longer mine. I didn't feel brave, I didn't need to. I'd felt like I was coming home and the sea would embrace me as its most loyal of disciples. Back here with the spray on my cheeks I feel peaceful for the first time since Mum's death.

I unscrew the lid of the urn, pausing for a moment to watch the fine jade seaweed splay like mermaid's hair around the base of the rocks before shaking its contents into the breeze. Reaching into my pocket, I pull out the letter I left for Sarah; the confession which shook her to the core when she read it. Ripping it to pieces, I toss it into the water, watching the scraps catch a wave and wash away.

I remember the words sealed in jam jars and cast into the tide when we were children. They'd held secrets to be discovered; innocent confidences to be shared. Secrets like those in my letter are different, they are given to the sea to keep, to hold safe in its depths. The sea is the best of confidents.

Next comes Mum's envelope of photos. I take each of them out, one by one, smiling at the memories captured there. I hold back one of Sarah and I buried up to our necks in sand, big grins on our goofy teenage faces.

The last of the photographs, yellowed by time, is the one of Mum sitting in the pub garden on a summer's evening. I flip it over. On the back in faded biro is written:

The Gang; London 1971 Exams over! Free at Last!
Michael, Nick, Jenny, Karen, Eileen and David.

I look at the men's names circled in crayon by me all those years ago.

I let it float away with the others, watching the water lap over the faces, watching them catch their last wave. It seems right they should be with Mum.

I retrace my steps back up the cliff path to Ross, who's waiting to get me back before lights out. It was good he managed to pull strings to be the one in charge of me for the day. At least he'll be able to combine the trip with a visit to see his kids in Bristol. From my conversations with him in the car, things are no better with Trudy. Although he said he's been seeing more of his first wife, Karenza, these days and to my mind seems a happier. I'm glad and hope he finds whatever it is he's looking for.

I'm used to the regime now and I'm a quarter way through my sentence.

I can't complain. The judge took into consideration everything that had happened to me and two years is fair for fraud given the fact I'm a solicitor or rather I was, and should have known better. I'll never be allowed to practice again of course and I can't say I'll miss it. The stupid thing is Maureen got everything anyway. Donoghue hadn't made a will before so once the will was set aside, as her only relative she inherited her estate.

I don't blame Ross for arresting me for forging the will or Sarah for telling him about my letter although God love her she lied about destroying it. It's one thing to keep a secret when you think someone is dead, quite another to pervert the course of justice once you know they're alive. At least he let the stuff on Jennings go and I suppose no one will ever know who was really responsible for his death, or whether ultimately it was down to Jennings himself. I never forced him to take the drugs or the booze that killed him.

Ross is leaning against the police car.

'You okay?' he says gently as he opens the rear door.

'I'm fine.' I smile.

As we climb the steep hill I turn to look out the back window towards the sea and the beach below and imagine Mum and I as we were. Eileen Penrose and her Claire.

In that moment I understand I'll always be her Claire and ghosts are just as much about the living as the dead.

THE END

A LETTER TO MY READERS

Thank you for taking the time to read **RAGE**. I have always been drawn to stories which interweave the simultaneous plotlines of many compelling characters; stories where innocuous decisions by one individual have profound and unexpected implications for another.

As a lawyer who has practised for many years in a small rural Cornish community I have witnessed first-hand the chaos that ensues when the toxic cocktail of fear, desperation and rage forces someone to take the law into their own hands. In **RAGE,** Book One in my **CORNISH CRIME** series, I explore how intelligent, rational women can, if the circumstances are right, make the calculated decision to break the law and when they do how the web of deceit they weave can affect their friends, family and the wider community and build a cage around them hard to escape.

I have always been fascinated by the schizophrenic character of the windswept Cornish peninsula my family has been lucky enough to call home for generations. Occupied by a cast of reluctant bedfellows, city-slick escapees and us locals who carry the remnants of our myth-ridden history etched on our backs like tattoos, it teeters between the bucket and spade domesticity of modern-day tourism and a superstitious past, riddled with Pagan traditions.

The resultant clash of cultures and sensibilities causes friction, resentment and drama. My aim, through my writing, is to explore what happens when these divergent worlds collide to expose a darker reality at odds with the picture-perfect landscape. Whilst I was lucky to enjoy a fantastically satisfying career as a lawyer I cannot now imagine anything more joyous than being able to sit at my desk and write knowing others might read and connect with my words. Cornwall has captured the hearts and imaginations of countless wonderful writers through the decades; their vivid images now woven into its rich tapestry. If I can add one colourful stitch I will be happy.

Would you like to read more of my work? **Then visit my website www.cornishcrimeauthor.com to join my list.** You will be given the opportunity to become a member of my readers' club and receive free downloads, sneak previews and fascinating insights into the characters and places featured in my novels. These goodies are exclusive to members and currently include a **FREE** novella in the **CORNISH CRIME SERIES,** *THE ROSARY PEA What's Your Poison?*

I look forward to meeting you there and on Facebook **(www.facebook.com/julieevansauthor).**

A final request...

If you've enjoyed this book I would be so grateful if you could leave a review on Amazon.

As an author, it is a great thrill to know someone has enjoyed your work, and it will help other readers find my books.

Thank you.

Julie